Lilac,
Great covers

Empire of the Space Cats

by

Stephen Colegrove

Book Two of the Amy Armstrong Series

Copyright Information

Cover design by Lilac

Find out more about the author and upcoming books
at the websites below:
stevecolegrove.com
amishspaceman.com

Also by the author:
The Girl Who Stole A Planet (Amy Armstrong Book 1)
The Amish Spaceman
The Roman Spaceman
A Girl Called Badger
The Dream Widow

Table of Contents

Cast of Characters

Amy Armstrong: A fourteen-year-old thief from 1995 California. Accidentally flung two thousand years into the future, she is trying to find a way back to her own time

Philip Marlborough: A seventeen-year-old boy from late nineteenth-century England also trapped in the future

The Lady: An ancient human cyborg and head of a business that specializes in trans-dimensional theft, who gives Amy Armstrong a ship

Sunflower: An orange shorthair tabby who worked for the Lady and accidentally brought Amy Armstrong into the future. His wife disappeared while on a similar mission. Bone strengthening and other cybernetic implants have changed his body from that of a normal cat.

Betsy Jackson: A male Jack Russell terrier who formerly worked for the Lady. Dim-witted and easily distracted. Bone strengthening and other cybernetic implants have changed his body from that of a normal dog.

Nick: A female sprite who formerly worked for the Lady in the gem-sorting department. Sprites are a bio-engineered species of five-inch-tall humanoids with transparent wings that allow them to fly.

Nistra: A former officer of the sauropod prison system. Ordered to help Amy Armstrong find a way back to Earth. Sauropods are a bio-engineered species of seven-foot-tall bipedal lizards, similar to a fat crocodile walking on its hind legs

Kepler Prime: Nistra's homeworld, secretly miniaturized by the Lady and installed as the power source for Amy's ship

Empire of the Space Cats

The ship was tired, but this was nothing new. She'd been tired as far back as she could remember.

Her birth had been happy and gay as births frequently are, with parades and fireworks and celebration. The curving track of the stars through the universe, the planetary gravity wells, the plotting of acceleration and warp vectors——all gleamed fresh in the deep, multi-layered sensors of her eyes. The first crew of cats, dogs, and humans climbed inside her and worked happily together. They were smart, honest, and dedicated to a single purpose: the first journey to another dimension. That's when everything fell apart.

The first captain was all right, the ship supposed. Called 'The Lady' by the ship as a sign of respect, she'd taken the ship and her crew across the galaxy and back again, stolen imperial crown jewels, and escaped battle fleets more times than a poona had lives. Although the crew realized that returning home was impossible, the captain pulled them all together and kept spirits high. The ship thought of the adventures they'd had and sprayed a smile of high-frequency electrons from her forward attitude thrusters. But then the most horrible and distressing thing that inevitably happened to organic beings actually happened: the captain died. Advanced polymers, replacement organs, and nano-electronics lengthened her life but could not stop the ultimate sentence of death that every biological organism carries over his or her head. The feeling of loss felt by the ship was the worst, most overpowering sensation she had experienced in her short time in the universe. She abandoned her crew at a pleasant garden planet and raced madly through the dimensions, not caring where she ended up or if her power motivators fused into huge chunks of useless carbon.

As the decades and star systems flew by, the ship thought of nothing but the death of her only friend. She pointed the silver needle of her nose toward a lonely blue star at the far end of the galaxy, intending to destroy herself completely. As blinding waves of heat rolled across her silver nose and tendrils of the star's powerful gravity reached out to rip at her, a faint radio signal vibrated the ship's hull; an impossible signal in the unmistakable voice of the captain. The ship turned at the last moment and skipped across the gravity well of the star like a stone on a lake. On a lonely station orbiting a nearby planet she found a young woman––the Amy Armstrong of this dimension. She had the same voice, same face, and same ingenious mind as the first captain, but with a different past.

The ship convinced the young woman and her strange companions to join her for a fresh round of adventures. When this new captain passed away from old age, the ship was sad but also knew what to expect, and what to look for. The ship crossed the dimensions, her transponders tuned to the right frequency, and found the next Lady, and the next. It became more difficult to find interesting corners of the galaxy, especially since galaxies weren't shaped that way. Over time, repetition and age pounded away at the ship like high-energy cosmic particles on her hull. While resting and receiving critical repairs at Phobos Station, she revealed to the current Lady the constant thread of her existence through multiple dimensions. After that, each Lady helped the ship search for a replacement.

Docked to the side of the asteroid with her core removed to act as power supply for the most recent Lady's gigantic home, the ship thought she'd finally get some rest. But no, thirty years later a hustle and bustle filled her corridors. Batteries were warmed up, storage rooms were cleaned and restocked, and the locking bolt around the astrogation core was removed. A pair of humans and a cat, dog, sprite, and lizard tumbled inside.

The ship yawned, her titanium skin shivering, knowing what would come next. Seconds later, a current of trasmat energy flashed through her entire being, sending the ship to another dimension.

From the way they shouted and jumped around the airlock, the two humans and their companions were as puzzled as bees in a bag. It was the same old thing to the ship. To her, the thousandth transdimensional jump was pretty much the same as the first. The ship yawned again. So tired ... once the transmat finished, she might as well go back to sleep.

AMY ROLLED OVER and stared up at the glowing white dome of the airlock's ceiling. She touched the dull pain on the back of her head and looked at her fingers——no blood, just strands of blonde hair and orange thread. The back of her prison jumpsuit had ripped, probably during the headlong dash out of the Lady's asteroid.

"Good gravy and mashed potatoes," she groaned.

"Sorry!" barked Betsy. "I do that when I'm scared."

A dark-haired teenager pushed the small brown-and-white terrier off his face, then sat up and brushed dog hair from the sleeves of his gray three-piece English suit. "Not the awful smell from your bottom," said Philip. "Amy means the huge bang."

An orange tabby squirmed out from under Amy's left leg. "Obviously a transmat jump," snarled Sunflower. "Was I the only one listening to what the Lady said two minutes ago? Because it was only two minutes ago!"

A huge green lizard in a white physician's coat sneezed and rolled onto his back.

"Stop shouting, cat," he said, and clutched his chest. "I think I broke a rib. Or two. Ow! Something's inside me!"

Nistra squealed and slapped his belly as a lump darted around the front of his coat, bounced around the front of his crotch wildly, and then sped down a leg of his blue trousers.

Amy raised a hand. "Where's Nick?"

"You get one guess," said Sunflower.

A tiny blonde woman with transparent dragonfly wings on her back flew from the trouser leg and buzzed circles around the scaly head of the sauropod.

"You could have killed me, you giant stinky glob of stinky snake meat!"

Nistra blinked. "I am not a snake. Also, you were not invited inside my clothes."

"That's right," barked Betsy. "He didn't invite you. I would have remembered if he had because it would have been weird. I would have said to myself, 'Hey, Betsy. That's weird!' And then I would have agreed with myself and said——"

"Shut up," hissed Sunflower. "How about telling yourself that?"

"But I'd have nobody to talk to!"

"That's my point."

Nick flew to the center of the room, ran her fingers through her hair, and straightened the short hem of her purple sequined dress. The tiny woman glared down at the figures sprawled on the floor of the airlock and wagged a finger.

"If any of you EVER say a word to anyone about me being in a sauro's stinky pants, I'll put a bee up your nose."

Sunflower shrugged. "You'll have to find one first."

"Shut up!"

Philip raised both hands. "Steady on, you two. We have more to worry about than Nick's journey into the depths of evil."

"But it's a pressing issue," giggled Sunflower. "Get it? Pants get pressed? I don't even wear clothes and that's funny."

Nick zipped down and buzzed above the cat. "You try it sometime!"

"Sorry, my schedule is full." Sunflower pretended to pull out an imaginary journal. "I can probably squeeze it in next month. Get it? Squeeze?"

"Ooo, you jerk!"

Philip cleared his throat. "To return to the situation at hand ... Despite the Lady's best intentions in giving Miss Armstrong this ship, she may have thrown us from the pan into the fire."

"Why would you say that?" asked Amy.

"It's simply a feeling."

"I'm hungry," said Betsy, and scratched his furry neck with a front paw. "That's a feeling, isn't it?"

Sunflower twitched the end of his orange tail. "Dogs and your food. Didn't you eat last week?"

"I guess. But when I'm bored, I get hungry. I'm bored!"

"You will not have this feeling for long," said the lizard Nistra. "The engines of this ship have stopped. The glorious Sauro battle fleet will capture and torture all of you for as many years as a poona has hairs on its tiny head. Believe me, that is a large number––I had to count them in basic training."

Betsy wagged his brown and white tail. "Hooray!"

"Idiot dog," said Sunflower. "Unless you like torture, that's a bad thing."

"Oh, no! I don't like torture. Wait––what's torture?"

"In my case, being around you."

"I don't think there's any need to worry about the battle fleet," said Philip. "If you hadn't noticed, we've crossed into another dimension. In fact, it could be a dimension in which sauros are extinct."

Nistra bared a mouth full of sharp teeth. "Or we may be as tall as houses, and jump around squashing humans and breathing fire!"

Sunflower licked a paw and brushed his orange forehead. "Maybe there was a transmat, maybe not. Maybe that huge bump was a compression wave from the Lady destroying the Sauro battle fleet."

Amy sighed and slid back against the wall. "We're in an airlock, right? This thing is a spaceship, so it has to be an airlock."

"That's as good a guess as any," said Philip.

White ovals in the ceiling illuminated the circular chamber. Deep indentations of various size were embedded in the pale walls, each containing a pair of crossed bars. The hatch that everyone had dove through had shrunk to a meter-wide silver disk covered with irregular handwriting: "Avetisman! Vakyom Deyo!" Dozens of other phrases were scrawled in black marker around the airlock. An arrow scrawled next to each phrase pointed to something on the wall——small yellow triangles or colored squares——as if someone were trying to describe the function of unlabeled buttons. On the opposite wall to the entry hatch was a large blue disc, this one covered with more black scribbles.

Philip squatted beside her. "How are you, Miss Armstrong?"

"You don't have to be so formal, okay?"

Philip grinned. "My apologies——simply a force of habit. Are you hurt in any way?"

"Only my feelings. I'm just looking at all the crap on the walls that I can't read. What does 'Antre' mean?"

Sunflower turned away from a four-way argument with Betsy, Nistra, and Nick. "That's 'entrance' in Cat French. Didn't you learn anything in school?"

"What school? I'm from California, Planet Earth! Hello?"

"Hello," said Betsy, and wagged his tail.

Sunflower sighed. "Sometimes humans are really, really smart and sometimes they're sooo the other thing. It's like meeting a monkey that can drive a hovercar——you expect them to know other things like how to order from a wine list, or when not to throw their poop at strangers."

"Thanks, but I'm not a monkey."

"Don't make fun of her," said Betsy. "You aren't good at Cat French, either. Remember how you failed that one class and they almost kicked you out of college? My dad had to talk to the professor and——"

Sunflower flattened his ears and hissed. "Shut up!"

"Actually, I can read a bit of Cat French," said Philip. "I had several years in Nick's room with nothing to do but leaf through books."

The small blonde woman buzzed around the teenager's head. "That's because you never wanted to do anything fun!"

Philip stood up. "Steady on, old stick. Now, each section of writing describes a nearby button. It must be a simple enough task to read each text and press the right ones to escape this room."

The teenager held out a hand, and Amy pulled herself up. "Which one says 'This way to Planet Earth?'"

A loud click shook the room and plunged everything into complete darkness.

"Great," said Sunflower. "Now we're going to die."

"I thought that's what you wanted," said Betsy. "You said it last week."

"Sure, but not like this, and especially not with your horrible dog-breath in my whiskers."

"We must get out of this compartment!" roared Nistra. "Suffocating to death in the darkness is no death for a sauro warrior!"

"It's good you're not a warrior, then," said Sunflower. "What's a good death for a prison secretary?"

Claws scraped along the floor in the darkness. "Choking on cat meat," growled Nistra's voice.

"Quiet," whispered Amy. "Did anyone feel that?"

"I feel rather light-headed at the moment," said Philip. "Is that what you mean?"

Betsy whined. "I feel light-everything!"

"Along with the power and lights, the artificial gravity has shut off," said Sunflower's voice. "Am I the only one who remembers we're in a spaceship? They normally operate in space. The clue is in the name."

A thump came from the ceiling. "Ouch!" squealed Nick.

"Those crosses in the walls are probably hand-holds," said Amy. "Everybody grab one before we start crashing into each other."

"Too late," moaned Betsy's voice. "Really ... dizzy!"

Amy felt her feet leave the airlock floor. She spread her arms, but in the absolute darkness couldn't see or feel a thing. Something bumped into her chest and she slapped it away without thinking.

"Hey! Bad touch!"

"Sorry," said Philip. "Take my hand, Amy. I have the wall with the other."

Amy stretched her arms toward his voice and touched the rough wool of Philip's jacket. A warm hand grabbed hers and pulled her slowly forward. Amy bumped into the wall with her shoulder, then felt around the smooth surface until she found a recessed handle.

"Got one," she murmured.

"Why do humans always whisper when it gets dark?" muttered Sunflower.

"You're whispering, too," said Betsy, his voice coming from above Amy.

"That's because I hate you."

"Maybe they're telling secrets," said Betsy. "Let's wait and see."

A gurgling sound came from Sunflower's direction.

"I think he's dying," said Betsy. "Save Sunflower!"

"I wish somebody were dying, but it's not me," growled the cat. "Everyone hold on while I get us out of here. By 'hold on,' I mean 'hold on.'"

A crimson light snapped to life at the far side of the airlock, illuminating the weightless friends with a dim red glow.

"Wizard" said Philip. "I'd forgotten about the light in your forehead!"

The red beam flashed in Amy's eyes as Sunflower turned his head, then swiveled back to the instructions written in black marker on the wall, one paw hooked inside a divot as he floated in mid-air.

"It says ... 'destroy aliens and die.' There's a number one next to a yellow button. Definitely not pressing that."

"Sorry, old chap, but I daresay you read it wrong," said Philip. "It's a cleaning procedure."

Sunflower touched the button with his paw.

"Nothing," he said, and slapped it again. "Work, you stupid thing!"

A loud thunk vibrated the darkness. A violent tornado of wet air plastered everyone to the walls and covered them with a mist that smelled faintly of bleach and raspberries.

Amy used the sleeve of her prison jumpsuit to wipe of strange chemicals from her face.

"Good gravy! I think it heard you."

"What's a 'toutouni?'" asked Sunflower.

"Not important," said Philip. "Read number two." The teenager whispered into Amy's ear. "I believe we were supposed to remove our clothing before the spray."

"Let's skip that one," said Amy. "Not happening."

"Number two, something about weapons, blah blah blah, nobody has any weapons," said Sunflower. "Where's number three? Okay, I see it."

The orange tabby pushed off the wall and floated across the room, the light in the middle of his forehead gleaming red. He caught another handle with a paw and shone his light on a section of scribbled text.

"Number three: urinate on your clothing, pot-heads."

"Definitely not!" said Amy.

"Good show, Sunflower," said Philip, squinting at the crimson-lit markings. "But a better translation would be: 'wear the new clothing, you pisspot.' Sorry, Amy!"

"Why would you be sorry? You didn't write it."

"Yes, well. One shouldn't use language like that in front of a lady."

"Good thing I'm not a lady, or you'd be in trouble."

"I'm a lady, too!" squealed Nick from somewhere in the darkness. "Don't you dare forget that, Philly-Billy."

Sunflower pressed a square button. A section of wall cracked open and a white glow illuminated a wide locker filled with jackets, trousers, and caps of different sizes, all crimson in color. Many seemed to take on a life of their own and floated out in the weightless environment.

"Cat clothes!" barked Betsy, still spinning through the air. "Ooo, dizzy."

"I'd forgotten about this," said Sunflower. "You remember what I said about cats and dogs never wearing clothes?"

"No," said Amy. "You've only mentioned it about a thousand times."

"Right ... well, this ship must come from a dimension where cats and dogs wear clothes."

"Katmando!" barked Betsy.

"Yeah, yeah, the Land of Dairy Queen and peace and love and all that," said Amy. "What does that have to do with us?"

Philip squinted at the writing scrawled in black marker next to the locker. "I see why Sunflower has got his tail in a kink. The scribbles say we can't enter the ship without a proper uniform."

"This is unbearable," whispered Sunflower.

Amy shrugged. "It's not like you're getting your fur shaved off or anything."

"No, but it's incredibly embarrassing!"

"Having your fur shaved off would definitely be embarrassing," said Philip.

"I mean, wearing clothes!"

"You'll get over it, Sunnie," chirped Nick as she floated near the ceiling, her tiny wings folded and motionless. "I, um ... I'm going to be sick."

Nistra folded his arms. "Very funny, tiny woman. You are sick because your face is small and ugly."

Sunflower looked up. "That's not funny and it doesn't even make sense."

"I'll show you ugly, you overgrown circus freak!" squealed Nick.

The tiny sprite shot down through the air toward the sauro, but the lack of gravity messed with her aim and she rocketed into the weightlessly floating Betsy. To be specific, she rocketed into Betsy's furry white belly. The Jack Russell terrier vomited a stream of bright blue spheres, the majority of which flew down to Nistra and smacked the lizard in the face like tiny turquoise marbles, only ones that smelled like acid and a new hovercar but were actually sticky goo. Nistra, of course, screamed like a baby lizard on his first day at lizard day care.

The remainder of Betsy's lunch that hadn't landed on Nistra floated around the weightless airlock like an exploded bag of alien peas. The inhabitants of the small space naturally shouted, squirmed, and squealed at being hit with even tiny amounts of the stuff.

"Good gravy!"

"Watch out!"

"What's wrong with you, Betsy?!!"

"Ow!"

Efforts to avoid Betsy's floating lunch in the weightless environment only made the situation worse, as the two humans, cat, dog, sprite, and sauro bounced around the chamber slamming into the walls and each other.

"Sunflower!"

Amy caught a handhold on the wall next to the cat, up high near the ceiling.

"The yellow triangle! The decon!"

The orange tabby nodded, his fur matted with blue liquid.

"Right! Toss me down there," he said.

Amy pulled her legs up to her chest to avoid an out-of-control Nistra. She held onto the wall with her left hand and grabbed Sunflower behind the neck with her other.

"Gently now," gasped the cat.

Amy waited as Philip tumbled by, then shoved Sunflower. The orange tabby flew through the weightless chamber and hit the triangular decontamination button with both front paws. A hurricane of mist squashed everyone to the sides of the chamber like bugs on a windshield. After a dozen furious seconds the process ended, leaving an eerie silence in the chamber.

"My word," said Philip.

"Blessed Saint Mittens and his three legs," whispered Sunflower.

Amy groaned. "Yeah ... what they said."

"Sorry," whined Betsy.

Amy looked down at her orange jumpsuit. "Man ... I've still got blue on me, Betsy."

"Sorry, Amy!"

"Hitting the button again," said Sunflower. "Just to be safe."

Amy held up a hand. "No!"

"Wait!" screamed Nistra.

The antiseptic fist of air pressed everyone against the walls once more.

"I say," murmured Philip after the process had ended. "Our reptilian companion looks quite unwell."

The color of Nistra's scales had faded to a light green. His cheeks bulged and tears streamed from his brown eyes.

"That cleaning crap is making him sick, I bet," said Amy.

The lizardman nodded desperately, but held both hands over his jaws and kept them clamped shut.

"I'm still sick," groaned Betsy, tongue lolling as he floated through the room.

Sunflower grinned, his paw still on the button. "One more just for fun?"

"Don't do it, cat," said Amy. "We've got enough problems without adding lizard lunch to the mix."

Nistra shook his head and wagged an index finger at Sunflower.

"Mmm mmm ... urgh blurgh."

"I think that means 'yes' in Sauro," said the orange cat, his paw over the button. "In fact, I'm sure of it."

"Stop it," said Amy. "Get us out of this airlock! After that, you two can fight a duel to the death or throw pudding cups at each other for all I care."

"Fine."

The cat turned to the wall and pushed off in the direction of the locker. He sifted through the pile of uniforms and hurled stretchy red fabric across the airlock.

"Dog ... male human ... other kind of human ... big human for the ugly sauro ... here's mine! Brave, beautiful cat."

Amy held up the red garments that Sunflower had flung at her. The fabric felt stretchy and springy like spandex, but shimmered in the light and had a strange weight to it. A black diamond and the number "42" were embroidered over the left chest.

"This is long underwear," she said. "This ship was created by geniuses from the future and you're telling me they wore long underwear all day?"

Sunflower pushed his furry leg into a pair of small trousers. "Not all day, silly human. They didn't wear it in the shower."

"I need a shower," groaned Betsy, his voice muffled by the uniform top over his head. "And breakfast!"

Amy slapped the wall of the airlock. "Attention everyone––I'm changing. Don't look or I'll kill you."

"Of course," said Philip, one arm out of his jacket. "Allow me to turn around."

"Nobody wants to see your hairless monkey body," said Sunflower. "We'd be blinded for life."

"Urgh blugh," mumbled Nistra, motionless and pale green at the bottom of the chamber.

Amy faced the wall and unzipped her prison jumpsuit. Getting undressed in zero gravity wasn't the

speedy, five-second procedure like on Earth: deliber-
ate, careful movement and a constant grip on the
hand-holds were required to avoid spinning naked
across the room in full view of everyone. Philip's jacket and tie floated past Amy as she pulled the stretchy
top over her head, and then stuck her legs into the
filmy trousers.

"Done!"

"One moment, please," said Philip.

Sunflower's red forehead-light flickered on the
wall. The cat shook his head and sighed. "I should
have gone to art school. Why didn't I listen to my parents?"

"But then you'd be an artist," said Betsy. "I'd never meet you and I'd never be your best friend!"

"Gotta have dreams. Don't forget your head covering, Amy."

A scrap of black fabric floated by her head and
touched the wall.

"I gotta wear a hat? Geez, this is worse than Girl
Scouts."

The thing Sunflower had thrown to Amy was
made from the same heavy, stretchy fabric as the top
and bottom. She twisted her long blonde hair behind
her neck, folded it on top of her head, and pulled the
black material over her forehead and ears, tucking
strands of hair under the edges like a swim cap.

"This is very Buck Rogers," she said. "You couldn't
get more Buck Rogers even if the airlock door opened
and Buck Rogers was standing there with his span-
dex-wearing girlfriend."

She glanced at Philip and burst into giggles.

"You look like a total space-dork!"

"Thank you," said the teenage boy. "I prefer the
term 'space pillock.'"

Sunflower squeezed his furry orange body into a spandex bodysuit and cap, the expression on his face as sour and disgusted as a cat climbing from a tub of water.

Amy giggled and covered her mouth. "I can't be-lieve it——Sunflower's even worse!"

"We shall never speak of this for the rest of our lives," said the cat. "Why don't you help Betsy before the idiot rams into one of us."

The terrier tumbled slowly through the center of the chamber, little legs waving madly and his head stuck inside a pair of red trousers.

Amy moved from hand-hold to hand-hold until she was close to grab the brown-and-white dog. She pulled the trousers from his head and helped him wear the uniform.

"There you go. A proper space explorer."

Betsy licked her cheek. "Thanks!"

"Ewww! Remind me to find you some breath mints as soon as possible."

"Hey, Amy! Find me some breath mints!"

"Not now. In the future."

The little dog blinked at her. "When?"

"Never mind. It was a joke, anyway."

"The joke is this uniform," said Nistra, his scales darkened to a normal deep green. "I refuse to wear it."

"Suit yourself," said Sunflower. "Or, don't 'suit' yourself. Ha ha ha——get it?"

Nistra shook his head. "I do not 'get it' from a cat."

Sunflower pointed at the lizard. "Aw, man! Life of the party, this guy. Am I right? You know I'm right."

He floated over to another section of black writing scribbled on the wall.

"Hey——this is how we open the door."

"What about Nick?" asked Amy.

"Don't worry, I found something her size."

The sprite floated near the open locker, pulling and fidgeting with a short tube dress of stretchy red material.

"This is awful. I want something in pink!"

Sunflower sighed, and pressed a red button above the exit hatch.

Amy covered her ears as a loud mechanical clacking vibrated the chamber and something rotated inside the walls, as if the airlock was the center of a giant clock. Pin-point lights around the exit hatch flashed through a kaleidoscope of colors, at last holding steady on turquoise. The hatch spiraled away and Amy shaded her eyes against the light.

"It's open," said Sunflower. "Go, go, go!"

He floated through the opening, followed by Betsy and the tiny sprite Nick, still pulling down on the skirt of her tiny dress.

Philip stretched out a hand. "Amy?"

"If you say 'ladies first,' I may have to punch you," she said.

Philip smiled. "I would never say such a thing. I know you too well."

He pulled Amy forward, giving her enough momentum to dive in slow-motion toward the glowing turquoise opening, her arms flat to her sides.

She floated into a wide tube illuminated by yellow rings of light. A faint purple discoloration on the curved metal walls changed and refracted as she floated by, like the sheen of gasoline on a puddle of water. A line of rubbery, rectangular plates stretched into the distance along one side of the tube––Amy guessed that would be the walkway and where "down" was if the ship had gravity.

She rubbed her nose and glanced back at Philip. "What's that smell?"

"Raspberry," he said. "Definitely raspberry."

"No ... Philip——your shoes!"

The teenager had traded his wool suit jacket and trousers for the spandex bodysuit, but had slipped his socks and leather shoes back on. As he floated away from the airlock, tendrils of black smoke curled from the footwear.

Sunflower floated nearby. "Fire. Definitely fire."

"I thought my feet were getting toasty," said Philip. "Ouch!"

The teenager ripped off his shoes and socks and tossed them back into the airlock, barely missing Nistra's scaly head. The sauro still wore his old clothes.

"How rude," he snarled.

Amy waved. "Wait! Don't come out!"

Streams of black smoke began to pour from Nistra's lab coat and trousers as he floated from the airlock. The lizard screamed and slapped frantically at the burning garments.

"Help ... someone help," murmured Sunflower as he spun in lazy circles.

Philip was closest to the sauro and coincidentally the tallest of the group. The teenager pushed off from a wall with his knees pulled up to his chest. He floated down to Nistra and kicked the lizard's bottom, sending him back to the airlock in a cloud of fumes. As every action has an equal reaction, Philip rocketed back up the tube. He would have risked brain injury or concussion, if Amy hadn't grabbed his leg.

"Wow. Philip's a hero!" barked Betsy, pumping his legs in a weightless doggie paddle.

"Yes," said Sunflower. "Thank you for saving the horrible, disgusting creature who wants to strangle us in our sleep."

"How did you catch my leg?" Philip asked Amy. "You're not holding onto anything."

"I stuck my feet to these rubbery pads on the side of the tube. Feels like glue after a second, but I can pull away with no problem."

Philip touched the gray material. "How peculiar. The substance feels almost like skin."

Sunflower yawned. "Woo-hoo, the ship is alive. It's so exciting that I'm about to fall asleep with my eyes open."

"You said that operators like you and Betsy don't have to sleep," said Amy. "And not to correct you or anything, but I don't think anyone said anything about the ship being alive."

"The Lady did," said Betsy. "She's the smartest in the universe!"

"Was the smartest," said Philip. "God rest her soul."

Sunflower shrugged. "Don't think she had one."

"We don't know that she's actually dead," said Amy.

"Mostly dead," squeaked the tiny sprite Nick. "After the power loss and decompression, her body is mostly in space, with a little bit here and a little bit there."

Sunflower switched his furry tail back and forth and stared at the group. "We don't know anything about anything right now. Where we are in relation to the galactic core, what dimension, or whether there's a Sauro battle fleet about to blow us into a million-billion pieces and then blow each one of those pieces into a million-billion pieces. All we know is that we're floating in a corridor and wearing stupid uniforms!"

"I know I'm hungry," said Betsy. "Does that help?"

"Calm down, Sunflower," said Amy. "The Lady was trying to help us, not send us to our deaths."

Nistra floated out of the airlock, this time in a stretchy crimson uniform and black skull-cap.

"As long as it is honorable, death is nothing to fear," said the lizard.

"Does that include burning alive?" asked Sunflower.

Nistra held up a scaly green claw. He opened and closed his jaws for a moment, searching for something to say. "I ... um, no it doesn't."

Amy pushed off with her legs and floated up the long tube to a junction with another corridor. Strange words were scrawled in black marker with arrows and a rectangular map. To Amy's left the corridor continued for a good distance, the circular rings of light fading into darkness. To her right the corridor continued to another junction.

Philip floated up and stopped by pushing against the iridescent wall. "A crude outline of the ship, I suppose," said the dark-haired teen. "Some of these scribblings I don't understand. To the right is the forward area of the ship, or 'anavan,' which includes 'Zon Domi' and 'Zon Manje.'"

"What are those?"

"'Domi' is sleeping and 'manje' is eating," said Sunflower.

Something thudded into Amy's back. She felt Betsy's paws on her shoulder.

"Let's go there!" he barked.

Philip pointed to the left. "This way lies 'Pouvwa,' 'Mote,' and 'Navigasyon.'"

"I'm guessing one of those is 'Navigation.'"

"Spot on. The others are 'Power' and 'Engines.'"

Amy shrugged. "It's not that hard. Pretty close to real French."

"Close only counts when you're talking about plasma grenades," said Sunflower. "Cat French is a dead language with grammar that's as clear as something from Betsy's rear end."

Amy planted her bare feet on the wall and twisted around to look at her companions floating in the center of the junction.

"Here's the plan––Philip and Sunflower will go with me down the long corridor. We'll try to get the power and the gravity back online."

"If that's even possible," sniffed Sunflower.

"Betsy will go with Nick and Nistra––"

"Officer First Class Nistra!"

Amy stared at the sauro. "Betsy will go with Nick and Nistra to the right. The Lady was supposed to have stocked this ship with food and water. It would be nice to check on those supplies, or at least figure out how long before we have to drink our own pee."

"Awesome!" barked Betsy, his legs churning in the zero gravity.

"This is unbearable," said Nistra. "I'm not taking orders from a dog!"

Amy crossed her arms. "Betsy is a highly-trained, trans-dimensional operative with implants dedicated to communication, combat, and information, and has titanium-strengthened bones. He can pilot an attack bomber, doesn't have to sleep, and can remember every single thing you've ever said to him. The Lady picked him from millions of candidates to work for her, and you think he's not qualified to float in front of you down a dark corridor? Think about the fact that he doesn't have to sleep before you say another word."

The sauro gulped and smiled thinly, his sharp teeth barely visible.

"Well ... as long as we're, um, going the same direction, I, uh, will probably do what he says. Definitely! Not probably."

"Skippy-dippy, green guy!" said Betsy. "Grab my butt and push. I'm starving."

Nistra shoved the terrier through the corridor, and the tiny sprite Nick buzzed after the pair. All three turned left at the junction.

"The other way!" yelled Philip. "To the right!"

A few seconds later, the trio floated past the junction.

"He only got picked by the Lady because of his dad," said Sunflower. "You know that, right?"

"I was trying to scare Nistra," said Amy. "And keep him out of trouble. I just hope they don't eat everything in sight, because I could literally inhale a granola bar right now."

"I think they'll open an airlock and get sucked into space," murmured Sunflower. "But that's life, or as we say in Cat French——'se lavi.'"

"You never say that."

"What's a granola?" Philip asked.

"It's basically oatmeal."

Philip frowned. "Horrid stuff."

Amy punched him lightly on the arm. "Don't knock it till you've tried it."

"I'm sorry——what does that mean?"

"Don't be scared of trying something new."

"I've definitely tried oatmeal. It's a substance of which I've had quite enough for several lifetimes, thank you very much."

Amy let go of the wall, staring at Philip as she slowly spun upside down in the weightless environment.

"Something wrong, Phil? You keep pulling at your pants."

"Trousers!"

"Right."

Philip turned red. "My apologies. It's simply that these garments are so awfully tight. I feel like an elephant squeezed into a sausage skin."

"I'm used to it. My foster mom always made me dress in a leotard and tights and work out with her. I guess you don't have Richard Simmons and 'Sweatin' To The Oldies' in jolly old England."

"Since I've never heard of those two things, you're probably right."

Sunflower shouted from a distance, his voice echoing on the corridor walls.

"Are you two lovebirds done making kissy faces or should I call the love police?"

"I'm going to kill that cat," growled Amy.

She rotated to face the wall, crouched, and rocketed down the corridor toward the orange tabby, arms straight at her sides.

"Call an ambulance," she yelled. "And a hearse—you'll need both!"

Sunflower floated above a black hatch circled in tiny red lights, mouth open and yellow eyes wide as he watched Amy somersault and land with a thud on the sticky black surface.

"That was good," he said. "Are you sure you haven't been in space before?"

"I took gymnastics for six years."

"In space?"

"Of course not!"

"Also, what's an ambulance?"

A strand of blonde hair floated past her face and Amy stuffed it inside her cap.

"An ambulance takes cats to the hospital who talk too much and get beaten to death by angry girls."

Sunflower nodded. "A meat wagon."

Philip stopped clumsily next to the cat, bumping his side and leg against the black hatch.

"A hearse transports the dead to their final resting place," said the teenager.

Sunflower shrugged. "Still a meat wagon."

The cat touched the center of the hatch. The red lights changed to blue, and the five-foot black circle spiraled open to reveal another section of gray corridor lined with glowing rings and scribbled handwriting in black marker.

Sunflower floated through. Amy grabbed the edge of the door and pulled herself after the cat.

"This is a very strange vessel," said Philip, from behind. "I've seen absolutely no writing or placards of any kind."

"Scribbles in Cat French," said Amy. "There, there, and there."

"I mean the original signs. The writing from Katmando."

"Who knows?" said Sunflower. "Maybe college kids pulled them off the walls for souvenirs."

The two humans and orange tabby glided through the darkened corridors of the ship, passing through multiple hatches and turning and backtracking, always following the direction of scrawled arrows to "Chanm Pouvwa."

Sunflower pointed at a dark gray hatch as he floated by.

"There's the toilet, if anyone needs to go."

Philip squinted at the writing. "'Chanm Vwayaj Dimansyon? It's the transmat room, not a toilet."

"Right," said Sunflower. "I, uh, read it wrong."

"That's how I can get back to Earth," said Amy. "The transmat room!"

Sunflower floated past the hatch. "Not without power, you won't."

Amy grabbed the sticky wall and stopped. "Wait! What's that sound?"

The other two grabbed onto the surface of the walls and froze. A sound like a faint sigh rolled through the corridor, and a breeze stirred the hair on the back of Amy's neck.

"Not to shock your tiny monkey brains or anything," said Sunflower. "But it's the ventilation system."

"Sounds like breathing," said Amy.

Sunflower rolled his eyes. "That's what ventilation is!"

"But it sounds real, like the ship is alive."

Philip nodded. "The Lady did mention something along that line."

"Superstition and old cat's tales," said Sunflower, laughing nervously. "What does alive even mean?"

Amy poked Sunflower's furry chest. "Not dead?"

"Ha ha. You monkeys are smarter than you look."

The small group continued further into the ship, and Amy was more acutely aware of faint wheezes and sighs from the "ventilation."

Philip pointed to another corridor as they passed. "That one says 'Navigasyon.' Could we find out where we are?"

"Power first," said Sunflower. "Nothing works without it."

The ventilation sounds grew slightly louder as they followed twisting corridors deeper into the ship and further aft.

"Can we stop for a second? I'm feeling dizzy," said Amy.

Philip held her shoulder. "What's wrong?"

"I don't know ... I just ..."

Amy touched the curved wall of the corridor to steady herself and felt a tiny electric shock.

"Ow!"

Her hand left a gleaming mark on the wall that quickly grew into an irregular splotch of white, like an overturned can of paint. The bright stain grew a meter wide and then shrank into tiny ovals, disappearing as quickly as it had come.

Amy stared at her hand. "That was weird."

"It doesn't change for me," said Philip, pushing against the wall.

Amy touched the bottom of her bare foot to the gray material. She yelped at the same electric shock, and watched the wall around her foot gleam with light.

Sunflower floated up to them. "Are you two playing around again?"

"Look," said Amy.

"Whoopee," said the cat. "Let's hope that's a good thing, and not an allergy. Could be nasty."

"How could I be allergic to the walls?"

"Turn that question around and you might be getting somewhere. Next you'll be asking why the air smells like raspberries."

Amy shrugged. "Space perfume for space girls?"

"Space girls? More like, space monkeys. I'm no expert on this old museum piece, but I think it's a chemical applied to the walls or the air to keep the ship from rejecting us."

"Poppycock!" said Philip. "A ship that's alive is one thing; a dyspeptic one is another."

Sunflower blinked at the teenager. "Tell me about poppycock the next time you find yourself in an air-lock full of flashing red lights and alarm bells and all you have in your hot little hands is half a bottle of raspberry lotion."

"Did that happen to you?"

"Absolutely not."

"Turn that frown upside down," said Amy. "There aren't any airlocks around here."

She followed the cat as he glided into a spacious junction of two corridors, lit by dim radial lights. Next to a silver, rectangular door was an arrow and the handwritten phrase "Chanm Pouvwa."

Sunflower swiped his furry paw across the door, and it whooshed up and away.

"Welcome to the power room," he said.

A light flickered, illuminating a closet with a metal toilet, a tiny sink with a spray nozzle, and a patch of neon-green artificial grass.

Amy stuck her head inside. "Does the ship run on poop? Wait—I don't want to know."

"It's a WC," said Philip. "A lavatory. But why the grass? Who would need that to … um, complete their business?"

Sunflower pushed them back and closed the door. "Nothing to see here! Don't ask questions about things you shouldn't be asking questions about."

The cat pushed off the wall and floated down the corridor to a large silver hatch.

"THIS is the power room."

"Pouvwa" had been scrawled in large block letters in several places on the wall around the hatch, with many black arrows pointing directly at it.

"Probably right this time," said Amy.

"Someone could cause a first-rate cock-up around here with a rag and a bit of turpentine," said Philip.

Amy nodded. "Yeah, Sunflower——why didn't the Lady put up real signs?"

"You know how it is," said the cat. "Nobody wants to do chores after a day of robbing dimensions and rocketing across the galaxy."

The door of the Power Room spiraled away to reveal a black, empty space.

"What is this——a bigger toilet?" asked Amy.

Sunflower floated inside. "Don't be ridiculous."

As the cat passed the threshold, the room throbbed to life. Bubbles in shades of green from neon to aquamarine formed on the glossy black floor and floated toward the ceiling, where they met an identical layer of bubbles floating down.

Amy watched Sunflower glide untouched through the green swarm.

"Wait!"

A sphere the color of Japanese green tea spun next to Amy's face. She slapped it away without thinking, but her fingers passed through the bubble.

She stared at Philip. "Did you see that?"

"Pardon?"

"The bubble that almost smacked me in the face!"

Philip raised an eyebrow. "I'm afraid I don't see anything, Amy. Apart from Sunflower's headlight, the room is completely dark."

"I'm either losing it or about to be covered in green bubble goop. With my luck they're totally radioactive, and that's going to do wonders for my hair."

Philip shook his head. "I'm sorry––goop? Radio–what?"

Amy sighed and pulled on her stretchy space top. "Never mind. It was a joke."

Sunflower had glided to the center of the room and floated above a seamless dome made of the same glossy black material as the floor, ceiling, and walls. Surrounded by glowing bubbles, the cat hovered above the dome tapping and swiping at the surface. As Amy floated closer, she saw glowing lines of text below his paws.

Sunflower glanced up at her. "The system recognizes me, and I don't see any critical problems. I'll try to wake the ship out of sleep mode."

"What's with all the bubbles?"

Sunflower slapped his paw at the squiggly mess of text like a pesky fly.

"Bubbles ... if you need to use the toilet, we passed one in the hallway. Shove your rear on the hole and go. It's easy to use, even for a monkey."

"The green bubbles floating everywhere! Don't you see them? It's like that scene from Willy Wonka, only with radioactive snot!"

Sunflower blinked for a moment, and then looked up at Amy. "Strange––it usually takes an hour to go space-crazy. Have you been punching buttons when I haven't been looking? Did you switch on the T.H.E.?"

"The what?" asked Amy. "Bubbles are coming from the walls, and you're asking me if I did something?"

Sunflower glanced around the room. "It's not working for me. Oh, well. Maybe the system gets confused if you have more brain cells than a poona."

"You said it was called 'thee'?"

"Not 'thee'––T.H.E.," said the cat. "Tee Aitch Eee, Total Happiness Environment. That's what one of Betsy's friends said it was called. The ship reads your mind and projects what you want to see in every room. Saves a lot of money in decorating. Spend enough time in space and you'll realize how important that is. Goes back to that 'space-crazy' thing I was talking about."

"How perfectly wizard!" said Philip. "That must be the reason the walls are so drab and gray around the ship."

"The ship can read my mind?" asked Amy. "Why would I think the power room of a spaceship would look like a toddler's birthday party?"

"Silly, isn't it?" said the cat. "But that's what your monkey subconscious thinks a power room should look like." He squinted at Amy and spoke slowly. "Do you know big words like 'sub-con-scious?'"

Amy ground her teeth. "Of course. Do you want to see a cat fly out an airlock?"

"No."

Amy floated above the orange cat and watched him scroll through glowing lines of data. She closed her eyes and began to daydream, her thoughts turning to home, to her foster mother, to the time they visited the fair last summer. She opened her eyes and yelped.

Philip floated over to her. "What's wrong?"

Amy pointed at the walls. "Everything's pink! We're floating inside a giant tub of cotton candy! It's flying everywhere." She covered her face and tumbled through the weightless environment. "It's in my hair!"

Philip grabbed a fistful of red fabric at her waist. "Don't worry, Amy. I've got you."

Sunflower used a back leg to scratch under his cap, and watched the pair of teenagers bump into the ceiling and slowly drift down.

"The ship won't respond," he said. "I can't bring any of the systems up to full power."

Amy peeked out from between fingers covered in pink floss. "The Lady said she fixed it!"

"I know. I was there too, remember? We're still alive. While that seems less like a good thing and more like a fresh version of Hell the longer I spend with you monkeys, the fact that the Sauro fleet hasn't blown us to bits means the new power sphere worked, at least for a short jump. One little fly in the fish tea, though——this ship hasn't been used for at least thirty years, probably longer. Enjoy that sweet taste of oxygen in the air, because it's not going to last forever. Understand what I'm saying? If this ship doesn't wake up, we're all going to the big litter box in the sky."

"Maybe she just hit the snooze button," said Amy. "Does a living ship have an alarm clock?"

"An interesting point. Honestly, I have no idea what you just said because I've stopped listening and I'm looking for the escape pod in the ship's diagram."

"Let Amy try something," said Philip. "She and the vessel seem to have a connection."

Sunflower shrugged. "Fine. Dance around the room and wiggle your hips for all I care."

In Amy's mind the black control panel had changed into a ice-covered silver dome in a whirling tornado of pink sugar. As Amy stretched out her hands and touched the cold surface, a voice spoke in her head——an older woman's voice with the deep tenor of warm milk and a pain that felt the same as biting into aluminum foil, only between Amy's eyes.

Sa ou vle?

Amy rubbed the bridge of her nose. "What's that sound? Who's there?"

"I don't hear anything," said Philip.

"The ship is talking to her, or she's space-crazy," said Sunflower.

Mwen domi. Ou ale.

"I don't speak Cat French," said Amy. "I don't know what you're saying."

I'm tired. What do you want?

"I'd like a cheeseburger and a strawberry milkshake, but if that's too hard, then I guess you could take me back to the dimension where my friends and family live and I could buy a cheeseburger and a strawberry milkshake there. I'm Amy Armstrong from Planet Earth, year 1995, et cetera, et cetera."

Sunflower sighed. "Lots of golf courses on Earth in 1995. Now ... not so much."

A burst of static sounded behind Amy's eyes, as if the voice had inhaled sharply.

Amelia Earhart Armstrong? How did you find me?

"I didn't find anything. The Lady gave this ship to me––gave you, I guess––after we came back from London. The Lady broke me out of prison for stealing the Sauro home planet––which I didn't do, actually–– but before the Sauro fleet attacked her asteroid."

I see. The future has created the past; the young has found the old. It is the way of things.

Amy glanced at Philip and Sunflower's confused faces. "Excuse me, um .. Miss computer voice in my head? Please speak aloud so that my friends can hear you, and I don't have this weird headache."

"Of course."

The entire room vibrated with the deep bass of the ship's voice, forcing the teenagers and Sunflower to cover their ears.

"Too loud!"

"Sorry," whispered the ship. "I haven't spoken to anyone since the last one took my heart away. I took a nap for a few days."

"A few days?" said Sunflower. "It's been decades since the Lady docked the *White Star* and built her asteroid base!"

"Day, years," murmured the ship. "When the galactic wind has warmed your skin for a thousand years, every photon is the same as another."

"I should write that down," said Sunflower. "Too bad I don't have pockets. Or a notebook. Or a pen. Now I don't even remember what you said."

"Forget the galactic life lessons and sarcastic cats," said Amy, floating above the control panel. "We have to find a way back to Earth."

The ship yawned. "Can't I take another nap? The one you let me have was so nice."

Amy's illusion of pink cotton candy darkened, and she found herself floating above the same black dome as Sunflower and Philip.

"I'm sorry," she said. "If there's even a tiny chance of getting back to Earth, I have to try. My family ... my foster mother was really sick. After that, you can take all the naps you want."

"As you wish, my Lady," said the ship. "Your word is my command."

Amy stared at Sunflower. "What did she call me?"

"A lady, I think," said the cat, gliding by with his paws outstretched. "But you're more of an undeveloped girl. Or a boy. Are you a larva? I don't know the words for human things."

"You'll know them when I beat them into your skull!"

"Always trying to solve problems with violence. No wonder you monkeys destroyed Earth."

"Amy is a lady and there's no question about that," said Philip. "That ugly space uniform does her no credit, and I hope we can soon find proper clothing."

Amy pulled at her stretchy red outfit. "Thank you, Philip. Always a gentleman."

A quiet snoring vibrated the walls.

"Here we go again," said Sunflower. "Sleeping like a fish."

Amy snapped her fingers. "Hey! Miss ... spaceship or whatever. Wake up!"

"Sorry," said the matronly voice, and yawned. "I thought I could have a tiny cat nap."

"Is that a joke?" asked Sunflower. "Am I being made fun of by a spaceship?"

"I think we should ask the ship to turn on the gravity," said Philip. "Floating around like a guppy in a fishbowl was fun for a little while, but by Jove I think it's turning my stomach."

"Great idea," said Amy. "Gravity please, Miss ship!"

"Request received," said the warm voice. "Power matrix on-line. Activating main engines; increasing thrust to one-quarter. Rotational impellers engaged."

Sunflower's eyes widened. "No, wait––"

The cat fell through the air and bounced off the black control dome, while Amy and Philip smacked onto the glossy floor beside him.

"––a minute," groaned Sunflower.

Amy sat up, rubbing her elbows and knees. "Ouch and double ouch."

"Sorry," whispered the ship. "It has been a few days since I had a crew."

Amy helped Philip to his feet. "No problem. What should we call you, anyway? 'Ship' just seems weird."

"I will respond to any name you choose, my Lady."

"Please stop calling me that."

"What honorific would you prefer?"

"Amy. Just call me Amy."

Philip spread his hands. "The question is, what should we call you?"

"I have no opinion in this matter. In the thousand years of my life I have been called Ship, White Star, Lionheart, Indomitable, The Beast, Bright Arrow, Avenger, El Diablo, Momma Boom Boom, Enterprise II, Chick Magnet, Etwal Blan——"

Sunflower groaned. "This could take a while."

"To recite the entire list would require twenty-three minutes and twelve seconds," said the ship.

Philip held up a finger. "What was the last one—— Etwal Blan? That means 'White Star' in Cat French."

"What you call 'Cat French' is the original language of my home, Katmando," said the ship quietly. "'Etwal Blan' is the name given to me by my parents."

"It sounds like 'Blanche,'" said Amy. "Let's call her Blanche!"

"Or ... you could just not call me anything," said the ship.

Amy pumped the air with her fist. "Blanche—— take us to Earth!"

2

Amy, Philip and Sunflower retraced their steps through the corridors of the ship, this time with gravity working and their feet firmly on the rubber walkway.

"I hope Betsy and Nick are doing okay," said Amy.

Philip nodded. "I know what you're thinking. Why don't we ask the ship?"

"Blanche, we have some friends wandering around inside you. Have they murdered each other yet?"

"Negative," said the ship calmly. "Is the elimination of their life signs your intention?"

"No! I mean ... no. What's their status?"

"Two organisms in the cafeteria are communicating at a high level of volume, apparently over the ownership of a marshmallow. One is a canine with bio-engineered implants, the other is an artificial, feline-created organism which according to my database is called a sprite. There is a ninety percent chance these are biological pests and not the friends you mentioned. Would you like me to vent the biological pests into space?"

"No!"

"It's quite easy, the venting. Cleanup is not an issue."

"Please. Don't. Kill them."

"Very well. Should I add these organisms to the official crew roster?"

"Yes! That one. Do that."

"A third bipedal is wandering through Corridor Five-B. This organism is also not in my database, but the outward appearance is a mutated humanoid variation of *Varanus komodoensis*. I suspect it may have been created as a horrifying circus attraction to sell tickets. Would you like me to vent this bipedal into space?"

"Tempting, but no. Add him to the crew roster."

"Are you certain? It looks quite nasty. I can smell something foul in the ventilation, even though it wears a prophylactic uniform."

"I'm sure. His name is Nistra and he's part of the group."

"As you wish."

Sunflower shook his head as he trotted beside Amy. "You're going to regret not venting him into space. That was your chance!"

Amy shrugged. "No matter how violent or disgusting and no matter how many problems they cause, everyone has a place in the universe."

"I was talking about Betsy!"

Amy grinned. "So was I." She froze in the middle of the corridor.

Philip walked a few paces and stopped. "What's wrong?"

Amy pointed at the walls. "We're in a redwood forest! I can smell the trees and hear birds. Don't you see the mountain jay? It's just flew down the corridor!"

"Of course it did," said Sunflower. "T.H.E. is back online. Right now, I'm walking along the Gold Coast. For you monkeys, that's the greatest beach on Tau Ceti and the most beautiful spot in the galaxy."

"Everything's changed to the green Yorkshire countryside for me," said Philip. "Apart from the metal deck below our feet, of course."

"Hatches and doorways always show up in T.H.E.," said Sunflower. "You can see corridor walls and the hand-scribbled directions if you stare long enough. Take my advice——don't stare."

Amy squinted at the clear blue sky between a pair of giant redwoods. The faint smear of a large arrow and the black scribble of "Navigasyon" floated in mid-air.

She shook her head. "This is freaking me out."

"No wonder," said Sunflower. "T.H.E. pulls from your own mind to create sights and sounds. Mittens knows what horrors are inside a monkey brain. A floor covered with mashed peaches or something equally awful."

"Can't we give it a new name? T.H.E. is too confusing."

"That is the new name," said the ship's voice. "The previous nomenclature was also deemed unsatisfactory."

"What was the old name?"

"Memory Environment."

"Ah. Yeah, I get it."

Amy and her two companions followed the path of rubbery black material through the forest. After several turns they stopped at a wide silver disc floating on-edge, quite a contrast among the trees and the rust-colored needles. Sunflower touched the metal disc with his paw, below the handwritten phrase "Chanm Navigasyon," and it whisked away to reveal a dark, circular doorway.

Amy followed the cat to the edge and froze, her hands gripping the sides of the opening with the white knuckled-fear of a perfectly normal person who doesn't want to jump out of a perfectly normal spaceship.

Below her feet, above her head, and everywhere around her spread the infinite emptiness of deep space, as if she stood in the open hatch of an airlock. Tiny stars glistened against the vacuum, like a sneeze of powdered sugar in a universe of black anthracite. In the center of everything floated a circular whirl of stars——a three-dimensional map of the Milky Way galaxy——and a low metal cylinder. A handful of cushioned seats floated in mid-air around the axis of the cylinder. Sunflower sat in one of the seats, tapping his paws on top of the cylinder and staring at a square holographic display that flickered above the surface.

"Give me an hour or so and I'll calculate our position," he said.

Philip stood beside Amy, staring at the scene with the same wide-eyed shock as her.

"My word," he whispered.

Sunflower glanced at the bewildered teens. "What's wrong? You're looking at the outside of the ship projected onto the surfaces of the room. It's a holo-screen system like in the corridors, just not as complicated. I'm beginning to think you crazy monkeys haven't even been to the movies. Stop staring and get over here."

Philip offered his arm, but Amy shook her head. She took a tentative step into empty space and her bare foot touched an cold, smooth, and invisible surface. She walked carefully over to Sunflower and the galactic map.

"One foot after another," murmured Sunflower as he stared at the holographic display. "Just like falling out of a tree, right?"

Amy crossed her arms. "One more monkey joke and I'm dumping a litter box over your head."

"Okay, okay! Don't get nasty."

Philip joined them at the table. "I suppose this is why the ship doesn't have windows. Absolutely no need, with projection machinery such as this."

Sunflower nodded slowly. "Mmm hmm. Like I said, I'm busy figuring out where we are in the galaxy."

"Why not ask the ship?"

The cat stared at Amy. "Seriously? Who asks for directions these days?"

"I guess male stubbornness happens in all species," said Amy. "Blanche, where are we?"

"Inside the navigation room, my lady," the ship said smoothly. "Twelve meters along the x axis from centerpoint, two meters along the y axis from——"

"I mean, in the galaxy."

"Which galaxy, my Lady?"

Sunflower snorted and tapped his paws on the flat top of the cylinder, causing a hurricane of white numbers to spiral out.

"You don't even know what questions to ask," he said. "How many galaxies do you think there are?"

Amy spread her hands and looked at Philip. "One?"

The teen shrugged. "Two or three?"

Sunflower pealed with laughter and fell backwards out of his chair. The cat held his ribs and rocked back and forth on the invisible floor, laughing uncontrollably.

"Two ... or ... three," he gasped.

Amy sighed. "Blanche——how many galaxies in the universe?"

"The current number of observable galaxies is two-hundred billion," said the ship. "Give or take two or three."

"Hilarious."

"Thank you, my lady."

Sunflower wiped tears from his eyes and climbed back into his chair. "This little discussion has been pointless, anyway. No cat or dog has ever left the Milky Way even with a ship from Katmando, so we might as well say there's only one galaxy. Ship, what is your maximum speed?"

"Three point five parsecs per hour," murmured the female voice. "This velocity is not recommended for more than one ESD, or Earth Standard Day, and may cause damage to systems. Normal cruising speed is two point one parsecs per hour."

"Holy Saint Mittens," whispered Sunflower. "No wonder the sauros could never catch the Lady! Do you know how fast that is?"

"I have a feeling you're going to tell me," said Amy.

"One parsec is thirty-one trillion kilometers. This ship can cruise at sixty-three trillion per hour! She can travel from Kepler to Tau Ceti in four days, a trip that takes a normal passenger liner an entire month!"

"If there's no traffic," said the ship. "And assuming we don't hit anything on the way."

"We're a thousand parsecs from Kepler 22 now," said Sunflower, tapping on his console. "From the readings, the Lady actually did what she said––we're in another dimension."

Amy hopped a little and clapped. "Great! Is it mine? Can we fly back to Earth?"

"That would be pointless. The SBD signal is weak, and the distance from the galactic center too far, meaning the year is around 1139."

"The medieval ages?" asked Philip. "Swords and castles and princesses?"

"More like the swords and plague and toothless crones," said Amy.

"1139 in standard galactic time," said the cat. "Only a few years after we left the Lady. What's that in Old Earth years? I don't remember the calculation. Ship, what's 1139 in Old Earth?"

"3322 Common Era," said the ship.

Amy sighed. "Okay, but what's SBD?"

"SpaceBook Decay."

"Sorry?"

"I thought I explained that already," said the cat. "I hate repeating myself even more than I hate explaining things. Haven't you heard about SpaceBook already?"

Philip glanced at Amy. "I don't recall anything specific in my readings. Is it a book about space? An encyclopedia?"

"Absolutely not. It couldn't be less like those two things if it tried."

"Please try to explain it," said Amy. "How does it decay?"

Sunflower sighed and turned to face the teenagers. "SpaceBook is a series of one million communication satellites spread throughout the arm of the Milky Way galaxy where Tau Ceti and Earth are located. We can use the date code from the repeated signals to determine the age of the galaxy. That's how I know this is not your dimension––the stations are farther apart and the galaxy slightly older."

"What if we travel to a dimension without Space-Book?"

Sunflower shook his head and turned back to the display. "There is never, ever a dimension without SpaceBook. Ask me about it again sometime. It's only the greatest crime ever committed against the universe."

"Don't be so dramatic! In the entire universe? You said there were 170 gajillion or whatever galaxies."

"It's a long story and I'm not sure you monkeys would understand."

Philip walked around the floating map of the galaxy, his arms crossed.

"Speaking as one of those 'monkeys,' now that our vessel has become operational––so to speak–– perhaps we should look into finding Amy's version of Earth."

"That's exactly what the Lady tried to explain before we left," hissed Sunflower. "Returning to the same dimension is like searching for a single strand of hair at a wig convention."

"Do cats wear wigs?" asked Amy. "How do you even know what that is?"

Philip leaned on the console. "However remote the chance, that strand of hair still exists."

Sunflower slammed a paw on the console and shrieked in anger. Silver, mechanical fingers sprouted from the "manos" bracelets around his wrists and the orange tabby furiously began typing on a glowing keyboard that appeared.

"I see," murmured Philip. "Perhaps we'll save that discussion for later."

Amy wagged a finger. "Sunflower! That's a bit rude even for you."

"I'm sorry. It's just that you were asking about a transmat to another dimension, and I pulled up the drive statistics. It's completely burned out––that's why I lost my temper."

"Maybe it's offline because the ship was asleep. Blanche, is anything wrong with your dimensional travel ... stuff?"

"Transmat," hissed Sunflower.

"Chamber integrity nominal," said the warm voice of the ship. "Drive links nominal. Demat and remat signal location fields nominal."

Amy whispered to Philip. "Is 'nominal' good or bad?"

The teenager shrugged. "Good, I think."

"Main drive offline," said the ship. "Recombinator offline."

"Ooo, that's bad," said Sunflower. "Bad, bad, bad. Ship––what's the physical status of the recombinator?"

"Recombinator is currently an irregular mass of carbon, plutonium, lithium––"

Sunflower groaned. "That's enough! Bad. Sooo very bad."

"What's a recombina ... doozie-thing?"

"It's in the name," said the cat. "It's part of the equipment that puts your monkey bodies back together in the transmat chamber when we return. If you're done with living and this plane of existence and everything, you should try to remat without a recombinator."

"Do not try it," said the ship.

"Can we fix the thing?" asked Amy. "Pull into the nearest galactic service station? Call triple-A?"

Sunflower blinked at her. "That's like asking a poona to change the oil in your hovercraft. The *White Star* is from Katmando, a dimension more advanced than anything you can imagine. Even if we had anything like a 'galactic service station,' whatever stupid dog mechanic was working there would break more than he could fix."

"Betsy's not here, so don't make fun of him. That's a rule."

"Perhaps we have a spare?" asked Philip. "In case this one breaks, as it has done?"

"A replacement for the recombinator is not present in my storage," said the ship. "However, if the analogue for a Cynthia MacGuffin can be located in this dimension, another recombinator has the possibility of being constructed."

"My head hurts," said Amy. "What's a Cynthia MacGuffin?"

"A traitor," growled Sunflower. "A cat who pretended to work for the Lady, but was just a spy. He stole a shuttlecraft and made it to Tau Ceti before I caught up to him, a hundred miles over the Painted Sea. I shot a missile into his main engine and the shuttle started to burn as it fell toward the water ..." He stroked the whiskers on the right side of his face slowly, his voice quiet. "Bright and orange, like a velvet sundown."

"Sunflower! Snap out of it!"

"Sorry. Luckily, the traitor only managed to grab a ... wait, that's it!"

"A recombinator," said the ship.

Amy leaned on the console next to the cat. "You just said that he's dead. How does that help?"

"We've traveled to another dimension," said Philip. "Perhaps this MacGuffin escaped with the plans. Perhaps Sunflower never existed to stop him. Perhaps another cat stole the plans."

"Maybe in this dimension, cats never left Earth," said Amy. "And humans are the true masters of the universe."

Sunflower bowed his head over the keyboard, his entire body shaking with silent laughter.

"Masters ... of the ... universe," he whispered, and wiped tears from his eyes. "That's a good one. I'll have to remember that."

The cat sighed and resumed typing with the thin metal fingers of the manos.

"Back to this MacGuffin," he said. "He's a litter box full of 'perhaps' and 'maybes,' but what choice do we have? It's going to take a couple of days in travel time to reach Tau Ceti, and I'll look into repairing the recombinator. Amy––since you're in charge, but mainly because the ship seems to like you, give the order to take us to Tau Ceti."

Amy pointed at the orange tabby. "Take us to Tau Ceti. That's an order!"

"Not to me. To the ship!"

"Oh." Amy cleared her throat. She didn't know what to do, exactly, so she spread her legs and put her hands on her waist like a pirate captain.

"Blanche, plot a course to Tau Ceti," she said sternly. "Maximum warp."

"Course entered and calculated," said the ship. "Estimated time of arrival: fifty-two hours, twelve minutes. One question, my lady: what is a 'maximum warp?'"

Sunflower giggled. "Just say 'cruising speed!'"

"Take us to Tau Ceti, Blanche," said Amy. "Cruising speed." She raised her right hand, then dropped it. "Engage."

"Apologies, my lady. I accelerated to cruising velocity seven point three seconds ago."

"Sure. I, uh ... That's fine, too."

***

SPRAWLED FACE-DOWN on the metal deck of the corridor, Nistra groaned.

The giant lizard climbed to his hands and knees and slowly stood to his full height of over two meters. He wiped a trickle of blood from the end of his scaly green snout.

"What kind of ship is this?" he hissed. "No warning for gravity activation. No announcement or alarm. Not even a beep."

The sauro muttered to himself as he walked on his clawed feet through the corridors, constantly pulling at his tight red uniform.

"Raspberries," he growled. "Nothing smells worse than raspberries. Not even cat ships are this disgusting."

He opened door after door in the living quarters, stuck his massive head into cabinets, and flung open lockers.

"Where are all the weapons?" he hissed. "The plasma rifles? Gun swords? Flail rods? If this was a sauro craft, you couldn't walk ten meters without finding six different ways to kill a cat. There's not even a plastic knife!"

Nistra stopped in the middle of the corridor and glanced left and right at a pair of circular hatches.

"One of these stinking doors must lead to the armory. Even better, a toilet. Those kebabs I had for lunch at the prison ... ugh. I'll have the cook shipped to the outer colonies."

The lizard chose a silver hatch with "Prive" scrawled across the metal in black marker, and pressed a clawed hand to the center. The hatch spiraled away. Nistra coughed and covered his snout at the heavy smell of dust. The room was dark, but he could see the faint outline of shelves.

As the sauro tramped inside with his heavy, clawed feet, the floor panels snapped to life and cast a white glow throughout the room. A wide collection of objects sat on shelves behind protective glass: a pair of gold rings, a necklace with a heart pendant, a plastic bottle with a faded label, a paper book with a torn cover. A yellowed square of paper covered in scribble had been placed in front of each object.

"What a worthless collection of junk," spat Nistra. "A museum for garbage! Who saves a brown skirt and a tiny crowbar? Who keeps old food containers?"

The lizard spotted a small black revolver on a lower shelf.

"Thank the egg––a projectile weapon! Against my thick hide it would be as useful as throwing a rock, but against cats and Centaurans ..."

He scraped his sharp claws across the clear protective barrier, but failed to scratch the surface or pry open the shelf. The sauro punched the glass and jumped away holding his fist.

"Cat's teeth!" he howled.

The lizard rubbed his bruised knuckles and wandered to the back of the room. He froze, forgetting all about his hand.

"Cat's teeth ..."

Images covered the back wall of the room: some paper, some plastic, most digital. Many of the plastic squares had lost their original brightness, but hadn't faded as badly as the scraps of paper, their edges curled up like dried leaves. Digital screens glowed faintly, as clear as the day they were saved to a memory device. Every photograph featured the same subject: Amy Armstrong.

In one, she and Philip held hands beside a leafy tree. In another she wore a bulky white pressure suit on a gray lunar surface, the white silhouette of the photo-taker reflected in the dome of her helmet. She wore a diamond-covered crown and reclined on a golden throne in one photo, a black-and-white cat on her lap and a German Shepherd at her feet. She stood beside gigantic waterfalls, majestic mountains, vast oceans, strange urban landmarks, sometimes with Philip, sometimes with another man, usually with cats and dogs of all stripes and colors. Nistra chuckled at a photo of Amy with her arm around a Sauro in a business suit. Both were smiling.

"Either a mental patient or he bought the human as a pet," he sneered.

The sauro leaned closer and scanned the hundreds of images on the wall.

"Something strange about this human female," he murmured. "In this photo she is missing a hand. In another she has both, but is older. Here she has a scar on the right side of her face and a metal arm, but in this one she has black hair, no metal arm, and no scar. In this image her leg has been replaced with metal, and in this one——"

Nistra gasped. "The Lady!"

The lizard scraped a sharp claw across the image of a half-human, half-spider creature. Her hair had turned gray, but her face was still recognizable as a very old Amy Armstrong.

Nistra stuck a thin claw behind the protective glass and pushed and prodded the plastic photo. After a bit of work it fell out.

The sauro picked the photo from the glowing floor. "Amy Armstrong is the Lady, the most powerful trader in the galaxy? How is that possible? I was just standing in front of her! Somehow, I will use this to my advantage."

Nistra searched his tight spandex uniform for pockets. Failing to find any, he sighed and shoved the photo into his pants.

"Now for some strategy," he mused.

The sauro searched the corners of the room, at last finding a black marker lying in a corner. He walked into the corridor, closed the hatch, and scrawled "Radiation" below the word "Prive," along with the galactic symbol for dangerous radiological substances.

"Magnificent," he whispered, inspecting his work.

The sauro glanced at the marker in his claw and thought about tossing it over his shoulder. At last he sighed and jammed the metal tube down the front of his trousers.

AMY FOUND Betsy and Nick in the kitchen.

Like the rest of the ship, the room was designed for both a weightless environment and artificial gravity. Food preparation counters and sinks in the center island had covers and emergency suction hoses, and floor-to-ceiling metal cabinets around the walls had locking handles to keep contents from flying out.

Sunflower stood in the doorway. "You're going to get sick!"

The object of his scorn was the wagging tail and rear end of a brown-and-white Jack Russell terrier, busily rooting around in a steel cabinet. The dog backed out, revealing a fuzzy head completely inside a plastic bag of marshmallows, like a toddler dangerously pretending to be an astronaut.

"Hey guys!" said Betsy, his voice muffled and white marshmallows bouncing around his head.

He shook his neck wildly, causing the bag to fly off and huge marshmallows to scatter through the kitchen. The terrier scrambled up to Amy, his snout and jaws covered in sticky white goo.

"Want a marshmallow?"

Amy had a sudden vision of picking dog hairs from her teeth. "Thanks, but no thanks. I thought you only ate once a week, anyway."

"Betsy has a weakness," hissed Sunflower. "The medical term is 'brain no workee.' He knows that the changes the Lady made to our bodies means we're on a restricted diet––remember what happened last time you ate a bag of marshmallows, Betsy?"

The dog blinked at him. "Uhhh ... what was the question?"

"You don't remember, do you? That's because you went into a coma and we had to replace every drop of dog blood in your stupid dog body. There's probably no dog blood on this ship, dog surgeons, or even any blood or surgeons, so you can stop eating or die. Take your pick."

"I'll stop eating. Thanks, Sunnie!"

The orange tabby rolled his eyes. "Whatever."

A hollow thump came from one of the cabinets.

"Where's Nick?" asked Philip.

Betsy glanced left and right. "She ... uh ... just flew away. She went to find you. Yeah, that's it!"

Philip crossed his arms. "Are you telling a lie?"

"Mabily?"

"Betsy!"

"Okay, I was telling a lie. Nick's up there. I had to lock her inside."

Amy pulled the handle. As the door swung open, a tiny woman flew out and buzzed around Betsy's head, causing the terrier to howl and spin in circles. Nick's tiny red dress was smeared with sticky marshmallow goo.

"The dog almost killed me!"

"You were stealing marshmallows!"

"They were mine!"

Amy grabbed both by the back of the neck and held them off the floor.

"Did you two have coffee this morning? You're fighting like cats and dogs."

Sunflower snorted. "Don't you mean like sprites and dogs?"

"Whatever. You're both are acting like children, especially Betsy."

"Don't be too hard on the dog," said Sunflower. "He wasn't born with all the advantages the rest of us have in life."

"Like a brain," piped up Nick, as she struggled in Amy's fingers. "Everyone knows marshmallows are for sprites, not dogs! We can't eat anything but candy and cake and ice cream and chocolate!"

Amy set Betsy on the floor first and then let Nick fly away. "That can't be true. Is that true?"

"Absolutely," said Sunflower. "Sprites were engineered to eat junk food. Unless, of course, you change the factory settings."

"Why?"

"I don't know. Maybe you want them to eat bugs and stuff. Dogs have gardens, too."

"No! Why design them to eat junk food?"

The orange tabby shrugged. "Because it was funny?"

Philip raised a hand. "I lived with Nick for a few years. It sounds preposterous, but it's absolutely true––a sprite's diet consists entirely of sweets. Apparently the cat scientists who developed the sprites thought all dogs were too fat, so they designed them to eat everything that was bad for a dog's diet. Also, the cats thought it was the peak of hilarity, imagining the tiny creatures swiping huge cakes from the mouths of their canine owners."

Sunflower held a paw over his nose and giggled. "Sorry ... that's still funny."

"Excuse me, Amy," broke in the warm voice of the ship from speakers in the ceiling. "But I believe a clarification is necessary. The food substance in question belongs to neither the sprite nor the dog."

Nistra stepped through the doorway of the kitchen. He saw the opened bag and scattered white cylinders, and stamped a clawed foot.

"Who's been eating my marshdevils?"

Philip and Amy looked at each other. "Marshdevils?"

"I told you that's what it said on the package!" yelled Nick.

Betsy stared at the floor. "I thought they were just marshmallows that tasted like a goat that died after eating another goat that died."

"No wonder these two were ready to kill each other," said Sunflower. "Marshdevils are disgusting sauro food. Eat a couple of those and you'll want to roast kittens alive."

"That's not true at all," said Nistra. "They must be steamed for the best flavor."

"Marshdevils or kittens?"

"Both."

Amy raised her hands. "Nobody's roasting or steaming anything. Nistra, you might want to change your thinking about kittens. We're traveling to a planet where you shouldn't say that out loud."

The sauro stared at her with his yellow eyes. "No! You don't mean——"

"That's right," said Sunflower, a purr in his voice. "Before you can say 'jackrabbit' we'll be strolling the cobbled streets of the City of Light, passing tiny cafes and bakeries, classrooms and martial arts dojos, all packed to the brim with cats living life to the fullest. For romance, tradition, and elegance nothing holds a candle to the queen of all conurbations, metropoli, and municipalities——Cheezburger, capital of Tau Ceti."

Betsy danced and hopped, flinging tiny white globs on Amy.

"Yay! We're going to have fun!"

Amy stared at Sunflower. "Seriously? There's a city called Cheezburger?"

"Not just a city, but THE City," murmured the cat. "Full of energy, parks, tea shops, intellectuals, poets, skyscrapers, monuments to great cats long dead, holoscreen celebrities, and lovers walking along the river at sunset. It's the center of cat civilization, and that means civilization period."

"But ... Cheezburger? That's a sandwich! Ground beef and cheese!"

"Is it? I guess you're right. I grew up with the name, so I guess I never thought about the actual meaning. The city really isn't named after the sandwich, though. Saint Cheezburger was the first cat to set foot on Tau Ceti. Remember the colony ship from Earth?"

"How could I forget? Philip told me all about it."

Nistra cleared his throat. "Kepler Prime has excellent dining and um, fighting arenas. Couldn't we visit there first?"

"The transmat drive is broken and the best idea for fixing it is somewhere on Tau Ceti," said Sunflower. "If this plan doesn't work, we're all stuck in this dimension."

The sauro nodded and raised a claw gingerly.

"What's a transmat drive? And what do you mean, 'this dimension?'"

Amy sighed. "You'll have plenty of time in the next two days to get caught up with all of that. In the meantime, please help Philip make a list of supplies and food on the ship. Sunflower and I'll see if anything else is broken. Betsy ... where'd he go?"

Nick hovered in the center of the room, the clear dragonfly wings of the tiny woman buzzing like a miniature lawnmower. The sprite flipped her blonde hair back and stared at her fingernails.

A thump came from under the sink. Philip pulled open a metal cabinet and Betsy tumbled out, gasping for air.

"I can't find the candy!"

Amy crossed her arms. "Nick?"

"I didn't do anything!"

Nistra pulled down on his red uniform top. "One more thing, um, everyone. I found a dangerous room full of radiation, which is also dangerous, so everyone should, uh, stay away."

"How do you know it's dangerous?" asked Philip.

"Warnings and symbols on the hatch," said Nistra. "If you wish to continue to live, don't open it."

"Sure, whatever," said Amy. "Time to get to work, everyone. We've got two days."

3

The ship flew through the vast darkness between the stars, spiraling on her axis like a silver bullet, her skin gleaming blue from deflected interstellar particles.

Six new inhabitants wandered through her corridors, poked and prodded at buttons, claimed rooms, decorated rooms, made lists, tugged at tight uniforms, stared at screens in the library, and searched fruitlessly for real marshmallows.

The ship had specialized sleeping quarters for cats, dogs, and humans but nothing for tiny sprites or gigantic sauros, so temporary arrangements had to be made. For Nick, this meant a plastic dollhouse on Philip's bunk, and for the lizard Nistra, a pair of heat lamps and a green plastic plant in a narrow closet that definitely still held brooms.

"Much larger than I'm used to," the sauro murmured as he stood inside the cramped space. He jabbed a claw at a large black splotch on the wall, perhaps the result of a long-dead crew member clearing his or her nose. "And over-decorated."

The room Sunflower chose was designed for cats, of course. The entrance hatch opened to a cozy space filled with carpeted, ceiling-height cylinders and narrow, chaotic shelves spreading up the walls. As Sunflower tiredly explained, it was very important for a cat to be "up high, where nobody can get you."

Betsy's room was a piled-up jumble of chew toys, half-repaired electronics, scratched holodiscs with missing cases, and a huge, circular bed.

Amy walked inside and covered her mouth.

"Good gravy, it smells in here!"

Philip followed her into the room. "I hope it's not the previous resident. Although the fragrance reminds me more of a wet dog than a putrefying corpse."

"It's great!" barked Betsy.

Amy watched the terrier bounce and somersault on the large bed.

"I expected more weirdness in a ship from the fabled dimension of Katmando. Like floating energy beds and spacey glass chairs and tables."

"We had all of those and more on my maiden voyage," said the warm voice of the ship. "The glass furniture shattered the first week and none of the crew could sleep on the energy mattresses."

"Why not?"

"The constant hum."

Philip claimed a room with two sets of human-sized bunk beds. Across the corridor was "Chanm Komandan," or Captain's Quarters, and Amy was pushed into ownership. The hatch opened to a small compartment with a Murphy bed, a sofa, and a desk that folded into the wall when the bed was in use. At the back of the suite was a closet with a shower and toilet. Everything was designed for efficiency of space, like the rooms on a submarine.

Amy slept fitfully the first night, with dark hills projected on the walls and a brilliant field of stars on the ceiling, as if she were camping in Carmel Valley. It reminded her too much of her family, and when she thought about them she thought about Lucia in the hospital, two thousand years in the past and a billion dimensions away.

"You know you can change it, right?"

Amy and Philip sat in the cafeteria with plates of scrambled egg, ham, and buttered toast on the table between them. At least, it looked like eggs and ham to

Amy; she hoped it wasn't something projected onto plates full of gray goo.

"Change it?" She shook her head. "How do I do that?"

"It's as simple as clearing your mind. Have you ever tried to think of nothing at all? I'm certain you know what I mean."

"Sure, sometimes."

"If you relax and focus on absolutely nothing you can change what's projected on the walls, I assure you."

"Thanks, I'll try it. Did you sleep well?"

Philip laughed. "Like a brick! I simply imagined my room in London, and Bob's your uncle––fast asleep."

"Why not Yorkshire?"

"Quite a few unpleasant memories, I'm afraid, but of course you know that."

"Right. How's the inventory of the ship?"

"Enough food and water for a year, at least. In addition, I found an apparatus that can transmute basic elements into food, as long as carbon and water are in high enough quantities. It's quite fascinating."

"Can it make gold? A girl can never have too much gold."

Philip jammed a fork-full of eggs into his mouth and swallowed. "Theoretically, it's possible. Realistically, I'm a teenager from nineteenth-century England with little mechanical knowledge who barely reads Cat French."

Amy rested her elbows on the table. "You're smart and quick on your feet. I'd say you're in the top fifty percent of poor little rich boys on this ship."

Philip looked down at his plate. "We don't choose our families or how we were born, Amy."

"I'm sorry." Amy reached across the table and touched his fingers. "Forget what I said. You're the BEST poor little rich boy on this ship. I wouldn't be here without you."

Philip grinned and held Amy's hand with both of his. "I sense a wry humor in your voice. You know I'd follow you anywhere, Amy, and be your eternal serv-ant, if only you ... um, I wrote a poem about you—— about us. Would you like to read it?"

Amy slapped the table and stood up.

"No poems! Soppy words and mushy faces might work on London girls, but I'm from California, and we like results. Show me this transmogrifyer slash al-chemy thing you were talking about."

"As you wish."

The pair cleaned their plates in the kitchen sink and walked through the corridor. Amy chomped on two pieces of buttered toast as she watched the red-woods projected on the walls and ceiling.

Philip waved her forward. "Follow me, please. The device is in my bedroom."

"No poetry," Amy mumbled, her mouth full of toast.

"I wouldn't dream of it. It's there because I was showing the machine to Nick before breakfast."

Amy sniffed. "Do you smell something? Redwoods aren't supposed to smell like chocolate. Did Hershey built a factory in the mountains?"

"Oh, no!"

Philip sprinted down the corridor like a shot from a starting pistol had just fired. Amy smashed the but-tered toast into her mouth and chased after him through the fake hologram of a redwood forest.

The sweet smell of chocolate and vanilla floated from a circular opening in the forest that led to Philip's bedroom. The teenager stood inside, staring at a silver cube on the top bunk of his bed and the huge pile of frosted cupcakes, cookies, and chocolate truffles around the humming machine. Many of the tasty confections had spilled off the mattress and onto the floor in a colorful mess of frosting and cake.

Philip spread his arms. "I never should have left Nick alone with the devilish thing. Look at this mess!"

Amy grabbed a cupcake covered in purple frosting from the floor and took a huge bite.

"I don't want to know what I just put in my mouth," she said. "But it tastes normal."

A pink-and-white dollhouse stood on the bed next to the silver cube. A high-pitched whine came from inside.

"Urgh ... ooooh ..."

Amy opened a window on the top floor. Inside, Nick rolled back and forth on a tiny bed and clutched her enlarged, spandex-covered belly.

"Are you going to have a baby fairy?" Amy asked. "You look pregnant."

"I'm not pregnant and don't call me a fairy!" screamed Nick.

"Not to be too forward or anything," said Philip, from behind Amy. "But sprites don't have babies that way, at least not with the default factory settings."

"Stop talking about me! I ate too much!"

"I think we have a case of a silly little sprite who's having a competition with a silly little dog to see who's being the most silly," said Amy. "Wouldn't you agree, Doctor Phil?"

"Most certainly, Nurse Armstrong."

Amy glared at him. "I'm a doctor, too! We're both doctors in this fake situation. You don't think women can be doctors?"

Philip turned red. "Not at all. It's just … sorry, I've made a royal cock-up of everything, as usual."

Amy laughed and elbowed him in the ribs. "I'm just messing with you, Phil. Good job on making this trans-whatcha-dingus work."

"Thank you," said the teenager, after a relieved sigh. "I showed Nick how to make a chocolate chip cookie. I don't understand how she could make all these other things."

"Instruction manual," groaned Nick.

"Ah, I see. She used the book that came with it." Philip waved at the mountain of pastries. "But what did she use for the basic element? Something must be broken down for the machine to convert it to the final product. Sweets, in this case."

"Instruction manual," coughed Nick.

"Yes, thank you," said Philip. "I understand how the process works. I just don't see anything missing. Pillows, perhaps?"

"Instruction manual!" screamed Nick.

Amy sniffed. "I think she converted the instruction manual to cupcakes."

"That's the worst thing she could have used! How am I supposed to change the machine to make anything other than cupcakes?"

Amy raised a hand. "Calm down, Phil. Look at it this way: it's either the best way to get rid of stinky socks, or the easiest way to kill a sprite."

The plastic dollhouse vibrated as Nick rolled back and forth. "Sugar rush," she moaned.

"I'll get a broom and maybe a mop to clean up," said Amy. She turned around at the hatch opening. "And not because I'm a girl and crap!"

AMY HELPED Philip clean the sticky mess from his bunkbed and floor, and then left the teenager in his room, trying to understand the strange device without any instructions. She wandered aimlessly through the living quarters at the bow of the ship, the central core of navigation and transmat, and the power plant and engine in the aft sections.

Philip had mastered the ability to change the memories projected on the walls around him, but Amy found it hard to clear her mind. Her life had changed too much in the last ... week? Days? Time had become as stretched and slippery as a wet noodle, just like her role in the universe. She had been just a simple teenage girl from California, but that felt like such a long time ago. A time when Lucia had a heart attack. A time when she'd tried to steal a golden Super Nintendo.

Amy found the special console in the middle of a giant stack of plastic shipping crates put on the ship by the Lady. The rectangular block of gold was sealed in a clear plastic case and floated in a shimmering field of blue energy.

"I should have taken that beating from M.K.," she murmured. "I'd still be in Pacific Grove. I'd be with my friends, I'd be there for Lucia, and I'd have normal clothes to wear!"

Amy pulled up on the tight red spandex around her hips.

If she hadn't tried to steal the gaming console, though, she would've never met Philip. Ah, Philip. Tall and handsome, with English manners––it would be easy to get starry-eyed and squishy over a boy like that. Amy wondered what he'd written about her in his poem. Probably some stupid mopey garbage about flowers and love and feelings.

Amy sighed and shuffled through the forest. "I'm just a normal girl," she whispered. "Why is he suddenly locked on to me like a guided missile? Warning—warning—beep beep beep, and BOOM."

"He is attracted because you are the captain, my lady," said the calm voice of the ship. "Not normal at all."

"What? Blanche, are you always listening?"

"Yes, my lady."

"I told you not to call me that. Anyway, I've only been the captain for a day. I'm pretty sure Philip liked me before that."

"He is the companion, and you are the captain. In centuries past and centuries to come, this is always the way."

"That sounds like some far-out, hippy-dippy crap."

"No fecal matter is involved. You are the lady of the ship, and he is the companion. In centuries past and centuries to come, this is always the way."

"I get the point—you think I'm great. I just don't know why HE thinks I'm great. Me, instead of other girls." Amy trailed her hand on the fake tree trunks as she walked. Instead of bark, she felt the smooth metal of the corridor wall. "Boys, you know? Can't understand them, can't punch them in the throat and shove them off a balcony."

"I do not recommend that your companion be injured in this way."

Amy sighed. "They're like lost little ducklings, you know? After puberty, they start harassing the first girl that doesn't hate them or call the police or shove them off a balcony. Happens all the time. The harassment, not the balcony thing. That was a total lie spread by Dan Wilson."

"The pair of you are linked through time and space and represent a measurable, dimensional constant of the universe. Your companion has affection for you, my lady, not because of a chance meeting, but because he has always known you, and always loved you."

Amy stopped and spread her arms. "I can't decide if that's the most romantic thing I've ever heard, or the worst! This is proof that I've gone space crazy—— I'm talking with a spaceship about boys!"

"My lady does not have a mental defect. I have helped her with many relationships in the past."

"Well, one of us has to have a defect, and it's not me."

Amy sighed and stared at the tops of the redwood trees where a golden eagle floated across the blue sky, his wings spread wide. The distant scream of the eagle notched up a few octaves as he transformed into a seagull, and the ocean roared in Amy's ears. To her right, foamy surf crashed on the beach, and to her left rose a forest of redwoods and a mountain range covered in gray twilight. A path of rubbery black tiles carved a straight line across the beach above the high-tide line.

Amy hopped up and down. "I did it!"

She ran through the ship looking for someone to tell about her success, and stopped at a vertical silver disc floating above the surf. The phrase "Do not enter upon pain of death" was scrawled across the front in black marker.

Amy touched the disc and stepped inside, trading the ocean scene for a dim space filled with carpeted cylinders and narrow shelves.

"Sunflower? Are you here?"

"Of course I am. It's my room," came the quiet voice of the cat.

Amy squinted at the ceiling, and saw Sunflower's ears above a shelf. "Why is it so dark in here? Why are you up so high?"

"I can see perfectly fine," said the orange tabby. "I'm doing important stuff and I don't want to be bothered."

"I figured out how to change the projections," said Amy.

"Fabulous. I'm sure your mother would be proud."

Amy slapped the wall, causing the shelves to vibrate. "My mother? You have no idea what my mother was like. Sometimes you're so full of it, Sunflower!"

The cat's head raised an inch, revealing a pair of eyes that flashed briefly in the dark. "I'm sorry, Amy. I didn't mean to say anything negative. Come up here and I'll show you something."

"Way up there? How?"

The cat sniffed. "Don't tell me you can't climb. You monkeys lived in trees for ages."

Amy scrambled hand-over-hand up the narrow shelves and came face-to-face with the orange tabby.

"The monkey jokes weren't funny the first time. Still not funny now."

Sunflower blinked at her. "Monkey jokes? I was stating a fact––your people lived in trees. What's wrong with that?"

"Ha ha, what a comedian. Where am I going to sit?"

"Lay on the top shelf. I'll extend it."

The carpeted board slid out a few inches. Amy pulled herself up to the shelf and lay on her belly facing Sunflower's "work area" in the corner.

The orange tabby lay on a thick square cushion in front of three holographic displays. The cat was using both of his artificial "manos" hands to type on a keyboard in front of the cushion, the needle-like fingers clacking rapidly on the plastic keys.

"This is a cozy little setup," said Amy.

"The only way to get things done. Or the only way to fall asleep while getting things done. This bed is super-soft."

"So ... whatcha doing?"

"I'm trying to get you home." An image of the golden, special edition console appeared in one of the displays. "Recognize anything?"

"That's the Super Nintendo you stole from me."

"What? It wasn't yours in the first place."

"I saw it first!"

The cat sighed. "Whatever. This block of gold is special."

"You bet your whiskers. That's why I was trying to steal it."

"Right, but the real value doesn't come from how many bananas or coconuts or monkey money you think it's worth——this object is the only pure material we have from your dimension. That's important. Pure elements resonate on a specific nano-frequency when bombarded with beta radiation from the transmat drive."

"English, please."

"If we can fix the recombinator matrix——that's a big 'if'——I can combine the nano-frequency with the SBD signal and send you back home. About eight seconds after you left, actually."

"Still not getting it."

Sunflower leaned toward Amy and spoke slowly. "Gold thing good. Take you home soon. Mmm-kay?"

"That's great! But what's this SBD signal?"

"I talked about that yesterday. Don't you remember? SpaceBook––the best and worst thing to happen to the universe. I know you come from a backwards planet, but do you know anything about the problems of communicating across great distances?"

"I guess. Radio waves travel at the speed of light, which is 671 million miles per hour. Even solar systems that are really close together on a galactic scale can take years to receive a signal."

Sunflower nodded. "The fastest postal ship still takes a day to travel between Tau Ceti and Gliese. Instead of doing that, we send a message in a few seconds by bouncing the signal through the SpaceBook network."

The cat typed on the keyboard using the spiky fingers of his manos, and an image appeared on the holoscreen. A transparent sail pulled a tiny white cube across the emptiness of space, like a sugar cube behind a gigantic handkerchief.

"SpaceBook is a vast system of communication drones powered by the solar wind, and scattered through the spiral arm of our galaxy like a cloud of dandelion seeds. One billion evil dandelion seeds. Messages pass from one satellite to the next, and we can bounce a signal through the network at hundreds of parsecs per second."

"That sounds awesome, not evil."

"Really? Watch this. I'll send a request for the latest weather report over Cheezburger."

Immediately dozens of colorful boxes cascaded over the screen and covered the image of the Space-Book drone. Neon advertisements for a can of something called "Jurg" were quickly covered with image after image of cats lying on shaggy pink carpet or playing with yarn.

Sunflower smacked the keyboard. "Look at that smut! It's a good thing kittens are banned from using SpaceBook. Some of these female cats probably came from good families, and that just makes me sick."

"Okaaay. Your hangups with yarn aside, it's just a bunch of ads."

"A bunch of ads? This obscene trash will take me ten minutes to delete. If it's not ads, it's status updates from cats that don't exist doing things that don't exist in places that don't exist!"

"Cats that don't exist?"

Sunflower rubbed his face. He sighed and began clicking at the ads on his screen, deleting them one by one.

"Honestly, we know very little about the Space-Book drones. Most of the ads are in Cat French, while others are in English, so it can't be from that far in the future, or the past. We really don't know where they came from. The reference books within SpaceBook list places that never were, cats that never lived, and planets we've never heard of. Some religious figures think SpaceBook is from the same dimension as Katmando. Others say it's an attempt by other dimensions to contact us."

"What about you?"

Sunflower sniffed. "The drones are cross-dimensional markers for navigation. That's how the Lady used them, and that's how we're going to use them to get you back to your dimension. Beyond that, I have no idea. I would guess that SpaceBook cost so much money when it was built that the original creators had to look around for commercial sponsors.

That's where all the ads and fake status updates came from."

"How can you use them for navigation? There are billions of dimensions."

Sunflower tapped at the screen filled with ads. "I don't know why it works, I only know it does. Space-Book has been around for thousands of years, even before cats left Earth. It's a trans-dimensional anomaly. Listen——this isn't the stone age. Dimensional travel has been around for a few decades, but only one-way. The Lady designed the transponders in my chest and all the chests of her operators to tap into the nearest SpaceBook relay. Otherwise, we'd never be able to return to her ship with a haul of treasure."

Amy shook her head. "I know that I'm talking to a cat inside a spaceship full of holographic walls that can read my mind, but this SpaceBook thing is too far-out."

The display beeped, and Sunflower clicked another key.

"Far-out or not, here's the weather report. Sunny and clear, as always."

"Thanks for the update. How long until we get there?"

"Twelve hours."

"Great. I need to check on that lizard the Lady made us bring on board. Hope he hasn't eaten anyone."

DETENTION OFFICER First Class Nistra, former staff member of the High-security Anti-recidivist Lengthy Penitentiary and proud member of the proudest race of laboratory-grown lizards in the galaxy, glanced nervously over his shoulder.

The cramped library contained three cubicles with individual keyboards and display screens mounted on the bulkhead. Nistra had chosen the furthest from the hatch, a screen partly concealed by the wall of the next cubicle, and had scattered an entire box of disgusting human breakfast cereal on the floor to serve as an early warning for intruders. Even with those precautions, the scaly reptile found himself staring at the closed hatch more than the screen.

"Who is the Lady?" he whispered to the display. "Reduce volume of answer."

"The Lady is the captain of The White Star," said the ship.

"Is Amy Armstrong the Lady?"

"That statement is correct. The human female named Amy Armstrong who is presently on board this craft is the Lady."

Video snapped to life on the screen, showing Amy leaving Sunflower's room.

"How? The Lady is hundreds of years old and half machine! I was in the same room with both of them."

"Amy Armstrong is the Lady."

"But ... who is the Lady? What is she?"

Hundreds of images appeared rapidly on the screen. Amy at a variety of ages, across a spectrum of backgrounds and activities. Young and old, happy and sad, full of life and with a changing amount of artificial limbs. At the extreme end of old age, her lower body had been replaced with an obsidian sphere and the artificial legs of a giant arachnid.

"The Lady is a pan-dimensional arrangement of DNA molecules into a female *homo sapiens* organism," said the ship. "The Lady resonates at the same universal background frequency as the nanites within my systems, and therefore, our co-habitance is most pleasing."

Nistra bared his sharp teeth. "What does that even mean?"

"It means I'm not allergic to her."

"If she's always the Lady, and the Lady is always the captain, what happens when she dies?"

The screen snapped to black.

"After a period of mourning, the search begins for a new Lady. Transmat across many dimensions may be required."

"How do you return from those dimensions?"

"The assumption underlying your question is incorrect. A return is neither possible or necessary."

Nistra scratched his chin. "Can anyone else be the captain of this ship?"

"The Lady is the captain of the White Star. If the Lady is not present other organisms could be considered, but only if they have an updated resume."

"Was that a joke?"

"Yes."

"So ... just to be clear, nobody else can be the captain except Amy Armstrong?"

"That is correct."

"Does this ship have an armory?"

"No."

"Weapons locker?"

"No."

"A sharp stick?"

"No."

Nistra glanced back at the hatch. "Does the Lady keep a log or a diary? Display the most recent."

The screen in front of the sauro displayed the wrinkled face and tightly braided gray hair of the Lady, the one who had exiled Nistra to this ship. For a long moment the Lady simply blinked at the screen.

"I don't know what to say," she murmured. "This is the hardest thing I've ever done. You've been the center of so many firsts in my life, along with so many lasts." The Lady bowed her head. "Without your skin and healing nanites, dear friend, I would have died long ago and joined Philip in that vast, inter-dimensional nothingness. I don't speak lightly of these matters. It was not an easy decision to transfer the stasis-frozen Kepler Prime in your power core to my new base."

Nistra pounded the console with his scaly fist. "What?!!"

"I feel like I've cut the heart from my own moth-er," continued the image of the Lady. "But no other path is open, no other energy source available to pow-er the interior of the huge asteroid we've found. You can't imagine what I can do with that many transmat chambers! The riches are limitless." The Lady touched the screen with a wrinkled palm. "Sleep, dear friend. You've deserved it."

The image of the old woman faded to black.

Nistra shook his head, his sharp-toothed jaws open in shock.

"Kepler Prime in the power core ... bless the egg, how is that possible?"

The hatch whisked open behind him, and the room filled with a loud crunch and crackle.

"What the H-E-hockey sticks?" yelled Amy. "Who spilled corn flakes on the floor?"

Nistra stood up and bowed. "I was looking for food and accidentally broke a container of the disgust-ing stuff. I am completely at fault, my lady."

Amy frowned and jammed her fists on her waist. "What did you call me?"

"Nothing, Amy! Uh ... Miss Captain! Captain Armstrong!"

"That's better. Why would you eat in the library, anyway?"

Nistra shrugged, looking sheepish. "It's a ... custom of my people?"

"Gross! Grab a broom from your closet slash bedroom slash pigpen and clean up the mess. Food doesn't belong in the library or on the floor. You might want to write that down, because it's a custom of MY people."

The lizard smiled with pointy yellow teeth and bowed from the waist.

"By your command."

Amy squinted at the sauro for a long moment, then shook her head and left.

"Whatever. I'm taking a nap."

4

Amy felt a warm glow on her cheek.

She lay under the pale blue sheets of a hospital bed, sunshine flickering from the open window and over her face. With half-open eyes, she watched the green leaves of a maple tree flutter in the breeze, the waving branches sounding like the crash of waves on a distant beach. She wished she could see the ocean.

"Too late," said a young woman's voice.

At the foot of the bed stood a fourteen-year-old Asian girl. Her bangs were as sharp and straight as the pleats in the skirt of her school uniform.

"Helen?" Amy whispered hoarsely.

"Too late," said a teenage boy.

Tony glared down at Amy from the left side of the bed, his jaw clenched.

"Always too late," he said.

Amy swallowed, trying to clear the sandpaper from her throat. "Late for what?"

Billy, Anna, Viv, and Eugenia rose from behind Tony and spoke all together.

"Too late!"

A heaviness pressed the mattress at Amy's feet. Her foster mother wore a hospital gown, her short brown hair was matted, and dark circles framed her eyes. Lucia stared at Amy and shook her head slowly.

"Too late," she whispered.

Amy lay back on her puffy hospital pillow and sighed. "This is a nightmare, isn't it?"

The individuals around the bed glanced at each other.

"Duh," said Tony. "What did you think it was?"

"Aren't you scared?" asked Lucia. "She's supposed to be scared. Boo!"

Amy pounded her fists on the bed. "I hate nightmares!"

She opened her eyes. A red light pulsed on the ceiling of the captain's quarters and a faint beeping came from the wall. Amy covered her face with both hands and let out a long, body-shaking groan.

"Apologies for the alarm, Miss Armstrong," said the ship. "We are approaching the L2 orbital boundary for Tau Ceti. You requested that I wake you before planetfall."

"L2 boundary? What's that?"

"A point in space around a gravitational mass where an orbit is the most stable. L2 is a common location for orbital stations, planetary interdiction forces, and duty-free shopping."

"Duty-free shopping? Was that a joke?"

"No."

Amy brushed her hair in the small mirror of the captain's bathroom, and pulled at her tight spandex uniform, trying to adjust it to feel less like a sausage skin.

"Ugh! Why do I have to wear this stupid get-up? I look like a reject from the drive-in theater!"

"My lady, you are not required to wear the prophylactic garments."

"Why not?"

"I am not allergic to you."

"What about the others?"

"I am allergic to the others."

Amy shrugged. "What else am I supposed to wear? That stupid orange jumpsuit from the prison smells like a farm and I didn't exactly bring a suitcase full of clothes with me. I didn't bring any clothes, actually. The lizards took my London dress, so that prison jumpsuit was all I had."

"No need for concern, my lady," said the ship. "Your clothes are here."

A section of the bulkhead slid to the right, revealing a walk-in closet four meters deep. Amy wandered inside, staring in wonder at the racks of clothing along the walls.

"Wow! Amazing, Blanche, but these aren't mine. I've never seen any of these skirts or dresses before."

"You are the captain and these garments have always belonged to her."

Amy rubbed the silky fabric of a white, long-sleeved blouse between her fingers.

"With so many clothes, at least a couple should fit me."

"All of the garments will fit, my lady."

"There's the power of positive thinking. You sound like my mom––that one fits you, this one looks fine, why are you girls so picky, blah, blah, blah."

Amy grabbed the bottom of her spandex top and pulled it over her head. She flipped through the rack of silky blouses and chose a white long-sleeved t-shirt that felt like it was made of cotton. She stuck her arms into the sleeves first and pulled it over her head. The hem of the blouse fell almost to her knees and the sleeves were a foot too long.

Amy waved the floppy arms of the blouse at the ceiling. "See what I mean?"

"The garment will adjust, my Lady."

"That's what they all say. Wait––what?"

As Amy watched, the sleeves, hem, and sides of the garment shrank into a comfortable, close fit.

"Calibration finished," said the ship.

Amy held up her wrist and stared at the cotton material. "Don't tell me this thing is alive or full of robots or aliens or anything. That would freak me out."

"As requested, this information will not be disclosed."

"Thank you. Ignorance is bliss and all that."

Amy stripped off her spandex trousers. After opening all the drawers in the room, she found tights and underwear in a drawer labeled "Kilot." Another drawer labeled "Jip" was packed with folded skirts. Yet another held vests.

Amy chose a pleated skirt in dark blue plaid—— similar to her school uniform——and a dark navy pair of tights. A pair of black Mary Janes shrank around her feet and completed the outfit.

Amy stared into a full-length mirror along one side of the small room, and shook her head.

"This skirt is way too long. I'm not in Sunday school."

The hem of the plaid garment swiftly rose from below her knees to a scandalous height that was probably illegal and that not even the trampiest of the trampiest cheerleaders would wear.

Amy pulled down on the hem frantically with both hands. "I'm sorry! Good skirt! You're the best."

The hem lowered to a respectable two inches above her knees.

"I would advise my lady to speak only in a positive tone about her garments," said the ship. "The clothing will protect against many dangers and hazardous environments, but is a brand with high self-esteem."

Amy looked down at her dark blue tights and rubbed the fabric. "Great ... I mean, great! These are the best clothes I've ever had!"

"My Lady is wise and thoughtful, as always."

"What about accessories?"

Several drawers clicked out of the wall and displayed carefully-organized rows of hair bands, barrettes, bangles, bracelets, rings, and necklaces.

Amy found a black ribbon to tie back her long blonde hair and a leather vest in the same color. The buttons were silver and the material worn. Four small pockets were sewn on the front.

Amy donned the vest and nodded at her reflection.

"Okay, Blanche! Off to the cockpit."

"I am not familiar with this term. Please proceed to the navigation room. The other crew members have already gathered there."

SUNFLOWER TURNED at the faint swish of the hatch.

"Hey, everyone——look who decided to join us."

Philip smiled and raised a hand to his forehead. "Amy, how are you? I see you found something fashionable to wear. Very smart."

Nick stood on Philip's shoulder and buzzed her wings angrily. "Why does she get new clothes and I have this dumb red uniform?"

"That's a good question," said Sunflower, scratching at his spandex bodysuit. "Maybe she thinks she's special."

"She IS special," said Philip.

Sunflower shook his head. "Not like that, lover boy."

"I think she looks nice!" barked Betsy, and chased his tail.

A gigantic blue planet covered in swirling clouds slowly rotated below the feet of Philip, Sunflower, Betsy, and Nick. The entire group seemed to float in mid-air around the low cylinder of the navigational control console.

Amy held her breath and walked across the invisible, holographic floor.

"I think it's funny that everyone cares so much about what I'm wearing when you're floating above an alien planet!"

"It's not an alien planet," said Sunflower. "That's my home world below us––Tau Ceti Epsilon."

Nick giggled. "Where a tiny little kitten grew up to be mean old cat."

"Whatever," said Sunflower. "Anyway, we don't care what you're wearing––we care about the stupid red uniforms that WE have to wear."

"I'm taking mine off!" barked Betsy. The dog grabbed his trousers with his teeth and fell onto his back, his legs waving in the air.

Philip placed a hand on his chest and bowed formally.

"I care what you're wearing, Amy, and you look smashing."

Amy smiled. "Thank you. See, Sunflower? Somebody cares."

The orange tabby covered his mouth with a paw. "Keep it up with the disgusting love talk, and I'll be sick all over these controls. That won't be good for the electronics."

"Please do not release fluid or remove assigned clothing," said the motherly voice of the ship. "The probability of my having an allergic reaction will increase exponentially."

"Can't be as bad as wearing this embarrassing gear," said Sunflower. "What happens when a ship gets the sniffles?"

"Allergic response can include sudden expulsion of pressurized atmosphere and the offending material through the nearest airlock," said the ship.

Nick buzzed around Sunflower's head. "She'll sneeze you into space!"

"Without protective equipment or encapsulation," added the ship.

Sunflower's red cap was halfway off his head. The cat sighed and pulled it down over his ears.

Amy looked around the table. "Speaking of dumping things into space, where's Nistra?"

"The crew member is located in his assigned room," said the ship.

"He's not happy about visiting a planet of several billion cats," said Sunflower. "There's a bit of history between sauros and us. The war and everything."

"Don't mention the war," said Philip. He winced and rubbed his side. "Don't ever mention the war."

Nick hovered over the table. "You're lucky he only kicked you!"

"I'm afraid that he was simply lashing out in anger at the prospect of landing," said Philip. "I happened to be the only person within arms-reach."

"Foot-reach, you mean," murmured Sunflower.

A sudden flash of yellow brightened the darkness above Tau Ceti's atmosphere.

"We're under attack!" barked Betsy, and scrambled behind Philip and Amy.

"Use your knowledge implant, you brainless twit," said Sunflower. "That was the beam from an orbital patrol station."

"Shooting at us?" asked Amy.

"Destroying an approaching asteroid. Tau Ceti is surrounded by a field of dangerous orbital debris. Let's see ... how can I explain this to the mind of a monkey? If rocks in sky fall down, many cats die."

Philip rubbed his chin. "Orbital weapons platforms? How many?"

"Hundreds, all dedicated to asteroid duty."

"Could they shoot at us?" asked Amy. "What if they hate humans in this dimension? What if lizards rule Tau Ceti?"

"They must really like cats, then," said Sunflower. "All the cat soap operas coming over the comm feeds look normal. No sauro overlords in sight." He peered closer at the holographic screen. "What? They made a fifth season of *SuperCat*? I haven't even watched the second season!"

"Permission for landing has been requested from the orbital master," said the ship.

Sunflower rubbed his paws together. "Now we're getting somewhere. I can almost smell the fresh fish, the bookshops, and tea bubbling on the stove of every cafe. I haven't been home in ages."

"Doesn't the Lady give vacations?"

"What's a vacation?"

Amy shrugged. "A day off? You know——a break from not working?"

"Not to operators like me and Betsy. There's the small matter of the billion dollars the Lady spent on implants and replacing our blood with blue goo. Until we work off that debt, no vacation."

"Orbital master has rejected my application to land," said the ship. "Orbital master has requested to speak to the officer of the deck."

"Who?"

Philip nudged her in the side. "That's you, Captain Amy."

"Okay, sure. Put him on screen. Or she. It. Whatever."

A holographic screen flashed to life above navigation control and displayed a grizzled black cat with yellow eyes. A chain with a large golden seal hung from his furry neck, and the cat wore a tiny version of the seal as a piercing through his left ear.

"Captain Armstrong?" growled the cat.

Amy touched her forehead in a casual salute, and immediately felt like a total dork for doing it.

"That's me––Amy Armstrong. Commanding officer of the deck or whatever."

The cat blinked. "What's the nature of your intended visit to Tau Ceti?"

"I ... uh ..."

"Tourism," whispered Sunflower. "Always say tourism."

"Um, we're just passing through," said Amy. "Want to hang out, see some stuff, maybe do some shopping. Never been to another planet before. It's exciting! Right?"

The cat stared at Amy for a long moment, and then looked to his left.

"The application for planetfall submitted by your craft lists the crew as two humans, one dog, one sprite, one cat, and one sauropod. Is that correct?"

"That's us. I mean, that's my crew!"

"I see," said the orbital master. "Given the restrictions on sauropod visas and the extremely high power signature of your vessel, I must reject your application for security reasons. An exit vector is being transmitted now. Do not deviate from the exit vector and do not accelerate over one-quarter light speed or you will be fired upon."

"Aw, come on!" yelled Sunflower. "That's the biggest pile of poona droppings I've ever heard. I haven't been home in years, you boot-licking fascist lizard lover! Maybe the sauros really did win."

Philip covered his mouth and leaned next to Sunflower. "Don't mention the war," he whispered.

The orbital master snarled, showing white fangs. "Who said that? Who's talking? I gave an arm to the regiment, you long-haired hippy!"

The black cat jerked down the fur covering his right arm and revealed the dull metal bones of an artificial limb.

"Put the camera on that lizard peacenik," he growled. "I want to see the face of that coward before I accidentally on purpose blow you out of the sky with twenty orbital cannons." He turned to the right. "Shut up, Lisa! I don't care how much paperwork that is!"

Sunflower jumped in front of Amy and stood on his hind legs. "I may have overstated things a bit," he said, paws clasped as if in prayer. "I was actually calling one of OUR crew a boot-licking fascist lizard lover. It was ... uh, the dog! Dogs, right? They're the worst and I hate them. Don't you hate them? What I mean to say is, how ARE you?"

Betsy ran circles around Sunflower. "What's a fash-isht?"

The jaw of the orbital master dropped and his yellow eyes bulged from his black, furry face.

"Sunflower of the Western Range? Impossible!"

Sunflower tilted his head. "Weird. Never been called that before."

"Really?" asked Betsy, and skidded to a stop on the invisible floor. "Sunflower isn't your name? Can I call you Slappy? I had a friend called Slappy, but he ran away. Wait——yeah, he ran away."

Sunflower rolled his eyes. "Dogs, right?"

"I'm speechless, Your Excellency," said the orbital master. The cat gulped and rubbed the official seal around his neck. "I apologize for my stupidity in delaying your travel. Orbital clearance granted. Where would you like to make planetfall, Excellency?"

"Cheezburger South. Much quieter than Capital Spaceport. I hate traffic and crowds."

"As you wish, Excellency. Please have your navigator follow the recommended atmospheric insertion we are transmitting now. I will forward news of your arrival to the capital authorities. If it pleases Your Excellency, a few extra orbits of the planet will give us more time to prepare for your arrival."

"Whatever works," said Sunflower. "I don't need a wheelchair or anything at the gate."

"Thank you, sir." The eyes of the black cat filled with tears. "Forgive me for being too forward, Your Radiance, but let me be the first to say, 'Welcome home.'"

"Sure thing, Bob or whatever your name was."

The black cat dipped his head. "Candice Doodlekins, Excellency. I am forever your humble servant."

"Whatever."

Sunflower slapped the console with his paw and the screen disappeared.

"That wasn't weird or anything," said Amy.

Sunflower shrugged. "Doodlekins is a common name. Not that crazy at all."

"I mean how he treated you like you were famous."

"What did you expect? I'm one of a handful of cats on this planet that work for the Lady. Of course everyone knows me!"

Philip rubbed his chin. "There's something more to this story. That official called you 'Excellency.' That's not a common greeting."

"I know what he called me because I was here and it was two seconds ago," said Sunflower. "There's absolutely nothing more to it, period, end of story. The rest of you can run around screaming with your underpants on your heads, but I know for a fact that everything's okay, everything's normal, and the galaxy will spin on."

5

The galaxy spun on.

Inside the navigation room, Amy and the others had an incredible view as the blue and white planet slowly grew below their feet. During several orbits, Sunflower pointed out natural landmarks and major cities. On the dark side of the planet, the gleam of urban lights came only from the extreme north and south of the globe.

"Nothing at the equator?" asked Amy. "It's like a brown and tan belt."

The orange tabby chuckled. "Everyone lives in the north or south. Only cats that are suicidal or stupid wander below fifty degrees of latitude. Like the old saying goes: 'fifty degrees, fifty seconds to live.' "

"It's a desert?"

"The worst. Water boils in the open and nothing survives, not even sauros."

Blue ocean and swirling clouds surrounded them as the ship curved to the south pole and entered the atmosphere with a flash of orange and red. The glow of re-entry faded as the ship glided over lush tropical islands and blue seas. Beaches covered in white sand passed below and the ship flew over a continent of thriving agricultural lands, vast fields of wheat, tiny red farmhouses, lakes reflecting the sun, and evergreen forests. The countryside gave way to vast, orderly suburbs and straight roads covered in tiny dots. Here and there, the peaked yellow roof of an Asian-style temple towered over the grid of streets and houses.

Amy squinted at the roads. "Are those cars? Cats drive cars?"

"You say that like it's impossible," said Sunflower.

"A formation of twelve atmospheric craft are vectoring toward us," said the calm voice of the ship. "Bearing twenty-three degrees, velocity nine hundred meters per second, weapons powered up."

"That's not good," said Philip.

Betsy giggled and rolled on the invisible floor. "Sunnie's in trouble!"

"I am not, you idiot," hissed the cat. "The Lady paid off those loans."

A rectangular hologram appeared out of thin air in front of Amy. On it flew a formation of black jets with stubby wings.

"Your wishes, my Lady?" asked the ship.

"Call them," said Amy. "See what they want."

"As you wish."

Nick flew circles around the group. "It's a trap! They're going to kill us and I haven't even lived!"

"More time won't change that fact," murmured Sunflower.

"Shut up!"

The holographic projection changed to a pilot in a bright blue helmet and oxygen mask. The pilot pulled down the mask to reveal the whiskers and white fur of a long-haired Persian cat.

He touched a glove to his helmet. "Commander Patricia Lee of the Royal Blues. We would be honored to escort His Excellency's craft to planetfall. Shall we guide you in, captain?"

"Yes, thank you," said Amy.

The formation of fighter jets split apart and roared past the nose of the White Star. All turned in a synchronized vertical loop and lined up on the port and starboard of the silver, barracuda-like ship as she sped over the urban landscape.

Philip shook his head as he watched the escorting fighters. "I think we're in a spot of trouble."

"Don't be a spoil-sport." Amy spread her arms wide as the streets and houses sped below the clouds. "This is fantastic! It's like we're flying."

"We ARE flying," said Sunflower.

"You know what I mean. It's LIKE we're flying, not that we're inside a ship that happens to be flying."

"I'm flying inside a ship that's flying," squeaked Nick, her dragonfly wings buzzing.

Amy pointed at a clump of skyscrapers on the horizon. "Is that Cheezburger?"

"All of this is Cheezburger," said Sunflower. "That's the downtown financial district."

"I see a lot of cats," said Betsy, his tail wagging. "Cats, cats, cats!"

"Of course. This is the capital."

Philip pointed down. "Betsy means on the port side. Look there, far below us."

"I don't see what you're talking about," said Sunflower. "All I see is the landing field at Cheezburger South. Somebody needs to clean it up, too, because it's covered in trash."

"That's no trash," said Amy.

Sunflower's green eyes widened as the landing field grew larger and larger.

"Holy Saint Mittens and his three legs," whispered the cat.

It was as if a hurricane had sucked up the entire population of the city and spit them into a single point––the open concrete plain of the spaceport known as Cheezburger South. A vast, multicolored host of cats covered the five square kilometers of the landing field, lined the roofs of the terminal and neighboring buildings, clogged the streets and highways, and surrounded the gigantic spheres of parked spacecraft like ants around fallen Christmas ornaments. A wide circle in the crowd of cats was the only available space to land, and the ship dropped slowly toward it.

"Sunflower," said Amy. "Is there anything you want to tell us?"

"RA-ther," said Philip.

The orange cat grabbed his twitching tail. "I, uh ... probably a music festival? Maybe a movie star in the landing pattern? Is that his ship behind us?"

"I don't see anything," said Amy. "Hey, look at those banners. The movie star's name is Sunflower, too."

As the ship descended closer to the cheering cats, signs with Sunflower's name and furry orange face waved and bobbed in the midst of the crowd.

"Apparently this cat is the spitting image of you," said Philip.

Sunflower covered his eyes with his paws. "Oh, no."

"Sunnie's a movie star!" barked Betsy. "Can I have your autograph?"

"I'm not a star, I'm not famous, I'm not anything! This is the biggest case of mistaken identity in the galaxy. We'll clear it up and have a good laugh about it later."

Betsy tilted his brown and white head. "Not famous? But you said——"

"I know what I said! I'm famous small 'f', not big 'f'! This is a hero's welcome, a celebration for a king, and I'm none of those things."

Philip nodded. "Honesty trumps sarcasm, at last."

"Prepare for planetfall," droned the ship.

Amy glanced down at the chairs around the navigation console. "How? These don't have seat belts."

Philip shrugged. "Perhaps we should hold hands? Group hug, as you Americans say?"

"Kum-ba-ya and all that crap," said Amy. "If you just want a hug, Philip, you can tell me. I'm a big girl."

"We're gonna die!" howled Betsy.

The terrier shot away at a run and collided head-on with the "invisible" wall of the navigation room.

Amy sucked air through her teeth. "Ouch. That had to hurt."

"Quite so," said Philip, and put an arm around Amy's waist. "Shall we get back to the possibility of hugging?"

Amy pushed his arm away gently. "No touching in front of the cats."

"No bodily contact or physical restraint is required," said the warm voice of the ship. "Warning of planetfall is given so that crew have time to finish a beverage, freshen up their appearance, or have a dental cleansing."

"My makeup!" screamed Nick.

The tiny sprite buzzed out of the navigation room like a frantic hummingbird late for the prom.

Amy stared at the mass of jubilant cats below her feet. "Sunflower, Sunflower. What are we going to do with you?"

The orange tabby groaned and held his furry head.

"Either we're in a rather nasty spot of bother, or we're not," said Philip. "There's no use blubbing about it, so I say we take it like a man and walk out with our chins high."

"You just used about fifty different idioms in those two sentences," said Amy. "And I think you mean 'take it like a woman.' "

"No, you mean 'take it like a cat––whiskers straight and tail high,' " said Sunflower. "You monkeys speak English like a brain-dead goldfish."

"Goldfish can't speak!"

"Exactly."

Amy laughed. "Ha! There's the Sunflower we all know."

The orange tabby trotted to the hatch. "You two lovebirds can stay here and make silly faces at each other all day long. I'm going to the airlock to change out of this disgusting uniform. There's a real city waiting out there, and real civilization!"

SOOKA BLACK paced on all fours in front of the battalion of cat soldiers. At the end of each turn, the nervous cat glanced up at the sky and the knife-shaped craft dropping toward him. The strange design reminded him of the story about a cat named Damocles with a sword hanging over his furry head, and this did not help Sooka Black's anxiety.

The packed line of Life Guards behind him stood on their hind legs with their backs straight, tails down, rifles on their shoulders, and red berets on their fuzzy heads. Behind them and on all sides of the circular landing zone, a vast multitude of cats had turned out to see the landing. The sound of their cheers created such a deafening, oceanic rumble that Sooka could honestly believe it was the entire population of Cheezburger.

Sooka grimaced as he trotted in front of the Life Guards, a black cape flapping over his back. His brown fur was covered with a tortoiseshell pattern and not a few white hairs, almost all of which were because of silly events like this one. Another case of mistaken identity, another scrounger trying to pass himself off as the Emperor, another schemer to drop off in the wastelands.

"Cats and dogs have more chance of living in peace and harmony than the Emperor coming back," Sooka murmured under his whiskers. "He's not going to fall out of the clear blue sky, you know."

The vast multitude of cats cheered even louder as the silver spacecraft glided down to the landing zone, and gasped and hooted as a dozen pairs of landing legs sprouted from the bottom of the hull, long talons spread like a giant hawk reaching for her prey. Instead of murdering everyone and causing general chaos as Sooka hoped would happen, the landing claws touched and spread on the concrete. The silver barracuda settled with a burst of steam, like a sigh at the end of an exhausting journey.

Sooka Black straightened his black cape and the golden seal of his office around his neck.

"Let's see how good this cat is."

A Life Guard with stripes on his red beret leaned toward Sooka.

"Sir?"

"Nothing, sergeant. Put your cats to attention."

"Already have, sir."

"Put them at MORE attention, then!"

The sergeant saluted. "Yes, sir! Sorry, sir." The cat turned to face the soldiers. "BAT-ta-lian-AAH! Tan-SYON!"

With a clatter of metal, the Life Guards switched their rifles to the left shoulder and back again.

The outline of a circle gleamed on the silver skin of the ship. The circle sank inside, rolled to the left, and a metal ladder dropped to the concrete field. On cue, the imperial brass band started up from somewhere in the crowd, playing the royal Tau Ceti anthem. A flight of twelve fighters from the Royal Blues rocketed overhead, red smoke streaming from their wings, as an orange tabby appeared at the open hatch blinking from the bright sunlight.

Sooka Black sucked in a breath. "Cat's teeth, that's good surgery."

AS SOON AS the hatch rolled open the cheering hit Amy like a brick.

"Wow," she mouthed to Philip. The tall, dark-haired teen shrugged at the noise, and jammed his arm into the sleeve of his wool jacket.

Sunflower stared at the crowd for a moment, and then climbed down the ladder to the landing field, followed by Amy and Nick. The buzzing sprite had redone her makeup and thrown on a tiny white gown she had found somewhere in the ship. Philip had finished changing into his gray English suit. He carefully descended the ladder one-handed with an unconscious brown-and-white terrier under one arm.

A line of cats in black armor with "POLICE" across the chest stood around the perimeter and kept the crowd from surging forward by hitting them with batons that crackled with blue electricity. A gray tabby squeezed through the perimeter and sprinted toward

Sunflower, only to be buried under a pile of police cats.

Amy felt like she was on stage at a rock concert in front of fifty thousand screaming fans, only she had no idea what they were screaming about, what she could do to make them stop, or even if making them stop was a good idea. It was very possibly the scariest moment of her life.

A solid rectangle of cats wearing maroon berets and holding black knobby rifles on their shoulders marched on hind legs across the open concrete. At the head of the procession was a brown cat with a cape and a medal around his neck.

The orange fur on Sunflower's tail stood straight out. He grabbed Amy's leg and tried to tell her something over the screams of the crowd.

Amy shook her head. "Can't hear you!"

The cat wearing the cape stopped in front of Sunflower and bowed to the concrete, his furry chin touching his front paws. Sunflower froze for a second, and then returned the gesture. The brown cat turned, walked a few steps, and then tilted and bobbed his head in a manner indicating that Sunflower and his friends should follow.

A cat with gold stripes on his beret shouted unintelligible phrases against the din of the crowd. The orderly rectangle of cat soldiers marched around the small group, forming a protective shell as Amy and her friends crossed the landing area and entered the chaos of a screaming, banner-waving feline horde.

Amy plugged her ears with her fingers against the noise as the cat soldiers escorted the small group through the mob, using the butts of their rifles to beat away the overly-enthusiastic cats. A collection of low white buildings and a large silver dome gradually appeared over the furry heads of the crowd and the up-raised banners of Sunflower, growing larger and larg-er as the soldiers pushed through. After ten minutes of walking, the soldiers guided Amy and her friends to a set of double doors at the base of the giant silver dome, which was guarded by a platoon of armored cat police.

The metal doors slammed shut behind Amy and her friends. They walked through a dim, green-painted corridor, empty of all sound apart from the faint scratch of paws on the floor.

"Where are we going?" she asked, definitely too loudly.

The brown cat at the front spoke over his shoulder as he walked.

"Thank you for that question, honorable miss. Please follow me for only a short distance."

"How much further?" asked Sunflower. "I'm dying for a drink of water."

"Yeah! Me, too!" squeaked Nick.

"Only a few meters, honored guests. Refresh-ments will be provided."

The caped official led them to a metal hatch, typed in a combination code, and passed through. The cat soldiers stayed behind in the corridor as Amy and her friends followed the brown cat through a dark and ap-parently unfinished corridor filled with cables and the smell of plastic and oil. The cat passed through a large, heavy-looking hatch, crossed a small white room, and stopped in a circular chamber lined with soft, low couches. Unlike the utilitarian spaces they had just walked through, this room gave the impres-sion of heavy, overwhelming luxury. The floor was covered in lacquered mahogany and the walls were painted deep green with mirrored wall panels.

The cat bowed to Sunflower. "Please rest in this place for a moment, Your Excellency."

A white cat wearing a red bow tie popped through a small door in the wall. A silver tray strapped to his back supported a half-dozen glass bowls of water.

Sunflower swiped a bowl from the tray and plopped onto a couch.

"The service at the spaceport is much better than I remember. The last time I was here I lost all my luggage and got fleas from an old tomcat."

Amy bent over and grabbed a bowl. "Don't you have cups or glasses? Maybe a straw?"

The white cat coughed and stared up at her with bright blue eyes. Amy could have sworn he shook his head a bit.

Sunflower flicked his tongue rapidly at the water in the bowl and laughed. "Don't be disgusting. This is Tau Ceti, not some back-alley diner on Alpha Centauri serving cheese sandwiches and pickles. You're on a civilized planet, so act like a civilized cat."

"I have to drink from a bowl?"

Philip lay the unconscious Betsy on a couch. "When in Rome, do as the Romans do."

"I'd rather be in Rome, now that you mention it."

The brown cat padded over to the dog on the couch. "Does this servant of yours require medical attention? We have canine doctors in the capital."

"Can't you hear him snoring?" asked Amy. "He'll be fine."

"You need a brain to have brain damage," said Sunflower.

Amy waved at Nick, up high near the ceiling. The tiny sprite buzzed down to the bowl in Amy's hands and took a long sip.

The brown cat bowed. "Now that we are in a secure location, allow me the opportunity to introduce myself."

Sunflower looked up from his water bowl. "You're Sooka Black."

"Your Excellency remembers his loyal servant?"

"Of course! You're the right-hand cat of the Emperor. I used to see you plastered across the magazine covers at the supermarket. That was before I got hired by the Lady, of course. Not much reason to go to the supermarket after that. Or come back, actually."

Sooka blinked for a long moment at Sunflower.

"The Lady? Supermarkets? I don't understand."

"What's not to understand? Everyone goes to the supermarket."

"Not you, sire. Never in a million years."

Sunflower squinted at him. "I know the Lady replaced most of the squishy bits inside me and that means I can't eat normal food, but how is that your business? Who do you think you are?"

"I'm Sooka Black. The billion-mao question is ... who are you?"

"I thought you already knew that. I'm Sunflower of the Western Range, apparently."

Sooka nodded. "Of course. Perhaps you would agree to a simple test to verify your identity?"

Amy laughed. "Airport security scan! Next, a flea dip."

Sunflower shook his head and sighed. "Whatever gets me through customs faster. The wait at the taxi stand can be massive."

The white cat appeared again through the small door with a small, pen-like device rattling around the silver tray on his back. Sooka Black flicked a paw, causing the "manos" bracelet around his wrist to sprout thin metal fingers, and grabbed the pen.

"By your leave?" he asked Sunflower.

Sunflower nodded, and Sooka touched the inside of Sunflower's paw with the end of the pen. The device clicked, causing Sunflower to yelp and jerk his paw away.

"My apologies, Excellency," said Sooka.

"These consular procedures are very strange," said Philip. "Perhaps we should have landed at the other spaceport."

Sunflower glared at Sooka and licked the bottom of his paw. "Maybe another planet entirely!"

Sooka Black stared at a small display on the pen-like device. "Again, I apologize for the intrusive test and my questions, sire, but it is necessary considering the prolonged period of your absence."

"Does everyone who goes off-planet get hassled like this?"

"Not everyone," said Sooka, and looked up from the pen. "Your DNA matches that of Sunflower, your appearance matches that of Sunflower, and your speech pattern, vocal tone, and vocabulary match that of Sunflower."

"Thank you, Captain Obvious, for telling me something I already know."

"One last test, if you please. A single fragment of information can prove that you are who you say you are, and not an imposter. Vast sums of treasure and entire departments of the intelligence service have kept this one fact a secret from anyone but the actual Sunflower."

"It's not about that cat from my junior year of college?" said Sunflower. "She promised she wouldn't tell. In fact, I think she joined another sorority."

Sooka Black shook his head. "No, sire. Tell me––who are your parents?"

Sunflower's whiskers drooped and he stared at the glass bowl between his paws.

"You know everything about me. You should know that, too."

"Please answer the question."

"My mother's name was Bocephus," whispered Sunflower. "My father went by many names, but most of the time he was called 'Amy.' The first ten years of my life, they drove from place to place, selling catnip and leather mugs from the back of the transport van that was also our home. My only friend was a mouse that lived under the passenger seat." He glared at Sooka Black. "Happy now? Thanks for bringing up the fact that I had a horrible childhood and hippy-dippy, catnip-smoking parents!"

Sooka Black's jaw dropped. The brown cat bowed low to the floor and touched his chin to his paws.

"Sire! Pardon this servant for ever questioning you!"

"Why does it matter who I am or who my parents are?" said Sunflower. "You're the second-most important cat in the Empire and I'm sure you have better things to do. Tell me if I've done something wrong or let us get in line for a taxi already."

"There is no need for Your Excellency to wait for a taxi," said Sooka Black. "It is true that I am the not the most important cat in all civilization. That would be Sunflower of the Western Range––the Emperor of Tau Ceti."

6

Standing on all fours on the couch, Sunflower froze into the spitting image of a stuffed animal Amy had seen in the Monterey Wax Museum, only he was a wide-eyed, open-mouthed orange tabby, not a pointy-eared bobcat. He failed to move even when Nick landed on his back.

"Does that mean I'm a princess?" asked the tiny blonde-haired sprite. "I've always wanted to be a princess!"

"You and everyone else in the universe," said Amy. "Welcome to the club."

Philip raised a hand. "I'd rather not be a princess. I've met several, and it's more bother than you can imagine."

"Fine. Apart from Phil here, everyone else is a princess."

"Yay!" squealed Nick, and twirled through the air.

Sunflower shivered and closed his mouth.

"Impossible," he said hoarsely. "Sassycat was Emperor when I left the planet. He'd only been on the throne a few months!"

Sooka Black trotted a few steps closer and squinted at Sunflower.

"Forgive me for being so bold, sire, but what happened when you boarded the *Andre Norton*?"

"The what?"

"RMS *Andre Norton*, the trans-dimensional warship developed by the Navy. You boarded the craft for a royal inspection and she disappeared in a gigantic flash of light."

"That couldn't have been me," said Sunflower. "I don't remember anything like that, and it's the kind of thing I'd put in my diary."

"But … where have you been for three years, Excellency?"

Philip cleared his throat. "His Highness suffered injuries in the accident, and unfortunately, memory loss. It was only by the greatest of efforts that he acquired another craft and traveled home."

"Exactly," said Amy. She leaned down to Sunflower. "We crossed through several DIMENSIONS where things are DIFFERENT from every other dimension."

Sunflower nodded slowly at Amy. "Other dimensions where things are different." His yellow eyes widened. "Oh! I get it."

"The Emperor has suffered injuries?" Sooka Black rushed to a wall and tapped several lighted buttons rapidly. A screen brightened and displayed a tuxedo cat wearing mirrored sunglasses. "Leave for Saint Tarder Hospital immediately!"

"Copy that," said the tuxedo cat. "Prepare for emergency launch, Your Worship."

Philip held up both hands. "There's no need to see a doctor. Sunflower's fine, apart from the memory loss."

"And bad attitude," said Amy. "Is there a pill for that?"

"What a pair of comedians," said Sunflower. "I hate hospitals and doctors and people that go to hospitals. It's the last place I want to be!"

The lights in the room darkened to red and a warbling came from the ceiling.

"No time," said Sooka Black. "Grab your harnesses!"

Orange webbing sprouted from the couches around the circular room. Sooka jumped next to Sunflower and helped him buckle the straps around his chest.

Strong vibrations shook the floor as Amy grabbed a seat on the nearest couch and threaded her arms through the orange belts. "This isn't a waiting room?"

"It IS a waiting room," said Sooka Black, fastening the buckles of his webbing. "A waiting room in an Imperial corvette."

Nick flew down and jumped into the breast pocket of Philip's jacket. The teenage boy snapped the safety webbing around his chest as the room began to shake.

Amy shrugged. "When in Rome ..."

Philip grinned and gave her a thumbs-up gesture.

The rumble below their feet grew louder, and Amy felt a heavy weight pushing her down into the couch. Steel building supports slid past the mirrored wall. Amy realized the mirrors were actually windows as the hangar dome dropped away, revealing mountains on the horizon and the still-crowded landing field below.

The room tilted and the engine sounds reduced in volume as they cruised over the brick buildings and puffing smokestacks of large factories outside the spaceport.

"Where are we going?" asked Philip.

Sooka Black waved a paw at the gleaming steel skyscrapers rapidly growing in the opposite window. "To the best hospital in Cheezburger."

"Change course immediately," said Sunflower. "I feel absolutely fine. Take us to the Imperial Palace."

"As you wish, Excellency."

Sooka Black unbuckled his safety harness and scrambled to the communications panel.

"I think Betsy's waking up," said Philip. He held the little brown and white dog on his lap.

"Ooo, my head," groaned Betsy, his eyes still shut. "The washing machine ... always the washing machine. Why, Dad? Why do you always use the maximum spin cycle?"

"Because he doesn't love you, that's why," said Sunflower.

Betsy shook his furry head with his eyes still closed. "That's not Dad, that's Sunflower. Why did you put me in the washing machine, Sunflower?"

"Dogs don't wear clothes," said Amy. "Why would they have a washing machine?"

"To clean puppies, of course," said Sunflower. "The little monsters are constantly smeared in filth, rooting through garbage, and sticking their noses into every dead poona they see."

Betsy opened his eyes in Philip's lap and stared up at the teenager.

"Philly-Billy! Did Sunflower put you in the washing machine, too?"

"Not at all. We're in some sort of flying craft. The confusion is understandable, since you hit your head rather hard today."

"He'd have brain damage if the Lady hadn't strengthened his bones with titanium," said Sunflower. "Should have replaced his entire head while she was at it."

Betsy climbed to the top of the couch and stared out the window at the city far below. "Where are we?"

Sooka Black puffed out his chest. "Cheezburger, capital of the empire."

"Whoa! Cool! I've never been there." Betsy stuck his nose on the glass and his breath fogged the window. "I hope they have marshmallows and I can eat some when Sunflower isn't looking. I also hope Sunflower didn't hear me say that."

"Don't worry, I never listen to anything you say," murmured the cat.

Sooka stood next to Betsy and looked carefully at the dog. "Perhaps we should land at the hospital, after all, sire. Your canine companion seems to have an altered mental status."

"Altered from what? That's the way Betsy's always been."

"Speaking of wacko mental cases," said Amy. "We left that giant lizard back at the ship. I hope he doesn't get into trouble."

Sunflower blinked at her. "What? You mean like getting his head stuck in a bucket or eating soap?"

Amy turned and looked out the window. She watched the peaked roofs and jade green tiles of the houses pass below her.

"Worse. I don't know, it's just a feeling."

NISTRA WIPED SWEAT from his scaly green snout and kicked the dome in the center of the power room.

"I command you to open! I want my planet back!"

"You're still here?" asked the matronly voice of the ship. "How may I assist you?"

"I've been trying to open this power dome for almost an hour! Do it for me."

"That course of action would not be recommended," said the ship. "As you lack the necessary security clearance to access the power core."

"Who has clearance?"

"Only Amy Armstrong, the captain."

Nistra slammed a green fist on the black dome. "Blast and double blast!"

"Secondary advisement: I do not detect the appropriate equipment for removing and containing a Class-M planet held in micro-stasis. A shopping bag will not suffice."

Nistra sighed and stuffed the plastic bag into his trousers. "How about a cardboard box?"

"That is also an insufficient container."

The sauropod nodded and paced around the large central dome, rubbing his clawed hands across the top of his head.

"I have to leave the ship, but I don't want the stupid human and her friends to abandon me. If only there were a small, critical component of that ship that I could take with me. A component that would keep the ship from leaving."

"You mean the keys?"

A small door opened in the power dome and a silver arm shot out. A keychain with a fuzzy rabbit's foot and a pair of glowing pink crystals dangled from the end. Nistra grabbed at the keychain, but the arm jerked back into the dome and the door clacked shut.

"You lack the necessary security clearance to possess the keys," said the ship.

Nistra stamped his foot. "Curse you, egg-sucking ship!"

The sauropod marched toward the exit hatch, his scaly fist raised to the ceiling.

"It is decided. I will leave you, ship, to face the innumerable threats and disgusting smells of Cheezburger, the capital of those foul, evil cats who are the eternal bane of my people. I may not return, but if I do, this sauropod will return as your new captain! And, if not as your new captain, at least with some sort of devious scheme to trick you into thinking I'm the new captain!"

Nistra gave a confident salute to the ceiling. The giant lizard marched out of the exit hatch and down the corridor.

"Exit's the other way," said the ship.

The sauropod turned on his heel and stamped the other direction.

"I knew that!" he snarled.

7

An irregular grid of roads crossed Cheezburger, connecting the peaked, jade-tiled roofs of the suburbs with high-rise apartments and the steel and glass skyscrapers of downtown. As the corvette flew toward the center of the urban forest, every inch of land seemed covered in squarish concrete buildings, all four sides marked with flashing billboards and bright advertisements. Many of the flat-roofed structures were dotted with tennis courts and soccer fields of pale artificial grass. Like a chrome-plated snake in the sunshine, a river curved through the eastern districts of the city, passing under bridges of concrete, steel, and suspended wire, the variety of architectural designs showing how the city had changed over time. A blue haze covered the eastern horizon--possibly an ocean or a huge lake--and snow-frosted mountains lay in the west. A square of forest sat in the center of the skyscrapers; an oasis of nature surrounded on all sides by concrete and steel.

Amy tapped on the window and pointed at the green square. "What's that down there? Looks like Golden Gate Park."

"Or Hyde Park, for that matter," said Philip, peering at the forest.

Sooka Black glanced through the window. "I assume you mean the Imperial Palace and gardens."

Amy stared at the brown cat. "The whole thing? It's a hundred acres, at least!"

"You may rest confident. It is the 'whole thing,' as you say."

His paws on the window, Sunflower shook his head in awe. "I've only seen the Imperial Palace on television," he whispered. "And I'm supposed to be the Emperor."

Amy smiled and leaned close to the cat. "I won't tell anyone."

The Imperial corvette banked through the tall buildings and cruised over a walled moat that separated the perfectly squared-off forest from the packed streets of downtown. Tiny figures crossed the moat on graceful, half-moon bridges made from darkly stained wood. A chalk-white wall topped with black clay tiles guarded the inside of the moat, and square wooden towers with multiple tiers of black-tiled roofs stood at each corner. As the corvette glided toward a patch of concrete and collection of wooden buildings, several ponds and small streams flashed in the sunlight. Irregular strips of garden and flowering plants showed through the trees, the fit and flow of which seemed to follow the openings and lines of the forest, rather than forcing a design upon nature. A multi-story pagoda covered in golden tiles rose from the center of the gardens with a white diamond painted in the center of the roof. A line of tiny figures marched ant-like along a path connecting the pagoda to the landing area.

"Hey! We're landing in a park!" said Betsy. "Are we going to play there?"

"If you wish," said Sooka Black. "This is the Imperial residence, where you will be staying."

"No way! Too expensive," said the terrier. "We can stay in a cat motel. They always have free breakfast."

"Please do not concern yourselves with money. We are honored to serve the guests of the Emperor in any way possible, and have spared no expense."

Betsy stared at the cat. "Does that mean 'yes' free breakfast or 'no' free breakfast?"

"Remuneration will not be required for any meal," said Sooka Black. Noticing that the terrier continued to stare, the cat cleared his throat. "Yes––free breakfast."

Betsy jumped and spread his legs. "Yee-haw! I always thought you cats were a bunch of stuck-up smarty pants with bad attitudes. But maybe that was just Sunflower, and everyone on Tau Ceti is really cool. This Emperor sounds like a swell cat, and I'm going to say thanks when I meet him."

Sunflower took a deep breath and sighed. "Somebody tell him."

Nick climbed out of Philip's pocket and buzzed through the air to Betsy.

"Sunflower IS the Emperor, you dink!"

"What? No, he's sitting right there. Hi Sunnie! Why is he shaking his head? Now he's giving me the secret sign to shut up. Now he's giving me the secret sign that means all dogs are stupid and can't understand secret signs. That's not true!"

Amy cleared her throat. "Nick is right. Sunflower is the Emperor of Tau Ceti."

"Really? That's weird," said the terrier. "He never said anything about it to me before, and I know all of his secrets. He even told me about that sorority party his junior year, and he's not supposed to tell anyone about that."

"Quiet, Betsy!" hissed Sunflower. "Let sleeping dogs lie, if you know what I mean."

"What? I always tell the truth! So anyway, at this party Sunflower and all these female cats–"

"Is there a dungeon around here?" Sunflower asked. "A tree to chain him to? Throw him into a puddle and I'll be happy."

Philip rubbed the brown-and-white fur on Betsy's back. "Let's focus on the present, Betsy, and at the present time, Sunflower is the Emperor."

"Period," said Amy. "End of discussion. Moving forward with our lives."

Betsy jumped down from the couch. "Cool! Does that mean I can be emperor, too? I want to yell at people and make them do stuff."

Sunflower rolled his eyes. "I'll put you in charge of the royal latrines."

"Cool! Wait——what's a latrine?"

"A closet full of rainbows and unicorns and bunny rabbits."

"Awesome!"

The entire room shook and the windows vibrated as the corvette touched down. Through the windows, the concrete landing pad was surrounded by dark wooden buildings and thick evergreen trees.

Sooka Black climbed out of his safety straps. "We've arrived. Please allow me to escort Your Excellency and honored guests to the palace."

Outside the airlock a solid formation of white, short-haired cats stood on all fours holding their tails straight up. The first two rows wore shiny black helmets that reminded Amy of samurai armor. All wore collars of twisted black and white cloth with a golden gem as a pendant.

Amy moved a few steps from the airlock and looked back at the glossy black hull of the corvette. At the bulbous front end of the craft, she recognized the windows of the observation deck. A faint buzz like a swarm of bumblebees came from behind her, and she turned back to the formation of cats.

"Aaa-tan-SYON! Forward LEFT!"

Paws swished across the concrete. The block of cats split into a pair of columns that faced each other, leaving room to walk between.

The buzzing grew in volume. A dozen white drones appeared over the tops of the evergreen trees and flew down to the landing pad. Shaped like half-domes with four horizontal propellers, the formation of drones split to the left and right and hovered behind the two columns of cats. A fanfare of music began to play from speakers on the flat bottom of each drone.

Betsy wagged his tail. "Awesome!"

A white cat with a gold star on his helmet walked up to Sooka Black and Sunflower with careful, measured steps. The cat bowed low to the ground and touched his chin to his paws.

"Welcome home, Glorious Emperor of the Flowering Pear Dynasty. Welcome home, Lord of the Northern Star and Wearer of the Red Diamond."

"How's it going?" said Sunflower.

Sooka Black whispered hastily in his ear.

"Sorry," said Sunflower. "Greetings, Imperial Commander Francine, Defender of the Palace and Wielder of the Golden Blade."

The white cat backed up, keeping his head low and facing Sunflower, and took his place in the column of cats to the left.

Sooka Black waved a paw forward. "Please, Your Excellency."

"Everybody's waiting for me? Okay, whatever," said Sunflower, and ambled between the columns of white cats.

Betsy jumped at Amy and put his paws on her leg. "Can I have one of those helmets? Please please please?"

"Hey!" Amy pushed the dog away. "Don't rip my futuristic space pantyhose! Just keep your mouth shut for a few minutes and we'll see."

Betsy nodded excitedly. "Mmm hmm mmm."

"Mouth shut means no sound."

The terrier dropped his head and followed Amy and Philip. The pair of teenagers trailed behind Sunflower and Sooka Black. Nick buzzed overhead, keeping a watchful eye on the flying drones blaring their triumphal music.

The white cats bowed as Sunflower approached. After all of the guests had passed they formed a column and followed at the rear, each cat marching on all fours to the music.

Sooka Black guided them along a path of gray stones that curved through a forest of what looked like maple and pine trees, across carefully trimmed lawns, and along the edge of a pond covered with water lilies, the petals of the flowers spread open and bright pink. A pavilion of lacquered wood stood in the center of the pond, and a line of irregular stepping-stones seemed to be the only way to reach it. The upper floors of skyscrapers loomed over the trees, but apart from that no sights or sounds of a modern city reached the palace grounds––no honking horns, rumble of traffic, or thunder of jet engines crossing the clear sky. Bright yellow birds chirped and hopped on the manicured lawns, dragonflies buzzed over the ponds, and a bird or strange insect droned *breem, breem, breem* from the trees. Every twenty meters, faint curls of smoke rose from bronze pedestals, adding a thick floral scent to the air.

Philip took a deep breath and sighed. "Quite refreshing."

Amy shrugged. "I don't know. I thought the future would be, you know, more future-y."

"As someone who has lived in the future for two years––specifically, Nick's apartment––I'm happy to have less of it, thank you very much."

Nick buzzed above Philip, her tiny hands on the waist of her white dress.

"Hey! You aren't complaining again, are you? Because one of the things I really don't like is complaining!"

"He is! He is!" barked Betsy. "I mean, Hmm mmm. Hmm mmm!"

Philip bowed to the tiny flying woman. "Quite the contrary. I'm very appreciative of the fact that you saved me from certain death. I'm simply observing that this is a very pleasant garden, with very clean, fresh air. Air that doesn't smell like stale Hostess Sno Balls."

Nick crossed her tiny arms and continued to hover in front of Philip.

"Complaining!"

"She's right," said Amy. "It is a little bit."

Philip smiled. "Now that you mention it, I love Sno Balls."

"Great," said Nick. "Ooo! A bird!"

The blonde-haired sprite turned a somersault and zipped across the pond.

Amy watched her fly and twirl into the distance. "She's not going to eat the poor thing, is she?"

Betsy giggled and trotted after Sunflower. "Don't be silly! Birds aren't junk food. Wait––unless it's a chocolate bird!"

"Thanks, but we're not in the Land of Dairy Queen."

"The worst that could happen is Nick will ask the bird too many awkward questions, and return as fast as she left," said Philip. "Shall we?"

The teenager offered his arm to Amy, and the pair walked together, eventually catching up to Sunflower and Sooka Black. The two cats were sitting in the middle of the brick path.

"That is correct, sire," said Sooka Black. "The palace and gardens were designed and build in the Fourth Dynasty by Emperor Scoodeloo, after the destruction of the previous residence." The brown cat waved a paw at a high slope in the forest. "That ridge is the overgrown wall of the original palace."

Sunflower shook his head. "Wow! You should totally clear it out and build a tennis court."

"A good idea, Your Highness," said Sooka Black. "Even though a modern recreational facility would clash with the Imperial philosophy of harmony with nature, I support your idea."

Amy cleared her throat. "The Emperor has been away for so long that everything seems new to him."

"Quite understandable. The subjects of His Excellency are absolutely overjoyed at his return."

"I got that impression," said Sunflower. "Half the cats in the city must have been at the spaceport. I haven't seen crowds that big since the Diet Jurg protests."

"Our happiness at your return knows no bounds, sire."

The small group left the pond and strolled under the shade of broad-limbed trees, the troop of white cats marching silently at the rear. They passed another wooden pavilion nestled under trees next to a low hill, and yet another in a clearing a few minutes later.

"I'm quite unfamiliar with Tau Ceti and hope you don't mind me asking," said Philip. "But how does one become Emperor? I don't think Sunflower's parents were royalty."

"An Imperial lottery is held after the passing of the previous regent," said Sooka Black. "The winner may choose a lifetime supply of fish, or a lifetime as Emperor of all cats."

"Wouldn't the Emperor get as much fish as he wants?"

Sooka Black nodded. "True, but we had to weed out the stupid winners somehow."

Amy stopped and leaned against a tall maple tree. "We should have called a taxi. Did you plan on landing as far as possible from the palace, or was it an accident?"

Sooka Black turned. "Pardon? Do you need assistance?"

"Amy was joking," said Philip. "But how much further is it?"

"My deepest apologies. It is only a short distance, honored guests."

The party approached a ten-meter gate constructed from a pair of massive, red-painted logs with three vertical planks linking them at the top. As they passed through the red gate, both Sooka Black and Sunflower stopped. The cats bowed, clapped their paws together, and continued walking.

"Is that a prayer?" asked Amy.

"Nothing as silly as that," said Sunflower. "It's to scare away evil spirits."

Sooka Black nodded. "Passing through the gate is a cleansing process; a gesture to show that we leave behind the foulness of modern life."

Amy clapped and bowed. "Hai-keeba or whatever. And that foul smell is Betsy, not me. I took a shower."

Philip bowed. "As did I."

"I already had my bath for the week," said Betsy. "Sunflower sprayed me with a can of soda."

"I don't know what planet you're from——"

"Kapetyn. It was the first planet colonized by dogs!"

Amy rolled her eyes. "Even there, I'm sure soda doesn't count as a bath."

"You haven't been to Kapetyn," said Sunflower.

The brick path through the forest widened to a four-lane boulevard covered in white gravel. Another tall wooden gate loomed ahead, requiring another round of bowing and clapping as the cats, dogs, and humans passed beneath the massive logs. The gravel-lined path turned ninety degrees to the right, and the thick forest opened to a plaza surrounded by plain yellow buildings covered in tiles of the same color. A golden, multi-story pagoda rose into the clear sky, its large doors perfectly aligned with the last gate. The drones stopped playing their processional music and buzzed away into the trees.

Philip pointed at the pagoda. "I've read several books on the Orient, and that looks just like a temple."

"Could be a palace," said Amy.

Sooka Black bowed his head. "Both honored guests are correct."

The brown cat led them to a stone basin, the edges lined with wooden cups on short sticks. The cat pushed down on a lever attached to a spout and poured clear water into one of the cups. He gave this to Sunflower, who dumped the cold liquid over his head and yelped.

Amy covered her mouth and giggled. "A cat pouring water over himself? What's next? Flying pigs?"

"Ha ha," sneered Sunflower. "It's not just water. It's holy water, blessed by the Imperial high priest of Saint Mittens."

"Oh, that makes all the difference."

Philip cleared his throat. "Sarcasm, Amy."

"Sorry."

"His Excellency is correct." Sooka Black poured a cup, doused himself with water, and shivered, throwing drops everywhere. "A cleansing with holy water is required to enter the palace."

Amy sighed. "Can I get a holy hair dryer? A sacred towel? I'm no girly-girl, but I don't want to walk around all day with wet hair."

Sunflower stared at her. "You're a female?"

"Nice one. You know you've used that joke before, right?"

"Amy, allow me to assist you," said Philip. The teenager poured water into the hand-held ladle. "Hold your head over the basin."

"Don't you dare!"

Philip winked. "Trust me."

Amy pouted for a second, and then leaned over the stone basin. Without warning, Philip gasped and pointed at the forest across the plaza.

"By the gods! Look——a squirrel!"

Sooka Black, Sunflower, and the entire troop of cats scrambled in a mad, chaotic dash across the plaza, tails twitching and eyes searching the trees.

"Where?" growled Sunflower. "I'm the Emperor. I get to chase it!"

Betsy hopped in front of him. "You've never seen a squirrel in your life. I'm a dog and the only one qualified to catch it."

"You can't even climb a tree!"

Water splashed behind them. The cats turned to see Philip setting an empty ladle on the edge of the stone basin.

"There you go, Miss Armstrong. All finished dousing you with holy water."

Amy bowed with a clumsy half-curtsey. "Thank you."

Sooka Black stared wide-eyed at the pair of humans. "It's a miracle! Your friend's hair is completely dry. The holy water has magically evaporated!"

Sunflower shrugged. "Mabily ..."

The troop of white cats gathered at Amy's feet, bowed low to the ground, and meowed with a stream of low, reverent tones.

Sooka Black turned to Sunflower. "Once we find this squirrel and destroy it, we'll consecrate your friend as a living goddess. Word will quickly spread over the planet of this miracle of disappearing water."

Amy shrugged. "Being called a goddess is fine, but no autographs, please."

Philip cleared his throat. "Quite. As it happens, I believe I was mistaken about the squirrel. It was simply a falling leaf. No need to over-excite yourselves about that."

Betsy growled. "A leaf that looks like a squirrel? Kill it!"

The terrier scrambled across the open plaza, jumping and biting at dozens of suspicious leaves on the ground.

"At least Betsy has something to do for the next week," said Sunflower. "Shall the rest of us——"

A high-pitched scream split the air. A tiny shape flew out of the forest and plunged into the stone basin, showering everyone with water.

"Nice one," said Amy, holy liquid dripping down her face.

Philip reached into the water and pulled out a fluttering Nick, her hair and dress completely soaked. The tiny sprite coughed and fanned her transparent wings with a sound like the outboard motor from Barbie's pink plastic fishing boat.

"Where is he? I'm gonna kill him!"

Amy shrugged. "Who?"

"That stupid bluebird! He laughed at me and called my dress ugly. How do you think I got so wet?"

Philip set the blonde-haired sprite on the edge of the stone basin. "You plummeted into the water, that's how."

The miniature woman stamped her bare leg. "No, I didn't! I was chasing him and he pushed me in! I swear I'm never making friends ever again."

"Finally, some good news," said Sunflower.

Nick crossed her arms and shivered. "And now I'm going to freeze to death!"

"It must be my birthday," said Sunflower.

"Ooo! I hate cats! They're so mean."

Amy pointed to the circle of wide-eyed cats around the basin. "Not a smart thing to say on a planet full of them." She untied the black ribbon from her hair and gave it to Nick. "Remember——not all cats are like Sunflower. Here, use this."

Nick wrapped the black material around her body in a makeshift towel. "How's it gonna stay in place?"

Amy pulled a bobby pin from her hair and slid it down the back of the ribbon. "Problem solved."

Philip picked up the sprite and guided her into a pocket of his jacket. "You can ride with me until you warm up."

"Are the honored guests ready to proceed?" asked Sooka Black. "Let us continue."

The brown cat led Amy and her friends across the plaza in the direction of the golden pagoda, as the troop of white cats filled their helmets from the pump and and poured water on their furry heads.

"What's the plan for today?" asked Sunflower. "If you say meetings, meetings, meetings, and more meetings I swear I'll burn this place to the ground."

"No meetings are on the agenda, sire. Would you like drinks and refreshment?"

Sunflower watched Betsy gallop across the plaza with a leaf on his nose. "Not really. I don't eat normal food."

"I assure you, Excellency, it is prepared by the best cat chefs and far from normal food."

"That's not what I meant. It's ... uh, it's not easy to explain. Anyway, I bet my friends are starving. I just wanted to know if there was anything fun to do around here. The Emperor gets all the cable channels, right?"

"Of course, sire. In that case, it is my humble suggestion that Your Excellency retires to his chambers for a rest. The Emperor may visit with his council in the morning, and if he wishes, may choose to hold court."

"Groovy."

"Sire?"

"Uh, the Emperor approves."

Sooka Black led the group toward the pagoda and passed through a simple gate of mahogany beams and plaster walls. A pair of gigantic red doors covered in hundreds of fist-sized brass studs creaked open, and on the other side Amy saw a dozen white cats in samurai helmets and lacquered black armor. All stood at attention on their back legs and held cat-sized assault rifles against their furry shoulders.

The humans and cats followed Sooka Black across a small plaza and through another red-painted, brass-studded door. The yellow pagoda loomed tall against the pale blue sky, but instead of continuing to the multi-storied tower, Sooka Black turned right and trotted through a wooden breezeway, the bright red beams covered with hand-painted nature scenes.

"Aren't we going to the palace?" asked Amy. "I thought it was the big yellow thing. Don't tell me it's not a real palace and made of cheese or something weird, because at this point I'd believe anything."

Sooka Black stopped and stared at her. "Cheese? Never in a million poona years. Ah, but I see the confusion. The Hall of Harmonious Justice is where the Emperor holds court, but does not sleep. That is the royal living area, which lies ahead."

The covered breezeway led them past dozens of rooms, the sliding doors wide open and packed with cats wearing necklaces of twisted black-and-white cloth, each bowing low and touching chin to front paws. A mournful plucking sound carried across the warm breeze, and as they passed a stone garden filled with tall and rounded limestone, Amy saw a tuxedo cat sitting behind a table. The cat wore an embroidered white robe and played a long, horizontal zither, his paws gliding over the strings of the lacquered wood instrument.

"A harp of some kind?" murmured Philip. "Odd to see a cat playing music on that."

"Odd to see a cat playing music on anything," said Amy.

Sooka Black opened a pair of sliding doors and led them to a chamber full of soft yellow couches and pillows covered in delicate embroidery of fish and bright flowers.

"Wow," said Sunflower, craning his neck. "Is this my bedroom?"

"This is simply a rest area, sire," said Sooka Black. "A small room where guests may meet with Your Excellency. Your bedroom and those of your wives are through a nearby corridor."

Amy and Philip looked at each other. "Wives?"

A door flew open and a packed mob of cats streamed into the room, all of different breeds and wearing collars of twisted yellow cloth. The deafening chatter and giggles of dozens of female voices filled the room, along with an overpowering cloud of many different perfumes.

"Sunflower, you're back!"

"Dearest Excellency!"

"We've waited so long!"

"You've so much to tell us!"

"Me! Me! Look at me, sire!"

The female cats pulled Sunflower toward the door through which they'd entered the room. The orange tabby simply grinned at his friends as they dragged him away. The wooden door slid shut with a bang, and the eager chatter and giggles faded to silence.

"You don't see that every day in the park," said Philip. "Unless you're the Emperor, I suppose."

Amy shook her head. "I hope Sunflower's going to be okay."

"The Emperor has been absent several years, and his wives are happy to see him," said Sooka Black. "There is no danger to his person."

Nick peeked her head out of Philip's jacket pocket. "His person? It looked like they were going to eat him!"

"It is not a custom on Tau Ceti to devour the Emperor."

"With that many females around, he may wish for death," said Philip. "Ouch! My ribs!"

"Sorry," said Amy. "My elbow slipped really hard."

A scratching came from the double doors of the entrance. Amy slid one to the side and Betsy tumbled into the room.

"Finally," gasped the brown and white terrier, his pink tongue drooping from his jaws. "I found you. We gotta help Sunflower––he's been kidnapped by a bunch of cats!"

"Can't kidnap the willing," said Philip. "Those are his wives."

Betsy stared at him. "Wives? Wow, the more I learn about Sunflower, the less I know."

"That's hard to believe," squeaked Nick.

"It's like that night at the sorority I've been trying to tell you about," said Betsy. "He snuck inside all by himself and the next morning––"

Amy held up a hand. "Too much information, Betsy. Right now, I'm starving."

Sooka Black bowed. "I will have food sent immediately," he said, and pushed through a tiny square door.

Amy plopped onto a soft yellow couch and stretched out, her arms above her head. "What an exhausting day, and it's not even over!"

Philip sat on a nearby cushion. "I agree. Quite an interesting development, what with Sunflower being the Emperor of Tau Ceti and all."

Amy rolled onto her side and closed her eyes. "So soft ..."

"The resources of a planetary empire should make it easy to find Cynthia MacGuffin," said Philip. "We should be able to repair the recombinator and return you to Earth in no time at all."

"Earth," murmured Amy.

"Hey, Nicky," whispered Betsy. "Want to go look for some real food?"

"They're bringing it to us, you moron," hissed the sprite. "Didn't you hear what the brown cat said?"

"That's boring human food. I saw some candy when I was looking for you guys."

"Bring it on!" squealed Nick.

The tiny blonde woman clambered out of Philip's pocket and buzzed through the air to Betsy. She plopped onto the dog's neck like a miniature cowgirl and grabbed his fur with both hands.

"Giddyup and go!"

The brown-and-white terrier scrambled through the double doors of the entrance with Nick on his back, leaving Amy and Philip completely alone.

Philip sat unmoving on his cushion and watched her for a moment. "Are you tired?"

Like a teenager paralyzed from the neck down, Amy kicked off her shoes with a flick of her ankles, and they thumped onto the soft carpet.

"A little," she murmured. "Confused at everything. Lot of things happened today."

Philip nodded. "The real Emperor is missing."

"Yep."

"What happens if he comes back?"

Amy brushed blonde hair out of her eyes. "That's a good reason to find this MacGuffin cat as soon as possible."

"What if MacGuffin doesn't exist in this dimension?"

Amy yawned. "Then we're stuck here. Not HERE here, but this version of the galaxy."

She felt the couch sink as Philip sat next to her waist.

"Quite a few 'what ifs' ahead of us," said the dark-haired teenager. "What if we find MacGuffin and fix the recombinator on the ship? What if we actually find your Earth, your 1995, your family? There's no way to return to my dimension. No way back to my family."

Amy opened her eyes. "I thought you didn't want to return, that it was a horrible life. What about all that stuff about staying with me? Are you taking it back?"

Philip turned red. "Not at all!" He took Amy's hand and kissed the back of her fingers. "There is no question when it comes to you and me, dearest Amy. There is no 'what if' in my heart."

"You've got a really strange look on your face," said Amy. "Are you going to murder me now?"

"No," murmured Philip.

"Why are you whispering?"

Philip smiled. "Because."

He leaned down to kiss her, his gray eyes the color of rain and his pupils wide and black. His lips were soft and warm on Amy's mouth, and she didn't push him away.

A few minutes later, the double entrance doors slid open with a bang.

"We brought food!" yelled Betsy. "Wait——what are you doing?"

The teenagers sat up quickly and scooted to opposite sides of the cushion.

"Nothing," said Amy, hastily brushing her fingers through her long blonde hair. "Not a thing."

"It didn't look like nothing," said Betsy. "Nothing is staring at a wall and I know because I do it a lot.

That looked like Philip was trying to eat you. It's a good thing I found some food!"

"They were kissing, you dink," said Nick. "Now we wait for the babies to come out." She flew up to Amy and poked her in the belly with both hands. "How long does it take? Five minutes? I can't wait that long!"

Amy turned red. "Stop asking me about that! I'm not having a baby. Not now, and not ever!"

Nick buzzed away from Amy's swatting hands. "She's mad! I think it means there's a baby. Where does it come out? Her ears are red. I think it pops out of her ears."

Philip cleared his throat. "If you don't change the subject, I believe that Amy is going to lose her temper. I also suggest not staring at her, because it's obvious what you're thinking."

Nick crossed her arms and pouted. "I'm not! Anyway, we found some candy made from honey, and some bags of sweet buns. I'll share them with you."

"As long as Betsy doesn't eat anything," said Philip. "He can only have ReCarb, the same blue spheres that Sunflower eats."

"I know, I know," said the terrier. "But can I put it in my mouth, chew it for a minute, and spit it out?"

Philip shook his head. "Once the camel sticks his nose under the tent, the body will soon follow."

Betsy spun around. "Camel? Where?!!"

Amy took a bag of buns from Nick. She opened the crinkly clear plastic and wrinkled her nose at the smell.

"Where did you get these?"

Betsy trotted up to her. "Behind a building. It's great, right?"

"Did you find this inside a big green can with a lid?"

"No."

Amy sighed. "Good."

"It was in a big metal box with a lid," said Betsy. "With a million cool smells and all kinds of things squashed together in black bags!"

Amy handed the bag of sweet buns back to Nick. "Thanks, but I don't eat garbage."

"Your loss," said Nick. The tiny blonde woman pulled a glazed bun half her size from the package and shoved her face into it. "Junk food is garbage, isn't that what you said, Philip?" she mumbled with a mouth full of sticky bread. "That's what I love! Junk food."

A lacquered door slid open, and Sooka Black trotted into the room at the head of a procession of tuxedo cats, each with silver trays strapped to their furry backs. Heaping dishes of food rattled and clinked on the trays.

Philip clapped. "Bravo!"

Sooka Black pressed a button on the wall and a low square of lacquered wood rose from the floor. The tuxedo cats tilted their trays and the dishes of food slid across and down to the table. The cats pushed cushions around all four sides and trotted out the same door.

"Please enjoy yourselves, honored guests," said Sooka Black, and turned to leave.

Amy raised a hand. "Wait! What is all this stuff?"

"My apologies. I had forgotten you are not familiar with our cuisine."

The brown cat leaned over the table and pointed at the various dishes.

"Slices of raw *pwason* from the royal lakes, un-cooked *somon* from the streams of the Amber Mountains, chopped seaweed in sesame sauce, buckwheat noodles with fermented dipping sauce, bowls of white rice from the imperial fields, *kribich* covered in spicy-sweet glaze, milk buns, potato and poona stew infused with onion, and a bowl of live *wouj*."

Sooka Black pointed to a large glass cylinder in the center of the table, filled with water and a swarm of goldfish.

Amy stared at the fish. "Live what? I've had sushi before, but goldfish? That's like a school prank you force on your worst enemy. Not that I ever did that or anything."

"The fish must be decorative and not part of the meal," said Philip.

Sooka Black shook his head. "No, no. Live seafood is a very popular dish on Tau Ceti, but I apologize––this must have slipped through by accident. I gave the cooks very specific instructions not to include live fish. It will be removed at once."

He clapped his paws. A pair of tuxedo cats appeared and carried off the heavy cylinder of water, gasping and sweating as they held it between them.

Amy glanced at Philip. "Cooks for live fish? They don't have to 'cook' anything!"

The teenager shrugged. "Perhaps they season the water?"

"That's exactly the case, honorable guest," said Sooka Black. "If you'll excuse me, I must retire. The day has been quite busy and I must deal with several matters." He waved to a door on the left. "Sleeping areas for each guest and washing stations can be found along this corridor. Attendants will be on duty at all times if you have need of anything."

Betsy sniffed at an orange slice of raw fish and looked up. "Need anything? I need a marshmallow!"

Sooka Black bowed. "Of course. What is a marshmallow?"

"Please ignore Betsy," said Amy. "He looks like a normal dog, but actually he can't eat any food at all, especially marshmallows."

"He's far from a normal dog," said Philip. "I suppose that means he's abnormal."

"Hey!" barked the terrier. "I'm right here!"

Sooka Black bowed and touched his furry chin to the floor. "As you wish. Have a pleasant evening and a comfortable sleep."

The brown cat left the room and slid shut the paneled wooden door.

"Ah," said Philip. "Here's one problem: they've forgotten the silverware. I don't see a single fork or spoon."

Betsy giggled. "Cats don't use forks."

Nick bit off a huge chunk of sweet bun. "Yeah, Philly-billy. You should know that!"

"I know that none of the cats and dogs that worked for the Lady used forks or spoons, but I assumed the cats of the Imperial Palace would have more manners."

"We didn't use forks because we're different, not because of manners," said Betsy. "She changed our insides. All we had to eat were the blue balls of Re-Carb, and you don't need a fork for that. You just need a mouth-hole!"

Amy held up a pair of silver chopsticks. "I bet we use these. You hold them together and pinch the food with the other end."

Betsy jumped onto a couch. "That's right! Cats always do things the hard way. It's like the opposite of how dogs run a planet."

Nick looked up from the sticky bun, her face and hair smeared with frosting. "Don't talk about Kapetyn at the dinner table! You'll make all of us barf like a fire hose."

Amy had no problems using the metal chopsticks, but Philip grabbed a piece of fish with the metal rods and immediately dropped it on the floor.

Amy patted him on the knee. "Use your hands. I won't tell anyone."

"Thank you, Miss Armstrong," Philip said, and grinned. "It's always good to have friends."

8

It was dark, stormy, and cold––three good reasons for Nistra to shrink into the collar of his trench coat. The rain poured over the brim of his hat, streamed from the gutters, and roared down the fire escapes. In the black slice of sky above the stinking alley, lightning flashed and thunder rolled.

Night had come quickly in Tau Ceti, along with the rain. The skies had opened up just after he'd snuck out of the spaceport, but he'd stumbled across an unconscious human lying behind a grocery store, and luckily the filthy rags fit the sauropod. Few similarities linked the giant reptiles and their cat creators, and a wardrobe was definitely not one of them.

He'd tramped halfway across the city to this damp alley that smelled of fish and the graffiti-covered green door lit by a bulb dangling from a chain. Luck had led him here––luck and accidentally glancing at a poster slapped on a dripping concrete wall. Between a concert poster and an advertisement for Slurm stood the smiling but obviously airbrushed face of a brown sauro and a critical message:

"Celebrate Galactic Food at the Toho District Cultural Festival! Sponsored by Rotarians 1443."

Nistra had pulled the scrap of paper from the wall and held it to his chest like a baby sauropod hugging a freshly stuffed cat.

The Rotarians were an exclusively sauropod organization with a charter to spread lizard culture throughout the galaxy. Laying naked in the sun all day or biting the heads off live poona might sound like Egg Heaven to sauros, but these "cultural" habits never became accepted by most humans, cats, or dogs,

despite the Rotarian outreach. The clubs quickly became a place for expatriate sauropods to meet and
complain about how bad life was on every planet
compared to Kepler Prime, even though all of them
knew it was an absolute lie. Life on Kepler Prime was
a constant parade of bullies sticking sharp things
where you didn't want them to be stuck.

A foot splashed through a puddle. Nistra watched
a huge figure move through the shadows at the opening of the alley, his steps measured and heavy. Rain
dripped from his scaly brown head and beaded on the
shoulders of his raincoat.

The sauropod stopped and pounded on the green
door with a huge fist, and then turned and stared at
Nistra with clear yellow eyes until the former prison
official looked away. Hinges squealed and a crash of
music and boisterous laughter filled the alley. Nistra
looked up to see the huge sauropod duck inside the
battered entrance. The door slammed and the alley
returned to the quiet patter of rain and swish from cat
traffic on the street.

Nistra clenched a fist. "Knock on the door," he
whispered to himself. "Just do it!"

The faint sound of lizard singing reached his ear-
holes. At first Nistra thought it came from inside the
club, but a pair of sauropods appeared at the head of
the alley and the singing grew louder.

The pair held each other with arms draped across
their shoulders and swayed from side to side, soaked
to the bone in their blue nylon track suits––a fashion
normally repellant to sauropods, but on a planet of
cats few choices were available. Both sauros wore zero-g football caps with the brims turned backwards.

The sauros stopped in front of the battered door
and stared at Nistra.

"Hello," said the one on the left. "Why's he standing in the rain?"

The sauro on the right hiccuped. "Maybe he's hungry."

"What?"

"That's what I do. When I'm hungry, I go outside and look for something to eat."

"I need to get inside but I don't have enough money," said Nistra. "Actually, I don't have any money at all."

"Is that true?" The sauro on the left walked up and put an arm around Nistra, leading him to the door. "Don't worry about anything. You just come along with old uncle Astra. We'll set you up."

"Can't let a fellow countryman go to waste." The other sauro bowed and almost fell over. "Whoops!"

"That's Plastra," said Astra. "He's had too much to drink."

Plastra bared his sharp teeth. "I have not!"

"Do you blame him? It's horrible, all these cats walking on the streets, driving cars, doing things in their cat buildings. It's like they own the place!"

"They do own the place," said Plastra. "Now who's drunk? That fermented pond water is giving you brain damage."

"It's not pond water; it's cat wine!"

"Same thing."

The sauro held onto his zero-g ballcap with one claw and thumped on the scratched green metal with the other. The battered door opened a crack and a yellow eye glared out.

"What's the password?"

Astra shrugged. "Dunno. Let me in or I'll slice your face off."

"Correct," said the eye.

A scaly green claw forced its way out, palm up, and Astra slapped a few crumpled notes into it.

"Three of you, so three hundred mao!" hissed the eye.

"Sorry," said Astra. He dug through the pockets of his nylon jacket and found another pink bill.

The door swung open and the two sauros pushed Nistra into a maelstrom of sound and smell.

Wide and muscular reptilian bodies packed the club, from the stools at the long wooden bar to the stage at the other end, where a band fronted by a sauro in a black vest and flat-brimmed hat growled a blues-punk tune into a silver microphone. A blue banner embroidered with the symbol of a gear and "Rotarians 1443" waved above the head of the lead singer, and framed photos of sauros with their arms around each other were tacked to the walls. The stink of spilled vine juice covered everything, along with the earthy smell of unwashed reptile, the odor of herbal cigarettes, and the ammonia stench of poona urine. The brown, hamster-like creatures scrambled through the wood chips of a terrarium fastened to on the far wall.

"Thanks," Nistra yelled to Astra and Plastra.

The pair of sauros nodded under the noise from the band, and pushed through the crowd to the terrarium. After paying the barkeep, the sauros each grabbed a poona from the clear enclosure and shoved the wriggling creatures into their mouths.

Nistra peeled off his dripping hat and trench coat and hung them on wall pegs near the door. He'd been stationed at the prison for so long that he'd lost the taste for live creatures. Artificial poona made from soybeans was much better for the digestion, mainly because it didn't squirm and squeak inside your digestive pouch for two hours.

A huge claw poked him in the shoulder and he turned. The brown sauro he'd seen earlier towered over him.

"We don't need the stinking army around here," growled the giant reptile. He fingered the silver insignia on Nistra's uniform jacket. "Especially not a desk jockey from the prison."

Nistra pushed the claw away. "Are you telling me to leave?"

The giant sauro grinned, displaying a mouth packed with sharp teeth.

"Yes."

The band stopped playing and everyone in the club turned to watch.

"Okay," said Nistra. "I get it."

He turned toward the door, but quickly lashed out backwards with his right foot, striking the crotch of the imposing sauro. The giant reptile screeched and doubled over. Nistra kneed him in the jaw, then grabbed the sauro's thick wrist and applied pressure to the nerve.

"Ow! Ow ow ow!"

The giant fell to the floor and tried to squirm away from the pain, but Nistra kept the arm high, increasing the angle of twist.

"Lemmee go!"

"Apologize," murmured Nistra.

"I'm sorry! I'm sorry!"

"Not to me. To the glorious army of the Sauro Republic."

"I'm sorry for saying bad things! The army is great!"

Nistra dropped the sauro's arm and straightened his jacket. "Right, and don't you forget it. Don't insult officers, especially ones from a prison. We have lots of training in nerve locks, and plenty of criminals for practice."

"Yes, sir."

Nistra felt the eyes of everyone in the club on him. He bowed.

"Good evening," he said. "I am Detention Officer First Class Nistra, formerly of the High-Security Anti-Recidivist Long-term Prison, otherwise known as H.A.L.P."

A scattering of applause and cheers erupted from the crowd of sauropods.

"Thank you," said Nistra. "Fellow Keplerites, you don't know how happy I am to see another scaly face after being trapped on a spaceship with filthy humans, a cat, and a dog."

The crowd murmured in disgust.

"I've come to ask for help."

Nistra held up the photo of Amy he'd taken from the ship.

"This foul human creature has stolen my planet and is using it to power her own starship. Does she care about the millions of lives she's putting at risk? Does she lay awake at night, wondering how to free the innocent sauros in her engine room? No! She seeks only her own personal enjoyment."

The crowd of sauros roared and stomped their feet. The entire bar shook with deafening noise until Nistra held up a hand.

"Treasure and glory await those who will help me attack the ship belonging to this human. I swear on the eternal Egg that I will not sleep until we have destroyed this half-grown pirate and her cowardly cat and dog slaves. Those who join me will forever bring honor to the homeworld!"

The giant sauro climbed to his feet and pumped his scaly fist high. "Let's destroy it!"

"Kepler Prime?"

"No, the spaceship! Smash it to the size of poona droppings!"

Nistra smiled and gripped the giant's shoulder. "I have a better idea, my new best friend. We're going to steal it."

THE PILLOW vibrated under Amy's cheek. A few seconds later, the panes of glass in her bedroom window rattled.

She threw off her blankets and ran into a hallway lined with red columns, the wooden floor cold and smooth under her bare feet. The pale light of morning shone through horizontal wooden slats high on the walls.

Doors opened in the hall. Philip, Betsy, and Nick peered out from separate rooms.

"Did you feel that?" asked Amy.

Philip stepped into the hallway. "An explosion, more or less."

Amy giggled and covered her mouth with both hands. "Are you wearing a nightgown?"

Philip's sleeveless white garment brushed the floor, an identical copy of the one Amy wore right down to the lace hem and neckline. The tall teenager glanced down and shrugged.

"Is anything wrong?"

"That's for a girl, not a boy," said Amy, giggling through her fingers.

Betsy jumped in the air and barked. "I told him but he wouldn't listen!"

"I'm not about to take sartorial advice from a dog, especially on a cat planet. Where I'm from, it's perfectly normal for a man to dress like this in the evening."

Amy walked up to Philip and tugged at his cotton dress. "Dear Philip, this isn't Victorian London. Where I'm from, this is a nightgown for girls. Do you want to be a girl?"

Wearing a tiny version of the nightgown, Nick flew up to Philip, her wings buzzing.

"That would be so cool! We could be best friends and dress up like princesses!"

The teenager turned red. "I certainly don't want to change my sex or become a princess in any way, shape, or form. Please excuse me."

He jumped into his room and slammed the door. It opened a second later.

"It was on my bed, if you wish to know!"

"He's right," said Betsy. The terrier scratched behind his ear with a paw. "Maybe the cats want him to be a girl?"

Amy held up a hand. "Changing the subject. What was that boom I just heard?"

Nick shrugged her tiny shoulders. "How are we supposed to know? Ask Furball. Here he comes."

Roused either by the slammed door or the conversation of his imperial guests, a brilliantly white and outrageously fluffy Persian cat approached from the end of the hallway, his tail waving lazily in the air.

"You can't call him that," whispered Amy. "It sounds racist. Or cat-ist."

Betsy tilted his brown and white head. "But that's his name." He raised his voice. "Hey, Furball––move it or lose it!"

The white cat scrambled down the hallway and slid to a stop next to Betsy.

"Yes? How may Furball help the honored guests?"

Amy rubbed her eyes. "I should have known. Furball, what was that sound we heard a few minutes ago?"

The white Persian bowed. "That was me, your honors, and I apologize. I had spicy kribich last night, far too many, and gave myself indigestion. I was a greedy, disgusting cat and the sound must have woken your honors."

"No, no. I mean the big explosion."

The cat bowed even lower. "The servant's litter box was full so I used the imperial closet at the end of the hall. I have damaged my family's name and will resign immediately. Farewell forever and I hope you never see this stupid and revolting servant again, unless it is to step over my bloated corpse in the street."

Amy sighed. "Don't resign or anything like that. I'm talking about the booming sound from outside. Did it come from the sky?"

The cat stared up at her with wide blue eyes. "The sky? Ah, yes! Your honor must be speaking of the atmospheric defenses. Any meteor that is somehow missed by the orbital satellites is targeted and destroyed by high-powered lasers surrounding the city. It is a common sound for residents of Cheezburger, and that is why I did not think of it at first. I have shamed the Furball family and will resign immediately. Farewell forever and please spit upon my bloated corpse if you––"

"Stop saying you're going to resign," said Amy. "You're doing a great job, and thank you for the information."

Furball bowed. "I live to serve, your honors."

Amy knocked on Philip's door. "It was just an exploding meteor!"

"Thank you, I heard," came the boy's muffled voice.

Amy went back to her room and washed up in the small bathroom. Someone had laundered her clothes overnight and placed them in neat triangular bundles at the foot of her bed. While she was changing, a white cat knocked on the door and delivered a tray containing rolls of smoked fish and rice, and a cup of hot green tea.

The cat bowed. "Honored guest, the imperial court will assemble in twenty minutes."

"Do I have to go?"

The cat's green eyes bulged. It stammered an incomprehensible reply, then sprinted down the hall, the empty tray clattering on its back.

Philip stuck his head out of his room and grinned at Amy. "I think that means 'yes.'"

A CROWD OF long-haired white Persians streamed through the imperial quarters, uprooting servants, soldiers, and guests and dragging them along like corn cobs in a flash flood.

Amy and her friends fell in behind a gray tabby in a red cape. The cat began to drone in a deep voice as he led the crowd in a chant.

Sunflower the mighty

Sunflower the great
Lord of the North Star
Leader of the state

He is the chosen one
He wears the crown
Emperor of the flowering pear
To him we bow down

Amy jogged faster and the tails of the cat servants whipped past her skirt. She caught up with Philip and the teenagers linked arms.

"Sunflower's not going to leave the palace," she whispered. "Not unless we drag him out by his ears. Would you give up all this if you were King of England?"

Philip shrugged. "As we say, a bed of roses is no place to sleep."

"Because of the thorns?"

"Precisely, my dearest."

The river of cats pushed Amy and her friends through the red-columned walkways of the imperial living quarters and toward the Hall of Harmonious Justice——the towering yellow pagoda in the center of the palace grounds. They crossed a plaza of carefully-swept concrete, the cats chanting verses to Sunflower, and climbed steps to a yellow door covered with a pattern of huge golden studs. Flying drones hovered in a ring around the pagoda with solemn processional music warbling from their speakers.

"Halt!"

A guard in a samurai helmet blocked the door and pointed his assault rifle at Betsy.

"Dogs are not allowed in the Hall of Harmonious Justice!"

"The what?" asked Betsy, his tongue lolling.

"It's okay," said Amy. "Betsy, can you wait outside? This won't take long."

"Could be hours and hours," said the guard. "At least two or three cat naps."

"I don't like the sound of that," said Betsy. "I'm a messy little dog and who knows what I'll get into."

"Quite so," said Philip. "Nick, please stay with Betsy. If he gets into trouble please come and find us."

"You guys owe me big time," said the tiny fairy. She buzzed down to Betsy and straddled the terrier's neck. "That means lots of candy!"

Betsy sprinted away with Nick hanging on, her transparent wings vibrating and one arm flailing the air.

"I didn't say you could run off!" yelled Amy. "And ... they're gone."

"It's just as well," said Philip. "Imagine the horrible scene if we'd forced them to attend a long-winded royal ceremony."

The pair re-joined the chanting parade of cats, following the crowd through massive doors into a soaring open space that made Amy gasp.

The roof of the pagoda rose high above her head, supported by many floors of wide crimson pillars, each covered with hand-painted scenes from Tau Ceti's natural world. A chalky haze that smelled of flowers floated high above, glowing white in a few narrow beams of sunshine that filtered through closed wooden slats. Embroidered tapestries hung around the walls of the ground floor, featuring cats fighting claw-to-claw with various enemies or leading long processions of other cats, including one from a spacecraft shaped like a gigantic silver football. A golden throne stood at the far end of the room on a raised dais, in front of a painting of a tree blooming with white flowers. A plain wooden chair sat on the floor below the dais and to the left of the throne. Cats of all sizes and colors packed every inch of space on the ground floor, and leaned over the balconies above.

Amy and Philip moved through the chanting cats––careful not to step on any tails––and found space at the back of the crowd next to the curved wall.

"Catchy tune," said Amy, humming along with the drone of the cats. "Someone should write a song about me."

"Anything would be more enjoyable than this monkish dirge," whispered Philip. "Especially with you as the subject."

The crowd of cats parted in front of the teenagers. Sooka Black appeared and bowed low.

"Please follow me, honored guests. Your place is by the throne."

Amy and Philip followed the black-caped official and stood where he pointed––to the right of the throne below the dais. The cat moved a few steps to the left beside the simple wooden chair that sat below the throne. He stood on all fours with his tail straight up.

Amy leaned close to Philip's ear. "What do we do now?"

Philip smiled. "What everyone does at court––we wait."

The chanting went on and on and began to grate on Amy's nerves. She decided that cats should never sing, and if they did it was probably a violation of the Geneva Convention or the galactic equivalent. Scientists could probably use this sound to unclog drains, she thought.

The ground floor and balcony gradually filled to the brim with cats of all shapes and colors of fur. A handful of late-comers shoved into the back, desperate to get inside as the heavy wooden doors swung shut.

A calico cat with a collar of braided white cloth spoke to the guards and squeezed through the gap in the closing doors. She trotted up the empty center aisle and whispered into Sooka Black's ear.

The caped official nodded. He stood and grabbed a giant spear from behind the chair, and began to slam the wooden shaft on the stone floor. The loud thumps echoed through the hall and the host of cats quickly fell silent.

"The emperor approaches," said Sooka Black loudly. "Pay your respects to the Lord of the Northern Star!"

The crowd of cats bowed as one, pressing furry chins to front paws. A fanfare of trumpets sounded from outside and Sunflower stumbled through the open entrance surrounded by a pack of giggling female cats.

The orange tabby wore a crown with a giant ruby and a bright yellow cape. He trotted with his wives up an empty path through the center of the crowd, giggling and laughing as much as any of the female cats, all of whom wore necklaces of twisted yellow cloth and walked in swirling clouds of perfume so strong that it caused a dozen cats to clutch their throats and pass out in their wake.

From the upper balcony, a black cat screamed out, "Long live the Emperor!"

The poor animal had leaned too far over the railing, however, and tumbled over the edge. The crowd ignored his uncomfortable landing on the very fat and very furry Minister of Galactic Trade, and eagerly took up the chant he had started.

"Long live the Emperor! Long live the Emperor! Long live the Emperor!"

Sunflower walked proudly through the cheers and climbed the steps to his golden throne. He plopped his rear on the bright yellow cushion as his wives lounged on the steps below.

Sooka Black thumped the giant spear on the floor. "Silence!" He waited a moment for the chants to die away, and then bowed to the throne.

Sunflower stared out at the crowd and took a deep breath. "I am Emperor Sunflower," he boomed. "Glorious Father of the Flowering Pear Dynasty, Lord of the Northern Star, and Wearer of the Red Diamond Crown. I'm very busy now, but thank you all for coming!"

He jumped off the throne and scampered through the crowd, his wives chasing after him and the entire host of cats staring wide-eyed as the Emperor and his giggling, perfumed troop disappeared through the slowly opening doors.

"You don't see that every day," said Amy.

Philip nodded. "Not even on a cat planet."

Hisses and murmurs filled the hall, and Sooka Black stood frozen with his eyes wide and mouth open. A furry mob surrounded him with questions while the majority of the cats rushed for the exit.

Philip rubbed his chin. "I don't quite understand. Why didn't he give a speech? Receive royal guests? Issue proclamations?"

Amy put an arm around his shoulders and sighed. "Where do I start? Okay. When a daddy cat and a mommy cat love each other very, very much, they want to make a baby cat. Or kittens, in this case."

Philip smiled and kissed her. "You're very funny. I don't know if there's a young lady in the universe quite as smart and beautiful as you."

"There's at least three or four."

"What do we do about finding this MacGuffin?"

"The who?"

Philip blinked. "The cat who tried to steal the plans for the recombinator matrix? The item you need to return home?"

Amy nodded and brushed cat hair from her skirt. "Where's Sooka Black? Maybe he's got an idea."

They found the brown tortoiseshell cat slumped in his wooden chair below the throne, staring blankly at the ceiling and ignoring repeated questions from the cats around him. The cats looked up and scattered as the teenagers approached.

Amy knelt beside the cat. "Sooka—are you okay?"

The brown cat straightened in the chair and smiled at Amy. "My apologies to you both. I was simply lost in thought."

"It's Sunflower, isn't it? He's not really good at this 'emperor' thing. It's because he lost his memory and all that ... stuff."

Sooka Black stared at Amy. "What? No, it's quite the opposite. I had hoped the emperor would return a changed cat, but he's following the same old patterns, spending all his time cavorting with his wives and smoking catnip." He eased out of his chair and slowly walked away, his tail almost dragging on the polished floor. "What they say is true——hope is for kittens."

Philip held up a hand. "Mr. Black! One moment, please."

"Yes? If you have any requests for specific food or accommodations, please see the head steward."

"It's more complex than a sandwich," said Amy. "We need to find a cat."

Sooka Black turned. "There are many cats on Tau Ceti, and many good cooks. Making human food is not as hard as you think."

Amy waved a hand. "It has nothing to do with food. Do you know a cat named Cynthia MacGuffin?"

"Not personally. Please excuse me for a moment and I will index his name."

Sooka Black trotted across the empty hall and disappeared into an alcove. Amy and Philip heard the faint tapping of keys, whispering followed by a long silence, and Sooka Black trotted out, his tail held high.

"No address or contact information exists for a Cynthia MacGuffin. However, his name is mentioned in a recent article on the theoretical physics department at Meowie University."

Amy giggled. "Meowie University? That's not real."

"It's the most respected institute of scientific learning on Tau Ceti. Kittens travel from all over the planet and even from Gliese to study there."

Philip clapped his hands. "Wizard! Let's pop over to this university and have a chat."

"My deepest apologies," said Sooka Black. "It's only a short walk through the downtown area, but unfortunately I can't allow you to leave."

Amy shrugged. "Why not? It's a free country, isn't it?"

"For cats, yes, but not Centaurans. Do you know the black market price for a matched pair of humans, both of breeding age?"

Amy's cheeks flushed and she jabbed a finger at the cat's nose. "You spying pervert! We didn't do anything!"

Sooka scrambled backwards. "Oh, no! I'm very sorry. I thought that two humans traveling together of opposite sex and the same age would be mates. This would always be the case with a pair of cats. I apologize if I have said anything offensive."

Philip put his arm around Amy's shoulder. "We're certainly a matched pair, and let's leave it at that."

"Right," said Amy. "But what's this about humans and the black market? I thought Tau Ceti was civilized."

Sooka Black frowned. "It is not as simple as one thing or another. The treaty with Alpha Centauri gives humans full rights and protection under cat law. Official and unofficial are two whiskers on the same cat, however, and catnappings, enslavements, and underground pet markets still take place. You will be safe while in the imperial palace, but outside of that anything could happen. A human in the midst of cat society stands out like a shaved tail, I'm afraid."

"I don't like the idea of being a pet," said Philip. "Again."

Amy grinned. "Newsflash! You're still Nick's pet, according to her."

"I suppose. As long as we take precautions, I don't see a problem. We're much taller than cats. In any case, who would kidnap us––sorry, catnap––while visiting a university campus?"

Sooka Black paced back and forth for a moment, then nodded. "I give my approval, with two conditions. One––you must take an escort from the palace. Two––if you aren't catnapped and actually return safely, you must promise to try and convince the emperor to change his ways and become a better leader."

"Done and done," said Amy. "How about Furball, the cat who delivered breakfast? He can be the escort."

Sooka Black bowed. "I will make the necessary arrangements. Please meet at the eastern gate in one hour."

"Now for a word with his glorious highness Sunflower," murmured Philip.

Amy watched Sooka Black trot across the wide floor of the hall and pass through the giant yellow doors.

"He's not going to listen," she said.

THE PARADE GROUND outside the Hall of Harmonious Justice was empty apart from a pair of cats in red berets walking slowing around the perimeter with assault rifles strapped to their furry backs.

"Exactly what I expected," said Amy. "Betsy and Nick nowhere to be seen."

"To be fair, the assembly was extraordinarily brief," said Philip. "If we follow the nearest screams and sounds of absolute pandemonium, we're certain to find them."

He took Amy's hand and held it firmly. The pair descended the marble steps outside the hall and crossed the parade ground toward the red-painted wood of the imperial living quarters.

"Do you really think we're a matched pair?" Amy asked. "We're kind of opposites. I'm a scrappy thief from California and you're a posh English lord."

Philip kissed her hand and smiled broadly. "Neither of which matter thousands of years in the future on a planet run by cats. Sense governs the heart, not sensibility, and my heart is yours, dear Amy. In any case, you're no thief. Didn't you tell the Lady that you'd learned your lesson?"

Amy used her other hand to dig into a pocket of her plaid skirt, and held out a golden necklace with a glittering pendant of a fish.

"I stole this last night."

"Left in your room by the previous occupant. Nothing to be worried about."

"It wasn't in my room. It was in Betsy's."

Philip sighed. "One wonders why a young lady would be rummaging through strange drawers in the evening hours, but since you've plainly admitted the crime, I can safely say there is nothing to worry about. Unless, of course, you're a somnambulist and burglar at the same time."

"A somna-what?"

"A sleepwalker."

"No. I was awake."

"In that case I freely admit that, in addition to being a foppish English lord, I am also a hypnotist. To remedy this thievery of yours will require quite a few private and extremely personal sessions."

"I want a second opinion!"

Amy tickled Philip under the ribs, ducked his outstretched arms, and sprinted through a covered breezeway of the living quarters. She turned a corner and hid behind a red pillar, covering her mouth to muffle the giggles. She screamed as Philip grabbed her in a bear hug and kissed her on the mouth.

The teenagers were far too involved with each other for the next few minutes to hear the footsteps.

"Look at that," said Betsy. "Leave them alone for five minutes and they're right back at it, doing that thing again. What was it?"

"Making babies," said Nick, sitting on the back on the dog.

Amy pushed away from Philip. "We are not! It was, um ... we were ...

"She was dying," said Philip.

Amy held up a hand. "Sharing chewing gum."

"I was helping her breathe," said Philip.

"It's strawberry," said Amy. "He likes strawberry."

Philip nodded. "Saved her life."

"Last piece in the universe," said Amy. "Oops! I swallowed it. Sorry, Philip."

Betsy and Nick glanced between Amy and Philip like the rapid back-and-forth of a tennis match, eyes wide and mouths open.

"They're lying," said Nick. "I smell a secret."

"What's chewing gum?" asked Betsy. "I bet I would love it!"

Amy stretched her arms wide and took a deep breath. "Doesn't matter. Gone. Left the building."

"I'm glad to see that the pair of you haven't caught anything on fire or caused any intergalactic incidents," said Philip. "Have you?"

Betsy wagged his brown and white tail. "Yes."

Screams erupted from the rooms nearby.

Nick buzzed up to Philip. "Talk later, leave now!"

"This way!" hissed Amy, pulling Philip's arm.

The two humans, dog, and tiny sprite ran hell-bent away from the commotion, stopping only when they reached the imperial bedrooms.

Amy brushed short white hairs from her navy tights.

"More cat hair! It's like we're on a planet full of them."

Philip slowed to a stop and rested his hands on his knees. he gasped. "I say, Amy," he gasped. "You're quite ... fleet of foot."

"Thank you, I guess. I've had lots of practice running from angry people. Betsy, what did you do back there?"

The terrier hung his head. "I had to go, and ... I thought it was a toilet."

"He pooped in the soup," said Nick.

"Oh my," said Philip.

Amy spread her arms. "I don't know whether to laugh or cry. I've never in my life been in a situation where a boiling pot of soup was an option for using the bathroom!"

"It wasn't boiling," said Betsy.

"That's not the point!"

Philip covered his eyes. "Let's not become mired in the details, please."

"Betsy did," giggled Nick, a hand over her tiny mouth. "His bottom is covered in soup!"

Philip waited for the chuckles to die down. "Be that as it may, we need to find this MacGuffin character so we can leave this dimension."

"Right," said Amy, wiping tears from her eyes. "Let's focus. Where's Sunflower?"

"I know where he is," piped Nick. "Follow me!"

The tiny woman buzzed through the breezeways like a pastel hummingbird, stopping here and there to glance through the horizontal slats of windows. She flew across a garden to a dark walnut building with a roof of curved yellow tiles. A pair of black cats in red berets sat on their haunches at either side of the entrance with cat-sized rifles strapped to their backs. As Amy approached, one of the guards stood on his hind legs.

"Halt!"

Amy spread her skirt and bowed. "We would like to speak with the Emperor."

The cats glanced sideways at each other.

"The Emperor is not to be disturbed," said the first guard.

"His Gloriousness is indisposed," said the second.

"What does that mean?" whispered the first.

"It means what you said!"

Amy spread her arms. "How long is he going to be in a state of undisturbment?"

The first guard sighed. "What does THAT mean?"

The second guard cleared his throat. "No schedule has been posted for the end of the Emperor's state of being indisposed."

"Are you being sarcastic?"

"No. The point of the thing is, you may not enter."

"Maybe they can't, but I can," squeaked Nick.

The sprite flew up to a tiny slotted window near the roof and squeezed inside.

"She can't do that!" said the first guard.

"It's no problem," said Amy. "I'll get her."

The first guard rubbed his furry black chin. "No! Definitely against the rules. Thomson, get inside and grab the sprite."

The second guard jumped. "Me? But the emperor said nobody's definitely allowed inside. I'm definitely a somebody, and I'll definitely get in trouble!"

"I disagree. You're definitely a nobody. If 'nobody' is allowed inside, that means you."

The second guard shifted his weight from one foot to the other. "Really?"

Female screams and a loud crash rattled the windows, causing the guards to grab their rifles. They reached for the door handle just as it slid open.

Sunflower stepped outside, walking on his hind legs and holding Nick in his front paws. His crown and cape were gone and streaks of pink and red covered the orange fur around his face.

"I'm busy, you clowns!" he hissed. "Find something to do in the city. One of those stupid duck boats that drive on land and water, or maybe a museum. How about the Zookiji Fish Market? Largest collection of seafood and motorized forklifts on the entire planet. Zoom, zoom—cats and fish flying everywhere. Never turn your back on a forklift—never."

He tossed Nick outside and slid the door shut.

"You can't stay in your room all day!" yelled Amy. "The emperor is supposed to care about his people, Sunflower. This is your chance to lead!"

Sunflower cracked open the door and scowled. "Chance to lead? This is my chance for a vacation! The planet's not going anywhere, is it? I'll get to that crap soon. Maybe tomorrow."

"What's that pink stuff on your face?" asked Betsy.

"Lipstick," said Sunflower, and slammed the door.

"Rather," said Philip. "I suppose that's put a cork in it."

"I thought lipstick went on your lips, not all over your face," said Betsy. "I don't think Sunnie knows how to use it."

Amy sighed. "Betsy ... you have a lot to learn about life."

The brown-and-white dog blinked at her. "Huh?"

"That's right," said Nick. "Make a list of what Betsy doesn't know and it would stretch across the galaxy!"

"You said that we were best friends and that you would be nice," said Betsy.

Nick sniffed and crossed her arms. "Who cares? I'm not your friend anymore."

"Truce cancelled!"

The terrier jumped and snapped his jaws at the tiny flying woman, who zipped away to Philip's shoulder.

"I'll stick a bean in your nose!" she squealed.

Betsy barked and chased Philip and Nick into the small garden. Amy ran after the terrier and held him on the grass with both hands.

"Truce is un-cancelled, by order of your captain. Looks like I'm going to have to separate you two. Who wants to come with us and look for this MacGuffin?"

Betsy and Nick both looked away sullenly.

"Okay. Who wants to stay here and spy on Sunflower?"

Nick windmilled her tiny pale arms. "Me! Me! Me!"

"No marshmallows around here anyway," growled Betsy.

Amy pointed at the blonde sprite. "Keep an eye on the glorious emperor of the cats, and don't get caught. Maybe he won't want to leave when the time comes––"

"Definitely won't," said Nick. "You didn't see what I saw. Just imagine all those wives!"

"He's still my friend and I'm not leaving without him, emperor of the space cats or not."

Nick saluted. "Aye aye, captain!"

The sprite buzzed away.

"That sounded very sarcastic," said Amy.

Philip sighed. "Indeed."

9

A flash brightened the sky south of the palace, followed by a roll of thunder. Amy stopped in the middle of the path and shaded her eyes from the morning sunshine.

"Another meteor, I suppose," said Philip. "Nothing to worry about."

"But it's the second one I've heard!"

The brown-haired boy took her hand. "I don't see anyone running around like scalded cats. It seems like a normal part of life here."

"Maybe it was an explosion of chocolate," said Betsy.

Amy shook her head. "For someone who can't eat normal food you sure think about it a lot."

"It's reverse psychology. I can't have it, so I want it!"

"That doesn't sound right. Somebody taught you those words."

"No, it's true! Mother got me to eat broccoli that way. She'd tell me and the other puppies how awful broccoli was and how we could never have it, so that's what we wanted!"

Philip shook his head. "Dogs eating broccoli? I've never heard a more peculiar thing."

"You realize that you're standing on a planet full of talking space cats," said Amy.

The teenagers held hands while strolling through the lush gardens in the eastern quarter of the palace. Random patches of purple and white carnations covered the open spaces in the forest. A handful of cats in conical bamboo hats wandered through the flowers, occasionally bending over the large plants with a pair of garden shears sized for their paws. In the next clearing, workers combed through beds of sand with long wooden rakes, as stone lanterns towered over their heads. Fences, bridges, benches, and tool sheds were all constructed of wood, stone, and thick bands of white rope, with no plastics or space-age materials in sight.

Amy and Philip stopped on a narrow bridge that crossed an algae-covered pond. Puffs of cold mist clung to the banks, under the low-hanging branches of evergreen trees. At the far end of the pond, a brown tabby slid silently across the water on a sliver of wood, lifting and pushing a long pole with his front paws.

"I thought cats were afraid of water," said Amy.

"He's a fishing cat, I wager."

"That's a joke, right? You know there really is a kind of cat called a 'fishing cat.'"

Philip smiled. "I had no idea, but it's a great example of the true spirit of the cats in this strange place. The contrast between the natural grounds of the palace and the streets of a very advanced city makes it clear that tradition is very important to them. No matter the changes in future technology, they see the emperor and this palace as part of their collective soul."

"Holy smoke, Phil——you sound like a college professor."

Philip shrugged. "I couldn't sleep very well last night, so I sat up thinking for quite a while. The bed was a bit too small."

"I didn't have to sleep!" barked Betsy. "I stayed in Philip's room and kept guard."

"Because of the Lady's modifications to his body and brain——such as it is——Betsy has little need for rest. Another reason the bed was too small."

A group of cat soldiers in red berets with rifles on their backs marched on all fours to the end of the foot bridge. The cats waited for the humans and dog to pass, and then followed at a respectable distance until they passed through a forest that faced the eastern gate.

A two-story block of mahogany beams and chalky plaster walls, the gate building was turned ninety degrees to the perimeter wall, as if to deflect someone or something trying to break inside. The massive, five-meter-high doors were made of the same dark wood as the gate, were covered in hundreds of polished silver bosses, and guarded by a pair of tuxedo cats in black samurai helmets. A white cat with a fluffy tail waited near the guards, licking a front paw. He caught sight of the two humans and the dog, and galloped forward with a spray of gravel.

"Greetings, imperial guests," he said with a slight stammer. "I am honored that you would choose this simple, worthless servant to guide you through the city. I will do everything I can to make your experience a pleasant one, and if you are not satisfied, I will immediately quit the imperial service and return to my family farm in shame."

Amy knelt in front of the cat. "This again? I don't know what you've heard, Furball, but I'm very low maintenance."

"It's true," said Philip. "Wait—what does that mean?"

"It means I'm not picky. Don't worry, Furball. Everything's going to be fine."

"Unless we eat some cheese!" said Betsy.

The white cat glanced back at the guards and shielded his mouth with a paw.

"Must you visit the city?" he whispered. "The danger of catnapping is very high, especially for young Centaurans like yourselves. Couldn't we simply walk along the street that circles the palace and return for lunch?"

Betsy jumped on Amy's back and rested his front paws on her shoulders. "I'll protect you!" he barked. "I'm not scared of cats."

Amy pulled the small terrier off her back and set him on the gravel path.

"No jumping!" She turned to Furball. "Thanks for the warning, but we really have to visit the university and find a cat scientist that works there."

"It's the entire reason we came to Tau Ceti," said Philip.

"Of course," said Furball. "How could I be so stupid? I have brought shame upon my family and will immediately quit the Imperial service! Farewell and if you never see me again it will be too early."

Amy held up a hand. "Stop it already; that kind of talk is getting old. I'm never going to ask you to quit, okay?"

"My apologies. Please follow me, honored guests."

One of the guards pulled a lever and the heavy red doors creaked open. The three friends followed Furball around a sharp corner and passed through another set of massive wooden doors. The sound, smell, and thundering vibration of the city burst over them like a tidal wave as soon as the tall doors began to crack open.

Beyond an arched, wooden bridge that crossed the imperial moat, cats of all shapes and colors trotted along the sidewalk or sat inside clear, bubbled cockpits of spherical cars that zipped through the streets like streams of colored pearls. The different types of hats, necklaces, capes, and backpacks worn by the cats in public was as much if not more than the variety of clothing worn by any crowd of people Amy had seen, and she'd been to San Francisco. The air was full of the heavy fragrances of licorice, rose petals, and raw fish. The bubble cars whooshed as they zoomed along the streets, and a constant, electric hum from the sky-scrapers made the tiny hairs on Amy's arms stand up.

"By Jove, it's amazing," said Philip.

On the face of a tall building across the street, a three-story video billboard displayed a giant pixelated kitten. The animal looked up from a bowl, his mouth and whiskers covered in milky green liquid.

"Jurg! It's not just for breakfast!" squeaked the kitten, loud enough to echo down the busy street.

"Aw," said Amy. "I don't know what that is, but I want to drink it."

"I doubt you would like it, my dear," said Philip.

He pulled her by the hand over the curved bridge and to the edge of the busy street.

"I'd like to try it, at least," said Amy.

Philip smiled. "As you wish. I hope you won't be offended if I watch from a safe distance."

A streetlight on the corner displayed a white circle instead of a green light. When the circle turned black with a dashed line, the stream of bubble cars slowed to a stop. As she walked with Philip over the yellow stripes on the pedestrian crossing, Amy stared at the cats inside their wheeled vehicles, who for their part, gazed back with equal amazement. Some looked up from books or video displays, some tumbled off their cushions, and others took out small silver cubes and held them up to their eyes like cameras, but most of the "drivers" remained curled up and fast asleep on the flat, cushioned dashboards.

Amy pointed at a cat inside a red bubble car. "That one's taking a nap, not driving!"

Furball stopped at the curb and looked up at Amy. "Driving? I don't understand this word."

The light changed to a white circle and the stream of bubble cars accelerated with a roar. The cats in their cars pressed paws and noses against clear windows and stared open-mouthed at Amy and Philip, even as their vehicles sped away and shrank into the distance.

Amy grabbed her skirt with both hands and held it down against the whirling breeze from the cars. "How can they stare at us and still drive? I saw one reading a book. There's another one sleeping!"

A bubble car whipped past. Three cats were curled up on the wide dashboard, each on a separate cushion.

"Ah," said Furball. "You think the vehicles are in manual mode, as on Alpha Centauri. Here on Tau Ceti we've had automatics for decades. It's as simple as telling the car your destination, then taking a nap or reading a book."

Philip clapped. "Wizard! Saves on the cost of a driver."

Amy watched a boxy yellow transport zoom by. On the side was the black-painted symbol of a mother cat carrying a kitten in her mouth.

"Does the system ever break down?"

Furball nodded. "Sometimes, but everyone stays home and watches soap operas on those days. Please, let us continue."

The white Persian led them along the sidewalk and through the downtown area of Cheezburger. Metal and glass skyscrapers towered overhead, darkening the streets and cooling the morning air with their shadows. From up close, Amy noticed that the sliding doors to the buildings were half the size of human entrances, with sensors that opened automatically.

"You'll need to watch your head here, Philip," she said. "Lots of low ceilings and doorways."

Philip squeezed her hand. "I'm feeling a headache already."

A stream of cats packed the sidewalk, trotting in both directions. Most simply stared at the two humans and the dog, but a few stopped and bowed low, touching furry chins to their paws.

"Hey, Furball," said Amy. "Why are they bowing? You said the city was dangerous, but I'm not feeling it."

"Some cats see my necklace and show respect to the imperial symbol," said Furball. "Most do not care. I assure you, the danger is still great."

They walked several long blocks through the financial district, passing banks, investment centers, and the stock exchange. The ground floors of these granite-columned institutions were filled with restaurants and cafes, each churning out fragrant clouds of steam that smelled of raw and cooked seafood, hot tea, garlic, and boiled rice. Some restaurants displayed long aquarium tanks in their windows, and Amy could see the waiters scooping out fish and serving them live to cats seated on cushions around a low table.

"Wow ..."

She stopped and tapped on the window of a shop filled with hundreds of food dishes in glass cases, along with the an aquarium packed with neon-colored fish.

"Where are all the tables? I see a bunch of cats wandering inside, but no tables. Do they only sell take-out?"

Furball turned and trotted back to Amy. "This is not a restaurant, but a business which sells plastic food to restaurants."

"Why on Earth would you need plastic food?" asked Philip.

Betsy wagged his tail. "It lasts longer!"

"The plastic food is used for display," said Furball. "It is also considered an art form by sad, lonely cats who collect the items as a hobby."

"Even the fish are plastic?"

"Indeed," said Furball. "Smaller restaurants use plastic fish in their front windows and keep the real fish in back to trick the customer. That is not a place you should eat."

The white cat turned up his nose and continued down the sidewalk.

"I want a plastic fish," said Betsy. "He can be my best friend!"

"Alas," said Philip. "I'm afraid we don't have any cat money."

Amy knelt down and rubbed the dog's furry neck. "Betsy, you can't be friends with a plastic fish. Did the Lady actually put a knowledge implant inside your head?"

"Sure!" said the brown and white terrier. "It falls out of my brain socket every few months. If I shake my head really fast you can hear it banging around."

The terrier whipped his head back and forth.

"Funny," he said. "Now I can't hear a thing. Ooo, dizzy!"

Amy grabbed the dog's head. "Stop that! How do we fix the implant?"

"Surgery. Or grab a piece of wood and biff me in the head. Sunflower came up with that one. Actually, Sunflower was the one who told me about the chip coming loose in the first place. He's really smart like that. None of the other dogs that worked for the Lady had problems like that."

Amy sighed and stood up. "Right."

"Back to the real world, eh?" said Philip.

Amy laughed and waved at the cats staring from passing vehicles. "The real world? I'm a cat celebrity in Cat-ville."

Furball blinked at her. "Catville is on the other side of town, honored guest. This is the financial district."

"Sorry. It was just a joke."

As they continued to walk east, banks and high-level businesses were gradually replaced by neon-illuminated shops selling electronics and toys. Huge video billboards covered the upper floors of the buildings and showed fast-paced, animated cartoons of cats fighting dogs and sauros. Boxes of plastic action figures were stacked high in the shop windows. Most were of cats and dogs, others were models of fighter jets and spaceships. Several figurines of humans were among the mix of plastic toys, all depicted as blank-faced dullards in animal skins. The long-bearded men gripped spears with their bulging arms and the toys of human women were big-breasted tarts in leopard-print miniskirts and too much makeup. Through the window, Amy could see the shop was packed with cats browsing the action figures, chatting to each other, and carrying the small boxes to the cash register.

Excited whispers came from behind her back.

"She's so young."

"I've never seen a Centauran in real life. You?"

"Me? Never!"

"I thought they'd be taller!"

Amy spun and the crowd of cats immediately behind her scrambled backwards with shrieks of astonishment. A few scrambled away and down the sidewalk as if they were running for their lives.

A black kitten wearing a blue backpack pushed through the crowd and tottered up to Amy on all fours.

"Momma! She's so pretty," said the kitten, his eyes wide and yellow. "Not like the movies."

Amy knelt in front of the kitten. "Hello, cutie. What's your name?"

A tubby calico cat rushed forward and scooped up the kitten in her front paws. Amy could hear the whining of the kitten and the angry yells of his mother as the pair disappeared into the crowd.

"Angela Dawn Snookums! Talking to a human. Do you know what kinds of diseases you could get from those disgusting things?"

"But I've never seen one. She was nice, momma!"

Amy sighed and stood up. The ring of curious cats on the sidewalk stared up at her, their eyes following her every movement.

"Looking for a song and dance?" Amy jerked her arms and legs robotically. "Greetings, catlings," she droned. "Take me to your leader."

Philip jogged down the sidewalk.

"There she is! Shoo! Shoo!"

The crowd of cats scattered from his waving arms and the barking Betsy nearby, although it was probably just Philip doing most of the frightening.

"Where did you two go?" asked Amy. "I stopped to look at something and the next thing I know I'm surrounded by a herd of cats."

"Did they ask for your autograph?" asked Betsy.

"No."

"Weird. I would have asked for your autograph."

"Sorry for leaving you, dear," said Philip. "Betsy tried to cross the street and if I hadn't chased after him, he'd be doggie pudding right now."

"Where's Furball?"

Philip pointed down the sidewalk. The white Persian waited patiently on a bench at the end of the block. He stopped cleaning his tail and bowed as the human teenagers approached.

"All finished, honored guests? May I purchase items for you? Sweets? A delicate morsel of Cheezburger's finest live octopus? Limited-edition human collectible figurines? The price is very high in this area, but the selection is very good."

"Thanks but no thanks," said Amy. "I was just window shopping."

Furball blinked at her for a moment. "I'm sorry. Does your village not have windows? Perhaps they are broken?"

"I don't want to buy a window. It's just a saying."

The cat nodded. "I see. 'Window shopping' means you don't want windows. So, if you actually wanted to buy windows, what would you say?"

"I'd say, 'I'm going to shop for windows.'"

Furball sighed. "That sounds exactly the same to me. Very confusing."

Philip held up a hand. "Please——let's table the discussion on idiomatic phrases. To be honest, I'm a bit parched from the walk. Perhaps we could find a cup of tea?"

"Of course," said Furball, and bowed deeply again. "I didn't realize humans drank tea. It's a very cat-like behavior."

Philip shrugged. "I'm English."

The teenagers followed Furball into a narrow alley packed on both sides with long lines of neon-colored vending machines. Faded advertisements and marketing slogans covered the front of the tall metal boxes, which hummed and rattled like dying air conditioners on a hot summer day. The white cat stopped at the second machine and studied a dozen cans viewable through a scratched window.

"Tea, you say?"

"Whatever is most popular," said Philip. "I'm not picky."

"And you, Miss Armstrong?"

"I guess I'll have a can. When in Rome, right?"

Furball blinked at her. "This is Cheezburger. I'm not familiar with the place you call 'Rome.'"

"Don't start that again! Get on with the tea machine thing."

"I hate tea," said Betsy, and pretended to spit in a puddle of water draining from one of the machines. Instead of spitting, his gesture unfortunately turned into a long strand of drool.

Furball pressed a few buttons and held his paw over a glass diamond on the front of the machine. A red beam flashed over his paw and a pair of narrow green cylinders thunked into the bottom tray.

Philip grabbed the first can. "Amazing! It's still cold. I've never seen the like, even in London."

The teenager pulled open the top of the green cylinder and tipped it toward the sky. He gulped down the contents while Amy studied the description on her can.

"What's 'somon' flavor?"

Philip sprayed green liquid across the alley and dropped the can. He bent over with his hands on his knees and coughed.

"Fish ... tea? Are you trying to kill me?"

"I wasn't! I'm sorry!" stammered Furball. "You said you liked tea. Of course I thought that was strange, but you said you liked it!"

Philip wiped his mouth. "It tastes like pond scum."

"Of course," said Furball. "That's the special ingredient."

"Who could drink this revolting poison?"

"I do. It's a very popular flavor!"

Amy handed her can to Furball. "I'll pass. Don't say you're going to quit blah, blah, blah. It was an honest mistake."

The white Persian bowed low. "I am deeply sorry."

Amy patted Philip on the back. "No need to apologize—our dear English boy will survive. How far to the university? I have a sneaking suspicion that we probably should have hired a cab."

"Whatever the honored guests desire, I will provide," said Furball. "The destination is only a short walk from here."

"Whatever I desire?" asked Amy. "I'd like a Diet Coke, but now I'm afraid I'd get Salmon Snapple."

"I'm not familiar with this beverage," said Furball. "We have international food stores in Cheezburger with products from Alpha Centauri. Would you like to take a taxi there? It is too far to walk."

"Nah," said Amy, and nudged Philip. "Ready to go, Phil? Don't you go dying on me."

"I'm fine," said the teenager, and straightened up. "Forward, forward. Always moving forward. Unless you see a toilet, of course."

"Gotta be more careful what you put in your mouth next time."

Philip nodded. "Of that, there is no doubt."

"Back to the crowds of cat-fans, then."

Amy turned and strode toward the sidewalk. A crowd dozens of cats deep packed the opening of the alley, all staring at the humans.

Furball scrambled in front of Amy and blocked her path.

"Please––I can take you another way. It will avoid attention."

"But I love attention," said Betsy, and wagged his tail.

Furball glanced at the crowd and the busy street. "Will all of these cats watching us, it is far too dangerous."

"Whatever works," said Amy. "Lead on!"

The two humans and Betsy followed the cat down the alley, across several side streets with little traffic, and into another narrow street packed on each side with open garbage cans.

Amy covered her mouth from the stench of rotting fish. "Ugh! This is the worst!"

Furball ran ahead of the group. "Walk faster. Faster!"

Amy followed him around a corner of the narrow lane and almost stumbled over the white cat, who had frozen in his tracks.

"Hey! Watch out!"

A few meters in front of Furball, three cats leaned against a wall of the dark, moldy alleyway. Two of the cats were completely black and the largest was a gray tabby with large white patches in his fur. All three wore black leather collars decorated with dangerous-looking silver spikes.

The gray tabby pushed off the wall and sauntered lazily up the alley toward Amy.

"My, my, my," he said in a lazy drawl, extending the vowels. "What we got here?"

"Stay back!" screeched Furball. "I'm in charge of the humans."

The tabby smiled and stood on his hind legs. He flicked his wrist and pointed a small silver pistol at Furball.

"Not anymore."

Amy giggled. "Look—the kitty found a gun. So cute! Are you going to shoot some mice?"

"I daresay it's more dangerous than it looks," said Philip.

The pair of black cats walked up to stand behind the gray tabby.

"Two humans is a huge wad of cash, boss!" said one. "We can finally buy a real gun!"

The gray tabby hurled the pistol at the cat who spoke. "You idiot! They can hear you."

Betsy barked at the cats. "What? It looked real to me."

Philip pulled back on Amy's arm. "An opportune moment to leave, my dear. Shall we go back the way we came?"

They turned and saw the way behind them blocked by another three cats in spiky collars.

"You're still outnumbered," said the gray tabby. "Hand over the two human boys and nobody gets hurt." He lowered his voice. "Also, if you have any tips on what to feed them, I'm all ears. The last one hated fish."

Amy stamped her foot. "I'm a girl, not a boy! The skirt didn't give you a clue?"

"I don't believe it," said the tabby. "You don't have two big things on the front like a human female. You're skinny like a boy, so I say you're a boy."

"I'm not a boy!"

One of the black cats giggled. "They sound so funny when they talk!"

"Real humans aren't like the ones you see in the movies," said Amy. "Real women don't look like action figures!"

The gray tabby shook his head. "I can't understand half of what this human is saying."

"It's not like the movies," said one of the black cats. "I like the movie Centaurans better."

Furball stood on his back feet and held up the official bronze insignia around his neck.

"These humans are guests of the Emperor, and you scalawags are upsetting them. Begone!"

At the sight of the imperial symbol, five of the six vagabond cats bowed, touching chin to front paws. The gray tabby dipped his head slightly.

"I recognize the imperial seal, and I will give you the honor of a cat-to-cat duel. If you defeat me in single combat, I will let you pass and give all the money in my wallet."

Furball rose on his back feet and held his front paws out like a boxer.

"Really?" he asked.

The gray tabby shook his head. "Nah. Get him!"

The alley exploded into a whirl of hisses, shrieks, and flying fur as all six hoodlums jumped at Furball with their fangs bared and claws out. The white Persian stayed on his hind legs with a posture like a tiny Victorian boxer, deftly side-stepping swipes from the thugs and punching each squarely in the nose with his curled-up paws. Bloodied and beaten, all six of the hoodlums scrambled away as if someone had thrown a bucket of scalding water at them. The alley became quiet again, apart from the buzzing of flies.

"Good gravy," said Amy. "What did I just see?"

"Bunch of cats jumping around, I think," said Betsy.

Philip clapped loudly. "Bravo! That was as good as any match of fisticuffs in Yorkshire."

Furball bowed. "Thank you."

"Why didn't you fight like the other cats?" asked Amy. "With claws and teeth."

"All servants of the emperor are trained in the secret art of 'man-style,'" said Furball quietly. "It is deadly, and only to be used when necessary. Please—— let us continue to the university before those gangsters return."

The teenagers, Betsy, and Furball left the alley and pushed through the pedestrian mob of cats packing the sidewalk in both directions. Several blocks later, the crowds thinned as they left the metal and glass skyscrapers of the financial district and entered a more residential area of high-rise apartment buildings constructed from yellow and orange bricks. A group of squarish white towers shone in the distance as they crossed an intersection.

"Is that the university?" asked Amy.

"Yes," said Furball. "That tower is the administration building."

Philip cleared his throat. "Many apologies, but I'm absolutely parched and need something to drink." He pointed at a nearby shop. "I'll just pop inside here and ask for something that isn't green."

The teenager put his hand on a wooden door with a large sign: "Happy Happy Joy Joy Human Café."

Furball scrambled to stand in front of Philip and spread his furry arms wide.

"Please don't! It's too dangerous!"

Amy peered at a wide display of photos below the sign. "Look at this ... I guarantee they have something we can drink."

Photos of human faces had been pasted on the door——each one with a jovial, ecstatic grin on his or her face——along with hand-drawn caricatures of people hugging cats. The collage was amateurish in design, but full of so much honest joy that Amy couldn't help but smile.

"Perfect place for a drink," said Philip.

Furball tugged at a leg of the teenager's trousers. "It's not what you think. These places are run by bad people. Gangsters like the cats in the alley!"

"I like gangsters," said Betsy, wagging his tail. "They talk funny."

Amy patted the dog's head. "Aww, Betsy——you mean they tell jokes."

"No! They say things like 'Beebedee bedeebee boobop bam! Like in the movies!"

"Amazing." She turned to Furball. "We're a block away from the best university on Tau Ceti. Could it really be that dangerous?"

Furball nodded vigorously. "Yes!"

"Really? You just beat up six cats and you're scared of this place?"

"Yes, yes, yes!"

Philip shrugged. "No worries. We'll have a nice, un-fishy glass of water and be off."

Amy stepped over Furball and pushed the door. "Good plan."

Inside was a tiny alcove as wide as Amy's shoulders. To the left of a locked door stood a sheet of thick safety glass with a slot at the bottom like Amy had seen at Bank of America. Taped on the inside of the safety glass were photos of four men and two women, with names scrawled below each in a cartoonish script.

Amy shook her head. "Cuddles? Sniffy? Princess? What's going on?"

Philip squeezed in beside Amy, his elbow pressing hard against her ribs.

"Hey! Watch it!"

"Sorry," said the dark-haired teen. "Barely enough room for a mouse in this cubicle."

"Your point is?"

Philip grinned. "Perhaps my point is ... you could sit on my lap?"

"One of us could leave. That's a better point."

"But I vowed to always be by your side, my love."

"By my side doesn't mean squashing me to death!"

Philip pouted. "Are you suggesting I take back my promise?"

Amy flipped her blonde hair and sighed. "No, don't do that. Come on, get in here."

Philip sat on the floor of the tiny closet and Amy settled on his lap. He squeezed his arms around her waist and looked over her shoulder as she read a list of instructions on the window.

"Happy Happy Joy Joy Human Café. Please respect the humans and they will respect you. Do not touch a human unless it touches you first. Do not approach a human from behind. Do not bring food from outside; human snacks are available for purchase. Do not bite or scratch the humans. Do not smell the tails of the humans––it upsets them. Do not ask the humans questions about religion, politics, the existential crisis of not being a cat, and don't make fun of their hairless monkey bodies. When your assigned time has finished, leave the cafe promptly."

"Crickey," said Philip. "Sounds like a zoo."

Betsy climbed on top of Amy. Furball followed the terrier inside and closed the door to the street.

"Now I know what a sardine feels like," gasped Amy. "Betsy, get your butt out of my face."

"Sorry!"

A calico cat wearing tiny spectacles above her whiskers walked behind the safety glass. She frowned and tapped on the window with the chewed-up end of a pencil.

"Is this a college prank?" she asked in a grand-motherly voice. "Can I help you with something?"

"Yes, please," gasped Philip. "A glass of water and some breathing room."

"The cover charge is five hundred mao plus one drink per person."

Furball gurgled and smacked the window with his paw. "Five hundred? But I'm a member of the imperi-al staff!"

The cat covered her mouth and yawned. "Ten per-cent discount."

"What?!!"

Amy patted Furball on the head. At least she thought it was Furball. Even breathing was a chal-lenge considering she was tangled up on Philip's lap and Betsy's tail kept swiping back and forth across her face like a windshield wiper.

"Don't worry! We'll pay you back," she said.

Furball shook his head. "It's not that, Miss Arm-strong. It's simply the principle."

"Whatever you do, please hurry up. Betsy and his sharp principles are about to tear a hole in my tights."

Furball sighed. "Four tickets and four drinks, if you please."

He touched the payment diamond below the window, and it flashed blue.

"Thank you," said the grandmotherly cat. "Enter to the right and ask your pets to please remove their shoes."

Philip chuckled. "We're not pets."

The elderly cat smiled. "I'm sorry––'companion animals.'"

The interior door clicked and slid aside. The jumble of humans, Betsy, and Furball fell sideways onto the soft carpet.

"Ugh! Smells like a locker room," said Amy. "Moldy socks and Irish Spring."

She stood from the carpet, brushed dog hairs from her blouse, and helped Philip to his feet. The ceiling in the cafe was higher than in the tiny entrance booth, and the dark-haired boy could stand without bending over.

"My word," he said. "What manner of drinking establishment is this? Even French pubs aren't this odd."

Colorful squeeze toys covered the beige carpet of the long room and childish drawings in crayon had been taped to the walls next to snapshots of humans. Wide, human-sized couches and cushioned chairs stood around the edges of the room, leaving the center open. At the far end was a counter with a sliding window and a door marked "Private."

All the toys and colorful decor made Amy think she'd walked into a day care center. Four adult humans lounged on sofas at the back of the room: two men and two women.

The men wore oversized t-shirts, baseball caps, and baggy cargo shorts that reached to their knees. In contrast to the sloppy, oversized apparel of the men, the pair of females wore tight plaid blouses and tiny jean shorts like it was some kind of country dance, their midriffs exposed and busts bulging like pairs of over-inflated balloons. All of the humans were bare-foot, and each held a cat on his or her lap.

"People!" squealed the women.

The blonde and the brunette dumped the cats from their laps and ran across the room to Philip. The English teenager held out a hand in polite greeting, but he was tackled like a ball-carrier at an American football match. The blonde woman grabbed him around the neck and the brunette wrapped her arms around his waist.

"You little darling!"

"He's so cute! Welcome!"

Dazed by the overpowering perfume and the pair of extremely busty ladies pressing their extreme busts against his person, Philip quite reasonably leaned back. "And ... good morning to you."

Amy crossed her arms. "Hello? Could you ladies please stop killing my boyfriend?"

The blonde squeezed Philip even harder and looked at Amy with big blue eyes.

"Killing him, honey? But I thought you came here for a hug."

"Yeah!" said the brunette, batting her eyelashes. "Everybody loves a hug."

Philip struggled to push the women away. "Actu-ally ... I don't mean to be any trouble, of course, but I'd simply like a glass of water that doesn't taste of fish. Nothing more, nothing less."

The busty brunette rubbed her cheek across his shoulder. "Poor boy! I bet you haven't had a hug in ages!"

An older man with dark gray hair approached Amy, his arms outstretched and a wide smile on his face. Amy ducked to the side and pushed against the man's chest, doing her best imitation of a Heisman Trophy.

"Watch your hands, mister! I know kung fu."

The man dropped his arms and smiled. "I'm sorry. Did we get off on the wrong foot? Let's start again. My name is Cuddles. My blonde ladyfriend is called Princess, and my other ladyfriend is Angel."

"Charmed," said the brunette, and gave Amy a big smile.

The busty blonde puckered her lips and kissed the air. "Love ya!"

"These girls are over the top," said Amy. "This can't be real."

"It's as real as rain," said Cuddles. "Have you been to a human café before?"

Amy shrugged. "Of course I've been to a café. Who hasn't?"

"Great!"

Cuddles wrapped his big hairy arms around Amy and she kneed him in the crotch. The older man squealed and crumpled to the floor with his hands clutching the front of his shorts.

"Why?" he moaned.

Amy jabbed a finger at his nose. "Rule number one—don't touch me unless I touch you first. Rule number two——see rule number one."

"But those are my rules," whispered Cuddles.

A young man with short red hair walked up.

"All right, all right, break it up. These kids are F.O.B. and have no clue what a human café is. Chill out, everyone. Princess and Angel——let go of the poor boy."

"Do we have to?"

"I think he likes it," said Angel.

The red-haired man shook his head. "Be nice. You don't want a spanking, do you?"

The young women sighed, untangled themselves from Philip, and shuffled away from the teenager with the very flushed face.

Cuddles groaned on the floor. "Thanks, Sniffy. I was getting confused there for a second, and you know what happens when I get confused."

"I do!" said Princess. "He pees everywhere!"

The redheaded Sniffy sighed and rubbed the bridge of his nose. "Tell me the truth—did everyone take your pills today?"

Princess hopped up and down. "I did!"

Angel clapped, jiggling her chest even more than Princess. "Me, too!"

Cuddles rolled over on the carpet and stared at the ceiling. "Do I have to? They make me feel funny."

Sniffy helped the older man to his feet and pushed him to the back of the room.

"No wonder you're talking back. It's in your contract; go do it!"

"I want a hug," said Betsy. "Who's ready?"

Princess squealed. "A dog!" She lifted Betsy from the floor and gave the terrier a huge kiss on the snout.

Amy looked around for Furball, but the white cat had disappeared. She turned back to Sniffy.

"Someone please tell me what's going on in this wacky house of horrors."

Philip raised a hand. "Not to be a bother or any-thing, but I'm still waiting for that drink."

"My apologies," said Sniffy. "Please have a seat. Princess, could you bring our guests three Centauran spring waters?"

The blonde woman pouted. "But we only have one case left!"

"Green water is fine with me," said Betsy, wagging his tail.

"Excuse me?" said Sniffy. "Do you mean tea?"

"No. I mean green water."

"Right," said Sniffy. "Two Centauran waters and one tea."

"Got it!" said Princess brightly.

She lowered Betsy to the carpet and jiggled through the door in the back.

Amy and Philip sat on a green couch. Angel sat beside Philip, while Sniffy plopped onto the floor and crossed his legs.

"Want a hug?" he asked Betsy.

"Sure!"

The terrier jumped into Sniffy's lap, tail wagging.

"This must be some kind of touchy-feely, hippie place," Amy said to Philip. "California is rotten with 'em. Crystals and runes and more Yanni than you ever wanted."

"What's a hippie?"

"The kind of person that runs a place called Hap-py Happy Joy Joy Human Café."

Sniffy laughed and scratched Betsy under the chin. "I'm going to guess this is your first visit to Tau Ceti. A human café is a place where cats play with humans without going to the expense of supporting their own pet. No judgement from the neighbors, no high cost of human pet food, no chance of police crackdowns or the landlord throwing you out of your apartment because of the smell. You might have noticed there aren't that many humans wandering the streets of Cheezburger. One reason is the high cost. A interstellar ticket from Alpha Centauri to Tau Ceti is millions of woolongs on the dodgiest of dodgy cat freighters, even if you spend the entire trip inside a box of Hamdingers. Also, the catnappings keep many humans off the streets."

"After everything I've seen today, it seems absurd to be shocked," said Philip. "But cats and dogs are supposed to be our pets, not the other way around."

Sniffy leaned forward and slapped Philip on the knee. "What a comedian! I'll have to write that one down. People say that's how it was in the old days, but I think it's just a bunch of superstition. Who knows, man––I'm not religious."

"The old days," said Amy. "You mean, the old days on Earth?"

"Earth? Nothing but dust on that dried-up rock. You've got a better chance of finding a swimming pool on Tau Ceti."

Philip glanced at Amy. "Because cats hate water?"

Sniffy chuckled. "You got it, sweet cheeks. They might secretly install a pool in their backyard, but just for the humans to splash around in. Cats like to watch their pets play."

"I know all about cats," said Amy. "We've got one at home. Had one."

Sniffy nodded. "Lucky. My family applied to host an interstellar exchange student, but didn't qualify. Lots of money in cat students. Not many jobs or industry on Alpha Centauri right now."

The door to the back room squealed open and Princess strutted out with three bowls on a tray.

"Ah," said Sniffy. "Here's your Centauran water."

Princess gave bowls to Sniffy and Amy, and stood over Philip with the last saucer in her hands.

The dark-haired teen watched Betsy lap water. "Perhaps I could have a glass?"

Amy nodded. "Me, too."

Princess giggled. "Don't worry, I'll show you."

The buxom blonde put an arm around Philip and sat on his lap. She took a sip from the bowl and held it to the teenager's lips.

"See? It's easy."

Philip drank all the water in the bowl.

"Yes," he said in a higher pitch, and cleared his throat. "Quite."

Princess hugged him tight with her cheek pressed against his face.

"You're a smart boy. Ow!" She jumped from Philip's lap and rubbed her leg. "Who pinched me?"

"Sorry," said Amy. "My hand slipped."

The brunette Angel giggled. "No, she grabbed your butt. I think she likes you!"

Princess grinned. "That's okay. I like her, too."

She sat across Philip's lap and sprang up again, this time with both hands on the rear of her jean shorts.

"Ow! That really hurt. You liked me too hard that time."

Amy studied the fingernails of her right hand. "It did? I should see a doctor."

"Perhaps you should sit next to Sniffy," said Philip.

The red-haired young man shook his head and laughed. "She's jealous, Princess. That's why she keeps touching you."

Princess blinked. "Is that so?" She plopped onto Amy's lap and gave her a wet kiss on the cheek. "Better now?"

Amy grimaced and made a rattling sound like a spoon stuck in a garbage disposal.

"Honey, you don't sound good," said Princess.

"Don't worry; it's my angina flaring up." Amy stared at Sniffy. "How long until we can leave?"

"The rules say until the bell," said Sniffy. "You can play with Angel and Princess and me until the bell rings."

"Pardon me for asking," said Philip. "But those aren't your real names, are they?"

"Of course not, but cats want us to use silly names, just like the humans in movies and the holoscreen. I'm actually Linda Palmer. I've been called Sniffy for so long that it sounds strange to say it out loud."

"My human name is Michael Chao," said Princess, and leaned close to Philip. "What's yours, honey?"

"Definitely not 'honey,'" said Amy. "He's Philip, and I'm Amy."

All three of the human hosts burst out laughing.

"How could your parents ..." gasped Sniffy between giggles. "How could they give you those names? Boys are called Amy. It's not a girl's name!"

"Watch it," said Amy. "I can feel my hand going crazy again."

Philip sighed. "We've already established that female and male names have switched places in the future. There's no point hammering it home."

Princess shifted on Amy's lap and stared at her fingernails. "I wish I could go home. It's been three years since I left Alpha Centauri."

"Why can't you?" asked Amy. "Too expensive?"

"That's part of it, but it's mostly the contract," said Sniffy. "She can't leave until after graduation. I'm in the same boat."

"Graduation?"

Princess nodded. "I'm studying astrophysics!"

"I'm majoring in human bioengineering," said Sniffy. "We're both on scholarships."

Amy shifted under the heavy weight of Princess on her lap. "I may be going out on a dangerous limb here, but I think it's going to be a while until either of you graduate with majors like that."

"Oh, this is just pretend," said Sniffy. "We don't act like this in class."

"Sure we do," said Princess. "The professors love it when——hey! Not again!"

The blonde jumped from Amy's lap.

"I think it's time to go," said Amy. She grabbed Philip's hand and stood up from the couch.

Betsy looked up from his perch on Sniffy's lap. "But I'm not done being hugged!"

"All right," said Amy. "Would you like choice number one: a foot in your rear, or choice number two: a pinch on your rear?"

Betsy blinked at Amy for a moment. "C."

"I thought so. Move it!"

Betsy squirmed out of Sniffy's arms and darted for the exit, Amy and Philip on his heels.

"You've still got time left!" yelled Princess. "My arms won't hug themselves! Hello?"

Sniffy sighed. He stood from the couch and brushed the dog hairs from his lap. "Save it, Mike. They're gone."

Princess plopped onto the couch next to Angel and crossed her arms. "People are so strange. Why can't they be like cats?"

Angel giggled and put an arm around Princess. "Right! Cats are like cats, so why can't people be like cats?"

Sniffy shook his head at the young women. "How many smart pills did you girls take this morning?"

Princess counted on her fingers. "One ... two ... four ... Wait! I have to start over. Two ... three ... seven ... is that a number?"

"Twelve for me," said Angel. She looked down at her chest and adjusted her open blouse. "This blouse is really cute. I think being cute is better than being pretty."

Princess laughed. "Right on, sister!"

Sniffy groaned and rubbed his eyes.

10

A dozen giant lizards stood around a long table in the basement of the Rotarian club, watching Nistra as he picked up and examined each of the weapons spread across the table.

A wide variety of illegal implements of death were represented, from combat swords to assault rifles. Each of the cat weapons had been modified with aftermarket triggers and grips to accommodate large sauro claws, and had been fitted with high-capacity energy magazines and illegal, overpowered capacitors for extreme damage.

"This is the best we could get with only a few hour's notice," said Astra, waving his scaly green arm over the table. "Tau Ceti has many restrictions on weapon ownership, even for cats. Sauro armaments from Kepler Prime are absolutely banned."

Nistra touched the scope of a small-caliber rifle. "Even this? I played with bigger weapons in saurogarten. It can't be useful for anything other than shooting *poona* from the front porch."

Astra bowed. "The weapon has a humble origin, Detention Officer, but the barrel and action have been replaced. It accepts a higher caliber of projectile."

"Still useless."

Nistra picked up a pulse rifle and held it to his shoulder. He stared down the sights and checked the energy in the magazine.

"This one's been in vacuum storage. That's fine if you want it to blow up in your face after the first shot."

From across the table, Plastra cleared his throat.

"As Astra said, it is the best we could do, Detention Officer."

The giant brown sauro standing next to Nistra slammed his fist on the table, causing all the weapons to rattle.

"Not good enough! We need better!"

Nistra held up a claw. "Thank you, George. George has appointed himself my right-hand sauro."

"These things take time," said Astra. "Ordering black-market weapons from the nearest sauro outpost can take weeks and might be confiscated. There's no guarantee they'll arrive safely, even if we ship them in crates of Salad Spray!"

Nistra shook his head. "We've got hours, not weeks. Those nasty humans could run back to their ship at any moment. If they leave without me, Kepler Prime is doomed and we're all stuck on Tau Ceti. I don't think any of you want to be brushing cat hair off your skin for much longer." He rubbed his scaly chin. "Who's the one with a cousin at the spaceport?"

Astra raised a claw. "Me, sir! He can sneak all of us into a shipping container at Cheezburger Central. None of the sensors will be able to see through it, and it's easy enough to bribe customs."

"Good," said Nistra. "Start the preparations for everyone to enter the container immediately. I will manipulate the weak-willed humans into landing at that field and accepting the cargo."

"Which of these weapons do we take?" asked Plastra. "We can each carry at least two."

Nistra leaned on the table with both arms and stared at the weapons.

"None."

Plastra's eyes bulged. "What?"

"Show some respect!" boomed George.

"Sorry. I meant to say, what––um, why would we leave these behind?"

"Because they're not powerful enough to help us," said Nistra with a sneer. "Also, this isn't a normal craft and doesn't have an armory. Any weapons brought inside the ship would probably set off alarms. I want to take over the craft, not find myself on the wrong side of an airlock."

George growled and pummeled the table with his fists. "Argh! Things are so hard!"

"You never told me why everyone calls you 'George,'" said Nistra. "That's not a sauro name."

The giant lizard smiled ferociously, showing rows of razor-sharp teeth.

"I took the name from a human I killed. He said George means 'great murderer' in human-speak."

"Was that before or after you killed him?"

George stared at Nistra blankly. "Before. I think it was before."

"Cool story, brother," said Plastra. "If we can't take these weapons, what's the plan?"

Nistra reached for a sturdy metal box in the center of the table. Warning stickers and "DANGER" in large red letters were plastered across the box, and it was sealed with a padlock.

Astra held up both hands. "Careful, sir! If you drop that——"

"Nothing will happen," said Nistra. "It's only dangerous to a few organisms."

He slammed the hilt of a combat sword into the lock, breaking it off. The dozen sauropods around the table jumped back and tried to claw up the walls.

"We're going to die!" screamed Astra.

Nistra lifted the lid of the box. "This is a substance deadly to cats, but will not set off alarms on the ship. I also happen to know that cats who have worked for the Lady have modified bodies. The changes that the

Lady made to their biochemical structure make her feline workers even more allergic."

The sauro reached into the box and held up a disc of Gouda cheese.

"Explosively allergic."

FURBALL WAITED on the sidewalk outside the human cafe, his fluffy tail curled around his feet.

"I see you've finished early," he said.

Amy brushed cat hair from the back of her skirt. "You were right, Furball––that place was a little bit creepy."

"I liked it!" said Betsy. "Can we go back? Can we go back now?"

Philip shrugged. "The water tasted fine, and the young women were quite enchanting."

"Really?" asked Amy.

"Did I say 'young women?' I meant to say the water was enchanting. That's what I meant to say, and the words were somehow turned around in my mind."

Amy laughed. "I know what's turning around in your mind." She linked arms with the tall teenager. "Forward! Into the valley of death."

"—rode the six hundred," said Philip, and grinned. "Let's hope we don't share the same fate as the light brigade."

"The what?"

"The light brigade. You just quoted Tennyson, didn't you? 'Half a league, half a league, half a league onward?'"

"Doesn't ring a bell. I studied burglary and petty theft in school, remember?"

"Poems are great," said Betsy, and began to sing. "I love turkey, I love chicken, Jurg Mix, Jurg Mix please deliver!"

"That's a commercial jingle, not a poem," said Amy.

The white spires of Meowie University towered against the blue sky as they walked through the streets of the college district. Businesses that catered to students lined the sidewalks: bookstores, tea rooms, music shops, and dozens of strange-smelling stores selling artistic prints and posters for dormitory rooms. Cat singers and human babies were the subject of many of the posters, the most popular being a blonde infant dangling from a branch above the slogan: "Hang in there!"

Cats with backpacks heavy with books crowded at the corner of an intersection across from the official entrance to the university, waiting for the light to change and the constant traffic of bubble cars to halt. Many did a double-take at the gigantic humans and their dog companion, and gave Amy and Philip more than enough space on the packed sidewalk.

Amy pointed across the street. "Hey––can you read that?"

An imposing sign made from concrete and orange brick stood on a grassy knoll. A few cats lay on the grass reading books.

"Inivisitat Chat," said Philip confidently.

"Peanut butter sandwich?"

Philip smiled. "Funny girl. You know it means 'Meowie University.'"

"My mother always said it's better to be funny than smart, and better to be good-looking than funny."

"How lucky that you're all three, then!"

Betsy whispered into Furball's ear. "Where's the sandwich? All I see are cats everywhere!"

The light changed and the crowd of cat students poured across the street, pulling Amy, Philip, Betsy, and Furball with them like a pair of department-store mannequins caught in a flash flood.

Oak trees covered the blue-green lawns of the campus, and cat students loaded down with backpacks trotted over concrete paths between the buildings. Furball walked inside the white tower of an administration building to inquire about Cynthia Mac-Guffin, and several cat students asked Amy and Philip for their autographs. A pair of black cats not much bigger than kittens posed excitedly for pictures with Betsy.

"I didn't know I was famous," said Philip, as he signed the front page of a history textbook.

"Sunflower is the famous one," said Amy. "We're just famous by accident."

"Ah, I see. Everyone thinks we're famous because we landed with Sunflower."

Furball scrambled out of the white tower and pushed through the small crowd around the humans.

"Make way, imperial business, make way," he shouted. "Please, honored guests––follow me."

Philip pulled Betsy away from the outstretched paws of the terrier's excited fans. He and Amy trotted after Furball as the white cat navigated a winding route through a maze of pale sandstone buildings covered in roofs of coffee-colored tile. A crowd of students followed at a short distance, whispering excitedly and taking photos of Amy and Philip with tiny cameras attached to their furry wrists.

The sandstone two-story buildings separated by trees and cultivated lawns reminded Amy of Stanford

University, only on a smaller scale and populated entirely with cats. She spotted a pair of dogs in the distance and passed three young men on the sidewalk, but they stared blankly at Amy's perky greeting.

"Hey, guys! I lost a cat around here. Seen any?"

Philip pulled Amy away from the puzzled humans.

"Very funny," he whispered.

"I know! That's why I said it."

Apart from a mass of antennae, satellite dishes, and strange white domes on the roof, the physics department looked the same as any other sandstone building on campus.

"We've found the right place, it seems," said Philip. "Now what's the plan?"

Amy shrugged. "Find MacGuffin, get recombinator, get back to ship."

"What if the chap doesn't want to give it up?"

"Then we go with Plan B," said Amy.

"And that is?"

Amy grinned. "Plan B is to come up with another plan. Honestly, we don't even know if this Cynthia MacGuffin has anything to do with stealing the recombinator."

Furball pushed through a low wooden door at the side of the building, and Amy, Philip, and Betsy followed him inside, the humans ducking their heads as they entered.

Amy expected low ceilings in a university for cats, but the lobby was open and stretched high above their heads to the roof. Windows in the opposite wall threw bright light on a large cone of aluminum in the center of the lobby, possibly the nose cone for an old rocket or landing craft. Sheer white walls on the left and right were studded with foot-long pegs leading diagonally to six round openings along each wall. A small cat emerged from one of the openings high above and ran gracefully down the pegs to the floor of the lobby.

"Please follow me, honored guests," said Furball.

He jumped to the line of pegs on the left wall and began to climb.

"Wait a second," said Amy. "How are we supposed to climb those things?"

Furball turned and blinked his blue eyes at her. "Like anyone. Don't you have steps where you come from? If you're scared, please stay here."

"I'm scared," said Betsy. "I'm staying here."

"Definitely not scared of falling," said Amy. "I'm scared of a cat doctor trying to put me back together if I pull a Humpty-Dumpty."

Furball blinked at Amy.

"She means if she falls," said Philip.

"I see. Please remain here and I will find this Cynthia MacGuffin."

The white cat scampered expertly up the diagonal line of pegs and disappeared into an opening.

"I don't trust him," said Philip. "Never had luck with a Persian cat."

Amy curtsied and pointed at the wall. "Boys first."

The tall teenager nodded and slowly climbed up the wall-pegs on his hands and knees, moving carefully from one wooden rod to the next. Amy crept after Philip, matching his pace. Halfway up the wall, she heard a scrabbling sound on the lobby floor. Something thumped on her back, and a calico cat wearing a backpack jumped over her head. The cat scrambled over Philip and disappeared into the next round opening with a desperate yowl.

"What on Earth?"

Amy shrugged. "Late for class?"

They climbed to the top opening ten meters above the lobby floor. A mob of cat students apparently waiting for them squeezed past and poured down the now-available pegs.

"No sign of Furball," said Amy. "Watch your head."

"Thank you," said Philip, his dark hair brushing the ceiling. "Don't worry. We'll find this cat one way or another."

"Should we put out a bowl of milk? Here kitty, kitty ..."

"I wouldn't recommend that. Cats in this time may very well hate that phrase."

"Good thinking. Here Cynthia, Cynthia. Here MacGuffin."

The teens walked along the cramped corridor, peering at nameplates and cracking open doors to stare into classrooms. Several cat students passed hurriedly, without taking the time to give the pair of humans a second glance.

Amy stopped at a door halfway down the hall. "Here it is––*Dr. MacGuffin, PhC. Theoretical Physics.*"

Furball trotted up to Amy and Philip from the far end of the hallway.

"I've already checked," he said dully. "The professor is not there."

Philip twisted the door handle. "He's right. Locked."

"Just because it's locked doesn't mean he's not there," said Amy. "He could be hiding."

"From who?"

Amy shrugged. "Students? A pair of scary humans like us?"

A distant thump and patter of steps came from behind a door across the hall. The wood-framed door squealed open and a fat gray tabby with white patches on his face and chest peered out.

"Freshman lecture is on the first floor," he growled. "Stop making such a racket!"

"Sorry," said Amy. "We're looking for Cynthia MacGuffin. Do you know him?"

"Of course I know him," huffed the old tomcat. "We shared offices in graduate school."

"Is he at lunch?"

The fat tabby cleared his throat. "Doctor MacGuffin has recently passed away. Thank you for your concern and please proceed to the building exit." He stamped his foot. "Well? Stop staring at me. Go on!"

"But we really have to talk with him," said Amy. "He's got something we need."

"A genius, a literal genius of a cat, has passed from this world and you're worried about term papers and grades? Why did we ever let Centaurans into this school? You're a shower of uncivilized monsters, every last one of you!"

The tabby slammed his office door.

Philip knocked on the glass. "Sir—we're not his students."

"I'm not opening it, so stop knocking," came the fat tabby's voice.

Furball twitched his fluffy white tail. "I suppose that's that. Should we proceed to the palace, or would you like to see the famous attractions of Cheezburger?"

Amy shook her head. "I don't believe him."

"Why?" asked Philip. "It's a big city, and bound to have many famous attractions."

"No! I don't believe the gray cat."

She pressed her lips to the gap between the door and the frame. "We really need to speak to Doctor MacGuffin. If we can't find him, we'll be stuck here forever! We're not students, not the police, and definitely not from the government."

The door opened a crack and the fat tabby squinted at them.

"You're not ... from the government?"

Amy shook her head. "Nope. Well, Furball is, but he's just our bodyguard."

"I'm your guide!" huffed the white Persian.

The door opened a crack wider. "Are you from the holoscreen?" asked the gray cat excitedly. "Is this 'Candid Cats'?!! I've always wanted to be on holoscreen!"

"Whatever that is, we're not from it. We came to Tau Ceti to meet Doctor MacGuffin."

"It's the only reason we're on this planet," said Philip.

The door swung open quickly. "Get in, get in!"

Every available space inside the small office seemed to be covered with stacks of yellowed paper covered in mathematical formulae. Books packed shelves along the walls and towered in huge piles beside a large cushion covered with cat hair. Boxes of wires, strange silver globes of various shapes, and blinking silver cubes took up space next to a greasy, dust-covered window.

The fat gray tabby sat on the large cushion and patted the fabric next to him.

"Please, have a lay-down."

Amy wrinkled her nose at the thought of adding more cat hair to the already-significant amount sticking to her skirt and black tights.

"Thanks, but I'll stand."

"As will I," said Philip.

Betsy curled up next to the tabby. "Not me. My feet hurt!"

"Allow me to introduce myself," said the fat tomcat. "I am Doctor Darlene Jackson, professor emeritus of physics at this university."

"Why did you say MacGuffin was dead?" asked Amy. "Did you bury him somewhere in this stuffy room? Maybe under these piles of paper?"

Doctor Jackson sighed. "No. I tell everyone he's dead because he might as well be. A single cat has little chance when standing up to organizations with vast power and resources, even if he is a gentleman and a scholar."

"Are you talking about the Lady?"

"Keep your voice down!" hissed Jackson. "Don't speak that name unless you want the sharp teeth of a trillion-mao corporation biting at your neck!"

"Sorry."

"No, I should be the one who's sorry. I could have stopped him from making these reckless choices. Cynthia was always a genius, but not the wisest cat I've known. He began researching quantum gates and dimensional theory years ago. Folly and useless! As anyone with any background in physics knows, there's no return from a quantum gate, and no way to test any route of return. Cynthia still thinks the possibility exists, and heard a rumor that the ... unnamed one ... had made her trillions by somehow returning from a trans-dimensional rematerialization. The stupidity! And now he's going to get himself killed for it. What's the point of research if you're too dead to do the research?"

"That's what we need to talk to him about," said Amy. "The rematerialization."

Jackson stared at the pair of human teenagers for a moment. At last he nodded.

"You will try to help him," he said quietly. "Behind your eyes, I see the feeling is genuine." He reached behind his ear and handed Amy a tiny silver disc. "Cynthia has fled to a research station near the equator. You will find the coordinates on the memory disc."

Furball jerked up from the cushion. "The equator? Nothing can survive the heat!"

Doctor Jackson shrugged. "Perhaps, but there is also nothing to bother a scientist trying to complete his research."

"Thank you," said Amy. "If we find him, we'll try to help."

Philip crossed his arms. "Pardon me for being presumptuous, Doctor Jackson, but how are you so confident of our motives? I suspect you have your own reasons——ones that you don't wish to reveal."

"What are you doing?" whispered Amy.

Philip shrugged. "After a two-minute conversation, he trusts a pair of strangers with the life of his colleague? I just don't see it."

Doctor Jackson licked a gray paw and settled on his cushion.

"I know you are good people for one single reason," said the cat. "She who shall not be named never, ever hires humans."

AMY STOPPED at the curb and waved at a yellow bubble car in the stream of approaching traffic.

"Taxi!"

The yellow sphere whisked by without slowing, a wide-eyed orange cat inside.

Amy shrugged. "Taken."

She turned to see Furball, Betsy, and Philip staring at her.

"What are you doing?" asked Furball.

"Trying to get a taxi. We have to get back to the palace, pronto!"

"That wasn't a taxi," said the white cat. "Even if it was, that's not how you get one."

Betsy wagged his tail. "Here's how we do it on Kapetyn!"

The brown-and-white terrier grabbed a pebble with his spidery 'manos' bracelet and side-armed it at a bubble car. The rock cracked on the clear windscreen, but the car sped on by with two cats staring at the terrier from the dashboard.

Betsy shrugged. "Taken."

"I'm surprised they didn't stop," said Philip.

"Exactly."

"And whack the living daylights out of you."

"Oh."

"Allow me to find a means of rapid conveyance," said Furball.

The white cat walked to an upright box that looked like a tiny blue phone booth and murmured into a screen. He strutted away from the booth calmly, and before he'd even made it back to the group, a black sphere screeched to a stop beside the curb. A curved door marked with "CBTB" in block letters swung up and open, revealing a padded interior lined in plush gray cushions.

Furball bowed. "Please enter, honored guests."

Amy pointed at the seat. "Too small. We need the extra-large, big-gulp sized taxi."

"I'll sit on your lap this time," said Philip. "Does that sound fair?"

"Definitely not! It doesn't work the other way around."

The teenager grinned. "I expect not."

Betsy scrambled into the taxi. "You can sit on my lap, Philly-Billy!"

"Dogs don't have laps, everyone knows that," said Amy.

She pulled the brown-and-white terrier out of the taxi, Philip slid inside, and Amy settled on top of him with Betsy in her arms.

Furball jumped up to the narrow, cushioned dashboard and pressed a button on the frame. The door lowered with a swish.

"Imperial Palace, north entrance," said the cat.

"Calculating," said a computerized female voice. "Destination: Imperial palace, north entrance. Pending charge: one hundred sixty mao."

Furball settled onto the dashboard and curled his tail around his feet.

"Start service."

The black sphere jerked away from the curb and sped into traffic.

"Arrival in eight point four minutes."

"Takes all the fun out of driving," said Amy. "Not that I've ever driven a car. I'm only fourteen and that would be wrong. I'd plow into a ditch and get grounded for two weeks. Not that it happened."

Philip shifted underneath her. "At least these horseless carriages are clean and swift. Not like the streets of London, that's as sure as mustn't. You've seen them first-hand, dear."

Amy wrinkled her nose. "Lots and lots of horse poop."

She brushed blonde hair from her face and wished she had a hair clip to replace the one she'd given Nick. As she watched the traffic of bubble cars around her, she noticed that several of the cat passengers in other cars were watching video screens.

"How strange," she murmured.

"Apologies," said Philip. "That's my pocket knife."

"No——all the cats are watching the same program. It looks like a public broadcast."

"Can we watch?" asked Betsy. "I like holoscreen. Is it *Jurg Force*? That's my favorite!"

Amy leaned away. "Stop it, Betsy! No licking."

Furball lifted his head and peered out the window.

"It's an Imperial broadcast! Quick——we must watch!"

He reached under the cushioned dash and pressed a button with his paw. A wide rectangle clicked up from the dash and Sunflower's face flickered to life on the screen.

"——and it's important to remember that I care about you, each and every one. Oh! Thank you dear."

Sunflower's head disappeared off-camera. He returned a few seconds later, his mouth and whiskers dripping in green liquid. The orange tabby let out a big sigh.

"You don't miss *somen* water until you haven't had it for months."

"I don't like this program," said Betsy. "Change it."

"It's on every station," said Furball.

"Why?" asked Amy. "What's the point?"

"Ego," said Philip.

"Like I was saying," murmured Sunflower on the screen. "Is this thing still on? Okay. I really appreciate what each and every cat is doing in my empire, from the littlest traffic cop to the biggest general in the navy. Although, if you really were the littlest traffic cop, you'd probably have a hard time stopping anyone." He chuckled. "Get it? Because you'd be tiny."

"Unbelievable," said Philip.

"My appreciation doesn't mean there won't be any changes," said Sunflower. "Lots of things to fix, lots. Where are my notes? Thank you. First on my list of various proclamations and new laws––no kittens in restaurants or movie theaters. If you want to yell and make the fur fly at home, that's your business. Leave the little monsters at home. Next: motorcycles are banned. Actually, change that. Any vehicle that makes noise is banned. The next cat to strap on a leather jacket and blat-blat down a residential street is going to be working in the equatorial mines until his nine lives are up. Mangos––I hate that fruit. Banned. Next––Mister Patti Mittens, algebra teacher at Hidden Valley High School, Western Range. If he's still alive, he's joining all you motorcycle guys in the mines." Sunflower leaned close to the camera. "I never cheated on that quiz, Mister Mittens! You'll have plenty of time to wonder why you sent me to the office instead of Tommy Applebottom––who actually WAS cheating––while your paws are blistered from digging up uranium."

"He's definitely lost it," said Amy. "He never completely had it, whatever it was, but it's definitely lost it now."

"Power corrupts," said Philip. "Absolute power corrupts absolutely."

Sunflower pointed a paw at the viewer. "When someone says 'thank you,' just respond with 'you're welcome.' The next cat to say 'no problem' instead of 'you're welcome' is going to have a problem. I guess the mines are going to be full at this point, so I can't send them to the equator. I'll make them into mango inspectors. Right! They'll have to look for mangos and eat them." Sunflower rubbed his chin. "Eventually, we won't have any mangos. Also, I now have the right to enter anyone's apartment and try on their clothes. If I like them, I get to keep them, and you get the honor of not working in the mines. Because the mines will be full, like I said."

"Good gravy," said Amy. "Should we kidnap this crazy kitty?"

Philip shook his head. "Too much trouble. I suggest we drop Furball at the Imperial Palace, grab Nick if we can find her, and head to the spaceport."

Amy nodded. "The ship can take us to the equator."

"I support this plan, honored guests," said Furball. "Although I would be happy to travel with you to the equator––an inhospitable, boiling wasteland covered with meteor strikes and fiery sandstorms that cook the flesh and rip it from the bone like a family of cats at a barbeque––I would be happier to die of old age without that experience."

Amy wagged a finger at the white Persian. "You're pretty smart for a waiter."

THE TAXI PULLED to the curb near the imperial palace.

Amy, Philip, and Betsy followed Furball through the north gate, after the samurai-helmeted guards scanned all of them with electronic wands.

"If you have any need of money, please use my name and the code I gave you," said Furball.

"All right!" said Amy. "Shopping time, girls!"

"I'm afraid you're the only girl here," said Philip.

Amy noticed Furball's anxious look, and laughed. "Just kidding. I would never do that. Wait a minute—— no, I would never do that."

Furball bowed. "Thank you."

"No problem." Amy covered her mouth in mock horror. "Oh no! Sunflower made that illegal. I'm going to the mines."

Philip put an arm around her shoulder. "I'll come with you, dear. I have a feeling we're all going there sooner rather than later."

"Sunflower the Merciless," whispered Amy.

Furball jumped in the air and looked around the gardens frantically. "The Emperor? Where?"

"Just another joke."

The white cat sighed and continued along the gravel path. "Too much joking with humans," he whispered. "Laugh, laugh, and laugh. Everything's funny until it's not funny.""

"What was that?"

"Nothing, honored guest."

Nick buzzed down from the roof of the imperial bedrooms as they walked up.

"What took you so long?" said the tiny sprite. "That was like a billion, billion hours and I had no one to play with!"

Betsy wagged his brown and white tail. "Sunflower's got a holoscreen show! Did you see it?"

Nick straightened her short pink dress. "Yes, and it's awful. He just talks to himself. There's no shopping or fashion or candy or anything interesting."

"We need to go back to the ship," said Philip. "Are you ready?"

Nick clapped her tiny hands. "Am I ever! I'll grab my stuff."

The tiny woman flew away with a loud buzz.

Philip knelt down to Furball. "Thank you for the help, my friend, and for defending us in the alley. I know it was your job to do all of that, but you did it well and in a professional manner."

"Exactly," said Amy. "What he said!"

The white cat bowed. "I am honored to serve. Please be assured that I will keep silent on the particular matters of this afternoon."

Amy tilted her head. "Sniffy and Princess?"

Furball bowed again. "The other matter of this afternoon. Your next destination."

"Ah, yes. Very good."

Furball sprang to his feet. "Now for selfie time! Pick me up."

The cat stood on Philip's shoulder as the group packed together. He held out a tiny camera attached to his paw and smiled.

"Look at my paw. Everybody say, goosebumps!"

"Goosebumps," said Amy and Philip.

"Bumpy goose!" barked Betsy.

Furball jumped down, bowed rapidly, and ran off with a spray of white gravel.

"He doesn't like long goodbyes," said Philip.

Amy shrugged. "What's a 'selfie?'"

11

Amy and Philip stood in the navigation room of the ship as the holographic projection of Cheezburger passed below their feet in a blur of skyscrapers and neon billboards. Amy still wore her white blouse, black leather vest, plaid skirt, and dark blue tights. At the ship's encouragement, Philip had changed into his red spandex uniform.

The teenager pulled at the cap stretched tightly over his hair. "This outfit is bloody frustrating, if you'll pardon my French."

"That didn't sound like French," said Amy.

"The uniform is required because of dander," said the motherly voice of the ship. "Human dander, cat dander, dog dander. I happen to find Miss Armstrong's dander not as revolting as others."

Philip winced. "What's revolting is that word, by Jove. Why do you have to use it?"

"Which word?" asked the ship. "Dander? Dander, dander, dander."

Amy squeezed him on the bicep. "She's got your number."

"This spaceship cannot be entirely mechanical. No machine I've ever met has made such jokes at my expense."

"The galaxy is a big place, Phil. I'm sure we'll find a planet of robots who tell jokes for fun at some point. I bet if we pried off the panels in the central processor of this ship we'd find a little old lady sitting behind an old-fashioned switchboard."

"That wouldn't surprise me. On the subject of prying off panels, do you think Betsy and Nick have murdered each other yet?"

"Both crew members are resting on their respective sleeping areas," said the ship. "No violence has been attempted."

The gray blocks of Cheezburger shrank below their feet. Even the suburbs disappeared under a haze of clouds as the ship increased speed and rose through the upper atmosphere.

"How long until we arrive at this research station?" asked Amy.

"Thirty-seven minutes," said the ship. "Do you wish me to increase velocity, captain?"

Amy stretched her arms above her head. "No, it's perfect. That gives me time to eat something."

"The point is moot because we may not have anywhere to land when we arrive," said Philip. "Furball mentioned that it's a wasteland."

"This MacGuffin cat went there, so it can't be that bad."

"We don't know if he survived the trip."

"The surface temperature during the daytime ranges from one hundred fifty to one seventy five degrees Fahrenheit," said the ship. "Exposed skin will receive third-degree burns, and materials with ignition temperatures in that range will combust immediately."

"Rats," said Amy. "Not bikini weather."

"That is correct, captain, unless your bikini is constructed of nano-polymer material and covers your body from head to toe."

"That sounds like armored pajamas, not a bikini."

"Do we have to wear protective suits?" asked Philip.

"The ship uniforms and the Captain's clothing will provide a brief moment of protection, enough time for crew members to either reach shelter or contemplate the futility of existence and where they went wrong."

"There's that humor again," said Philip.

"Who cares?" said Amy. "My clothes are totally cool. Get it? Cool. Ah, you don't get it."

Philip shrugged. "Another joke?"

"I have plotted an orbital insertion and planetfall at night, making environmental protection unnecessary," said the ship. "Analysis of weather patterns in the equatorial region reveals a high frequency of dust hurricanes and lightning storms during any point of the solar cycle, night or day. Navigation through these events would present a challenge, even for me. These are the constraints of your request to make planetfall at this location."

"Any suggestions?" asked Amy.

"I suggest the captain conclude her business and leave as soon as possible."

"Can't disagree with that," said Philip. "I don't want a third-degree sunburn."

A bright circle of sky appeared in mid-air and Nistra stepped inside the room, the ship's uniform stretched tightly over his muscular reptile body.

"Greetings, friends! I see you have returned."

Amy watched the sauro walk gingerly over the clouds and atmosphere projected on the floor.

"You know that's not real, right? The floor is still there."

The sauro smiled razor-sharp teeth.

"Of course, of course. I was ... walking in this strange way to show respect for the captain."

"You just made that up!"

"No, I didn't."

"So Nistra, old chap," said Philip. "Did you have fun scrounging through our valuables while we were away from the ship?"

Nistra stared at the teenager. "I didn't!"

Amy shrugged. "Which is it——you didn't have fun, or didn't go through our stuff?"

"I never did that thing. Both!"

"Don't confuse him, old stick," said Philip. "A reptile his size would have less than a teacup of brain matter. That's a fact of natural science."

Nistra raised a sharp claw. "Ah, but sauropods are engineered life forms, so your old rules no longer apply."

"Great," said Amy. "What exactly did you get up to while we were gone?"

"Sleeping. Eating. Sleeping. Staring at the wall of my closet. Sleeping. Eating."

"What a great story. You should write a book."

The lizard grinned pointy yellow teeth. "The captain is very wise in noticing my talent for narrative. At the prison, I wrote articles for the weekly newsletter, *H.A.L.P. Mandatory Entertainment,* and co-authored a manual on torturing political prisoners and non-blood relatives."

Amy stared at the giant reptile. "I was joking!"

Nistra's smile changed to a sad frown. "Oh."

THE SHIP ROSE into orbit like a salmon leaping over a stream, her silver skin reflecting the swirling clouds over Tau Ceti's south pole. The blue seas around the southern continent faded over the edge of the planet, and the ship flew over a continent of cracked brown wastelands, vast deserts wider than the Sahara, and the ragged, broken-glass shape of mountain ranges.

The silver craft passed over the terminator and into the darkness of night, when half the planet rested from the fierce solar rays. Instead of the brilliant web of street lamps that they would have seen over Cheezburger at night, the equatorial region was covered in dead shades of gray and swirling dust hurricanes hundreds of miles wide.

"Approaching planetfall of Tau Ceti Epsilon in four minutes ten seconds," spoke the ship through the crew broadcast system. "Destination is nine degrees forty-three minutes north, one five-five degrees five minutes west."

Amy and Philip raced through the corridors from the kitchen to the navigation room.

"Made it!" yelled Amy, slapping the hatch.

Philip jogged a few meters behind her, holding a large sandwich.

"No fair. I was eating this sausage bap! At least, I think it's a sausage bap."

Amy pouted. "What's the matter––can't eat and run at the same time? Ow! No pinching!"

Philip chased her into the navigation room where a dark, arid landscape was projected into their minds by the ship. The pair of teenagers turned quiet as they watched the bleak mountains and deserts pass below their feet.

"How can anything live down there?" whispered Amy.

"I doubt that anything can," said Philip.

"Two minutes to planetfall," said the ship. "Which crew will be disembarking, my Lady?"

Amy shrugged and looked at Philip. "Everyone?"

The hatch opened and Nistra walked carefully over the floor.

"What's happening?" asked the reptile. "Have we landed?"

"Ninety seconds until planetfall," said the ship.

Amy stared at a gray desert and mountain range far below her feet. "Have you contacted the research station?"

"I have, my Lady, but have not received a response from station personnel. The automated landing system is active, although on a low-bandwidth, obscure channel. An eighty-one percent chance exists of nominal planetfall."

Philip glanced at Amy. "What happens in the other percent?"

"Sixteen point four percent chance the station blast doors have frozen shut, creating a barrier we shall hit at fifty meters per second. One point five percent chance the landing system is transmitting false data, and we impact the surface. One point one percent chance that another craft is docked, not registered to the landing system, and which we shall hit at fifty meters per second. Point nine percent the power core fails and we impact the surface. Point seven percent——"

"Thanks, Blanche," said Amy. "We get the picture."

Nistra held a scaly hand over his heart and bowed from the waist.

"Captain, I have arranged for a delivery of sauropod food at Cheezburger Central. If you could pre-approve the loading of this large container, I would be most grateful."

"Sure, whatever," said Amy. "If we don't die in a giant fireball in the next ten seconds we can talk about your stupid crates of marshdevils or whatever."

"No crew member would experience death by fire," said the calm voice of the ship. "The primary impact would disable my kinetic dampers, inflicting internal injuries and organ failure as every crew member struck a forward bulkhead. These injuries would be fatal before any secondary combustion. To put it simply, your insides would be goo."

"What about our outsides?"

"Also goo."

"Thanks for that comforting thought." Amy hugged Philip around the waist and stared up at his face. "Any last words?"

Philip took a bite of the sandwich in his hand. "Dear, I want you to know——"

"Yes?"

"I absolutely love——"

"Yes?"

"——sausages. This one is perfectly wizard!"

Amy sighed. "Nice."

The rocky, gray and brown landscape below their feet grew larger as the ship descended, revealing numerous craters from meteor impacts on the desert surface. Ahead of the ship, the dull, broken peak of a mountain loomed tall in the night sky.

Amy and Philip held each other tight and Nistra grabbed the edge of the central console as the ship approached a square of four flashing lights at the base of the mountain. A horizontal smear of red appeared between the bottom pair of lights and grew into the rectangular, red-lit opening of a hangar. Two lines of blinking lights framed a runway that stretched deep into the mountain.

"The door's open, so that's sixteen percent at least," said Amy. "Right, Blanche?"

"No questions, please," said the ship. "I'm concentrating."

The opening of the hangar flashed by, and the ship quickly slowed to the pace of a sprinting human. She followed a series of green lights to a wide, open area cut from the rock and rotated a complete circle, pointing her silver nose back at the hangar entrance.

"Good show!" said Philip. "We've arrived."

"I'm just happy to not be a puddle of goo," said Amy. "It's like Christmas!"

Large blocks of machinery surrounded the sides of the turn-around area, some with black hoses that looked like they could be for refueling and others with claw-tipped arms retracted into sleeves.

"Nothing moves here," whispered Nistra. "Living or dead."

"Hard for dead things to move," said Amy.

The reptile shrugged. "Sauro children play a game with a dead poona. It is more fun with dead cats, but such are the times. Two teams fight for the corpse. If the dead cat bounces across a line, that team gets a point."

Philip rubbed his face and sighed. "How quaint."

A large purple craft stood at the other side of the rock-walled cavern. Twenty meters long and shaped like a hunched-over cockroach complete with articulated metal legs sprouting from the sides, the ship was connected to the machinery by a dozen large cables and corrugated hoses.

Amy pointed at the ship. "Tell me that's full of giant cockroach people and I'm not stepping one foot outside."

"It's a cat cruiser," said Nistra. "I do not see any weapon pods, so the owner is probably civilian."

Philip nodded. "Perhaps it belongs to Cynthia MacGuffin."

"No response from the craft," said the ship. "She's either unregistered or doesn't want to talk to me. Cat vessels are like that."

"Someone has to be here," said Amy. "Scan for life forms, Blanche."

"I detect no mobile heat signatures in this area or on the Cetean craft, my Lady. Analysis of biological material in the atmosphere and environment indicate that at least one, if not more, biological entities have been in this immediate area in the past ninety-six hours."

"What kind of biological material?" asked Philip.

"Cat hair," said the ship dryly. "Lots and lots of cat hair."

Amy pumped an arm. "Super! Let's go."

"Cat hair," said Nistra, and shivered. "If the captain pleases, I will stay with the ship."

Amy crossed her arms. "I do NOT please, you big baby. What if there's a fight and nobody's around to protect me and Philip?"

"Hey!" said Philip. "I can protect me and Philip. I mean, you and me."

Amy pushed a finger into Philip's chest. "If you're protecting me, who's protecting you?"

"Sorry? Oh, I get it. Yes, we definitely need him."

"But I want to stay by myself," said Nistra. "Being alone is the only hobby I have left!"

Amy pushed the sauro toward the door. "Nope, coming with us. Forward march!"

"What about Betsy and Nick?" asked Philip.

"The specified crew members are still sleeping in their quarters," said the ship. "Would you like me to wake them, captain, thereby adding their expertise on food, fashion, and repurposed garbage to the group?"

"Not when you put it that way. Let 'em sleep."

"Additionally, a scan of the weather patterns indicate that a major hurricane will strike the present locality in twenty-six minutes."

"Are we safe?"

"Inside this facility, that is a correct statement. The blast door was designed for these frequent storms. As long as it remains in place and we are not forced to leave, the captain and crew members will be safe."

"Got it."

BOTH PHILIP and Nistra grumbled mightily about wearing their stretchy red uniforms outside the ship.

"It's for safety," said Amy, as she climbed down the ladder from the airlock. "You heard what Blanche said about this place."

Philip followed Amy down the ladder and joined her on the deck of the hangar. "Do you have any extra clothes lying around? I wonder if some of those could be tailored to fit me. It shouldn't be that difficult to make a pair of trousers."

Amy fanned her skirt and grinned. "You don't need trousers, Phil—I'll make you into a little princess. I bet your closet back home is full of ribbons and bows and pretty lace dresses."

"I don't have a home anymore. The Lady saw to that, didn't she?"

"Sorry. I didn't mean to bring it up."

Philip shook his head. "Forget it. Apology accepted."

Nothing moved in the hangar or made a sound apart from the footsteps of the two humans and the sauropod as they walked over the polished rock floor. Even the machinery was deathly silent, and nothing chirped, hummed, rattled, or buzzed. The three intrepid explorers wandered around the side of the purple cockroach spaceship to an automatic sliding door. This led to a corridor illuminated with red lamps in the ceiling and lined with horizontal rubber pipes. Below the pipes stood a long line of numbered yellow barrels, some of them leaking an oily black liquid.

"Honey, I'm home!" yelled Amy, and listened for the echo. "Nothing. This is the welcome I get." She glanced at Philip and Nistra. "What? It's a joke."

Philip shook his head. "It's a bit of an odd thing to say."

"Yes," said Nistra. "On Kepler Prime we call this a 'crime of attempting cave ownership.' The victim is taken out and beaten, then strangled, then beaten, then burned alive, then strangled, then thrown off a cliff."

"Victim?" asked Amy. "Don't you mean 'criminal?'"

Nistra held up a fist. "On Kepler Prime, we punish the victim. Praise the Leader!"

"Great. Nobody strangle me for taking the lead and trying to find this cat, okay?" Amy strode down the red-lit hallway, her arms swinging wide. "There's always a map somewhere. Here's one! Nah, just cobwebs." She froze. "Wait——are there spiders in space?"

Philip put an arm over Amy's shoulder. "We're not in space, dear, but I'm sure whatever made that cobweb is massive and has fangs the size of houses."

The floor of the corridor vibrated from a distant thud.

Amy stared at Philip. "Was that a meteor?" she whispered.

The corridor shook twice more.

Philip shrugged. "Perhaps the storm?"

"Too soon for that," said Nistra.

The lights in the ceiling clacked off in sequence starting with the furthest down the corridor and covered the two humans and sauropod in complete darkness. The shivering impacts came again with a regular, steady beat. A sinister voice breathed through the air——cold, distant, and absolutely alien.

"Smelllsss," hissed the deep and sibilant voice. "We hopesss it tastesss good, yesss, doesssn't we?"

Amy grabbed for Philip in the darkness and hugged him tight.

"Spiders don't eat people, do they?" she whispered.

"I don't think it's part of their diet."

"Good."

"I also don't want to find out."

"Is that why you're pushing Nistra in front of us?" whispered Amy.

"You're as perceptive as you are beautiful."

The roar of a lion blasted their eardrums, and all three turned and fled. In the darkness, however, it was difficult to remember which way was which.

"This is a wall!" yelled Amy. "Where am I?"

Philip reached through the darkness and grabbed something. "I've got your hand, Amy. So dry and scaly. Also, dear, you need to cut your nails. Very sharp."

"What?"

Amy's fingers brushed across a wall and touched a flat button. She covered her eyes as the glaring lights in the ceiling snapped back to life. Between her fingers, she saw Philip and Nistra holding hands with their eyes squeezed shut.

She giggled. "What a cute couple!"

Philip and Nistra opened their eyes and sprang away from each other.

"Amy, I thought it was you!"

"Number one: don't ever tell a girl she has skin like a lizard. Number two: I should probably buy some hand lotion. Is there a Walgreens in space?"

Another thud vibrated the floor behind them.

"No, no, no!" roared the deep voice. "Lights off, you morons. Lights off!"

A Siamese cat stood erect in the middle of the hallway wearing a pair of gigantic metal boots. His fur was mostly tan--apart from his dark brown ears, face, and paws--and the cat held a white megaphone in front of his mouth.

The cat lowered the megaphone and shrugged.

"Boo?"

Nistra screamed and took a few steps back, until he noticed that he was the only one frightened.

"Sorry. Reflex."

Amy brushed a strand of blonde hair over her ear. "Let me guess--you're the galaxy's worst shoemaker?"

The cat shook his head.

"A nasty cat-robot experiment? Victim of a horrible boating accident? A cat stranded on this station for so long that he's forgotten how to love?"

Philip sighed. "What about the obvious, dear?"

Amy raised her index finger. "I know! This place is full of weird space gas which causes us to imagine a half-cat, half-robot monstrosity, who will trick us into either fighting to the death or kissing each other in front of a pack of space Romans wearing togas."

"Dear heart, you do have an imagination," said Philip. "This is Doctor Cynthia MacGuffin."

The Siamese cat jumped in surprise, causing the metal boots to thump the floor. He gripped the megaphone with both paws and held it out in front of himself like a pistol.

"Where did you hear that name?" he asked. "There's nothing on this station of value, so turn around and head back to Amber or whatever space dump you came from."

"Your boots might fetch a pretty penny," said Amy. "But strange as it sounds coming from me, we're not here to steal anything. We need to speak to Doctor MacGuffin."

The cat lowered the megaphone.

"You're not pirates? Bounty hunters?"

"As cool as it sounds to be a space pirate, no, we are not."

"Imperial Revenue Service, that's who you are. I knew it was a bad idea to toss that shoebox full of receipts into the river. I swear that bathrobe was a legitimate business expense!"

"We're not from any government organization," said Philip. "We met with your friend Doctor Jackson, and he gave us your location. We want to ask you a few questions and then we'll be going."

The cat sighed. "That's what they all say. Just a few questions, buddy, just a few. Just a few years of post-graduate work where some other cat takes the credit. Just a few years of teaching bonehead science to freshmen cats. Just a few mortgage payments, few loans from the bank, few back-stabbing research assistants. I've had it up to my whiskers with just a few!"

Amy held up her hands. "Whoa, now. We didn't come here to upset you. Sorry if that's happening."

The cat shook his head. He dropped the megaphone and pulled his feet out of the giant metal boots.

"I should be the sorry one," he said quietly. "I don't get many visitors. For obvious reasons, the strangers that do show up at this remote station are not very nice."

"So you ARE Doctor MacGuffin!"

The cat bowed. "The one and only."

A loud clatter came from the far end of the corridor. A pair of cats slid around a corner and scrambled up to the group on all fours. One was an orange tabby and the other was a white shorthair with calico patches. Both had black, cat-sized rifles strapped to their backs, ready to fire over their shoulders.

"Stop!" yelled the orange tabby, the muzzle of his rifle wavering between Philip and Amy. "It would be majorly uncool to hurt Doctor Cynthia. Like, WAY uncool."

"He's totally the smartest cat ever," said the patched calico, speaking with an older female voice. "The Doc wouldn't hurt a fly."

Amy held up her hands. "We're not doing anything. We just want to talk."

The tabby pointed his rifle at Nistra. "Well, man ... why'd you bring one of those things? All they like to do is kill, man."

Philip shrugged. "In case we met other things that like to kill?"

"Amy and Bocephus, put down your weapons," said Doctor MacGuffin. "It's fine. These humans and their sauro slave are not here to harm anyone."

Amy pointed at her chest. "Amy? That's my name."

The three cats burst into peals of laughter.

"Whoa, hang on a second," said the orange tabby, wiping away tears with a paw. "These humans think they can write anything on a birth certificate. How can you call a girl Amy?"

The calico female nudged the cat. "Don't make fun. Words can hurt, especially when it comes to names."

"Sorry." The tabby bowed. "I'm Amy, and this is Bocephus––my partner on the beautiful journey of life we call ... uh, life, man."

"Wow, way cool," said Bocephus, and kissed him on his furry orange cheek.

"Charmed, I'm sure," said Amy.

Philip bowed. "Philip of Marlborough. The sauro beside me is Officer Nistra."

Amy the cat nodded. "Totally awesome. Don't go aggro and kill us all or anything, okay?"

Nistra blinked slowly. "I will do my best to restrain myself."

Doctor MacGuffin waved a paw down the corridor. "Enough formalities. I suggest we escape to the upper floors. These lower levels are dank and smelly, and only useful for scaring the nine lives out of pirates."

MACGUFFIN STASHED the megaphone and boots in a closet and led the group to an elevator. Dark and empty floors flashed by the elevator's window as they rose through the mountain. The only signs that anyone lived here at all were one floor of machinery and a bright level packed with rows and rows of green plants.

"Ask me your questions," said Doctor MacGuffin. "Or should we stare at our paws like a bunch of half-wits?"

"We're here for your recombinator matrix," said Philip. "Or the plans."

MacGuffin slapped a red button and the elevator jerked to a halt, throwing everyone off-balance.

"You scoundrels! Apprehend them!"

Amy the orange tabby shrugged. "I don't know what that word means, dude. We can do some fascist gun-pointing stuff, though."

Bocephus nodded. "Heavy."

"They're from the Lady, you morons! I stole the recombinator from her."

"The what?"

"The shiny blinky thing!"

"Right, right," said Amy the cat, and pointed the muzzle of his rifle at the two humans. "Hands up, human dude and dudette and slimy space pig!"

Bocephus aimed her rifle at Nistra. "Space fascist!"

The lizard shook his head. "I am certainly a fascist, but to call me a pig is very confusing. I am nothing like a pig. It is the one species of mammal that I am absolutely not similar to. We are cloned in vats, while the pig gives birth to live young."

"Shut up, space pig!"

Amy held up her hands. "We're not from the Lady."

MacGuffin shook his furry head. "Why did your boyfriend say he wants the recombinator matrix? I should have shut the blast doors and let your ship explode on the surface!"

"No way you could have done that, Doc," said Bocephus. "You were taking a nap."

Amy the cat nodded. "Snoring like a space pig. I could hear it from my room."

"Quiet," said MacGuffin. "I suppose we'll send them outside to die like the others."

"Cool deal," said Amy the cat. "Violence is against my religion."

"I know, right?" said Bocephus. "Bad karma."

Amy and Philip glanced at each other. The pair leaned down and jerked the rifles from the harnesses of both cats.

"Whoa!"

"Stop it, human dude!"

Doctor MacGuffin groaned and fell to the floor in a furry pile. "You idiots! Now we're the ones going for a morning stroll of death. My research is ruined!"

Amy set the rifle on the floor of the elevator. "We're not working for the Lady. See? We're not here to hurt anyone. The recombinator on our ship is damaged, and we thought you could help us repair it. Otherwise, we're stuck here."

The Siamese cat nodded. He pressed a button and the elevator jerked upward.

"Why don't you ask the Lady? She knows more than I when it comes to transmat technology."

"It's complicated," said Philip. "At first we thought she was trying to kill us, and then she sent Amy to prison."

"We don't even know if she exists in this dimension," said Amy. "The recombinator burnt to a crisp during our transmat."

Doctor MacGuffin's eyes widened into huge yellow globes in the center of his furry brown face. "You're from another dimension? Blessed Saint Mittens and his three legs! Come to the laboratory. Come! I have to take samples!"

The Siamese cat slapped another button on the control panel.

"Samples are fine," said Amy. "As long as I don't have to pee in a cup."

"Don't be disgusting, this isn't Alpha Centauri," said Doctor MacGuffin. "I have a micturition machine."

Amy raised an eyebrow and looked at Philip. "I'm not going to lie––that sounds worse."

The dark-haired teen nodded. "Quite."

12

The door of the medical closet flew open. Amy leapt out with her hands up and entire body shaking.

"Ew! Ew! Ew! It touched me! Why did it have to touch me?"

With a white surgical cap over his furry ears, Doctor MacGuffin stood in front of a large display and watched a stream of blue numbers pour down the screen.

"The machine is simply doing its job. Did you expect to lift your leg and spray on a plastic fire hydrant? You won't find dog methods in a professional laboratory."

"I expected a cup!"

Philip cleared his throat and pointed at Amy's rear. "Ah, dear? Your skirt has somehow become lodged behind ... in your ... unmentionables."

Amy pulled her skirt up and out from her tights and flattened the plaid fabric with both hands. "Sorry. I was too busy being assaulted by the space cat scientist!"

MacGuffin glanced up from his screen. "We're not in space. Next! The sauropod."

Nistra shifted his weight from one foot to the other. "Do I have to?"

"Um, yes," said Amy. "If the captain and her boyfriend have to be assaulted, then space pig has to be assaulted."

"Please don't call me that. I find it offensive."

"That's why I used it!"

"It only stings a bit when it clamps down," said Philip. "Try not to struggle. That only makes it worse."

Nistra sighed. The giant lizard squeezed his wide shoulders into the closet and closed the door. A few seconds later, the door rattled and everyone heard a muffled yelp.

Amy shook her head. "So tell me, mister space doctor—are we going to live?"

"That's not what the test was about," said the cat, concentrating on his screen. "Please give me a moment and don't touch anything."

Amy wandered around the small room, peering into cabinets packed with strange silver tools and jars of goopy biological samples. All the surfaces in the room had been painted white and were polished to gleaming perfection, even the floors and cabinets.

Philip watched her move around the room for a moment, and knelt beside Doctor MacGuffin.

"Can you help us repair the ship?"

The Siamese cat stared at the graphs on his display. "Interesting, interesting. Absolutely nothing abnormal here. Both within human norms, but there IS one data point that concerns me." The cat jumped to another screen nearby. "From the radiation scans I did earlier, your mate is transducing on a nuclear level between several quantum planes."

Amy spun and yelled from across the room. "What's that about mates?"

"Nothing, dear," said Philip, and turned back to the doctor. "What does that mean in plain English?" he whispered.

The Siamese cat sighed. "Let me explain in terms that a Centauran would understand." He shook his head. "No, that's too hard. Try to imagine a chunk of rotting meat or whatever you monkeys eat for breakfast. You're holding it in your paws, about to eat it, then it disappears. Then it appears again, then it disappears. Think of that happening a million times a second."

Amy slammed a drawer. "Who's a piece of meat?"

"Certainly not you, my dearest," said Philip loudly. He turned back to MacGuffin and lowered his voice. "She's not a piece of meat."

"That's not the point. Your female mate is vibrating on a frequency that is so high, it's virtually undetectable. I say virtually, because I'm the most brilliant cat scientist in the history of cat scientists, and I've studied trans-dimensional phenomena for years."

Amy walked up to the pair. "What's this about vibrations?"

"Nothing, dear," said Philip. He stood and kissed Amy on the cheek. "He said you're very special."

Amy flipped her blonde hair behind her shoulder. "Duh! I'm the prettiest and smartest girl in the galaxy."

Philip bowed. "Never a truer phrase was spoken."

Doctor MacGuffin looked Amy up and down. "Although your accent is strong, you have a grasp of the English language. You've also learned to shave and wear proper clothing. I suppose that does elevate you over the hairy, mountainous drabs of Centauran humanity. Not something I'd brag about to my grand-kittens, however."

Amy shrugged. "I didn't come here to be insulted. Get to the point––why did you steal from the Lady?"

The cat stepped back from the display and rubbed his eyes.

"Because she was the only person able to harness the power of dimensional travel; it's as simple as that. A decade ago I became convinced that the million SpaceBook drones were not from our galactic timeline, and held the key to dimensional travel. Not just leaving, but coming back. Ten years of exhaustive research led me nowhere, until a colleague pointed out the Lady and her vast business in buying and selling treasures and precious antiques. I studied the signals between her asteroid and the SpaceBook network and discovered the connection. The rest was simply a matter of passing the test to become an 'operator' and finding the right moment to steal her technology. The price on my head and living in these horrific surroundings are my punishment."

"How did you escape?" asked Amy. "In our dimension, Sunflower destroyed your ship in the atmosphere above Tau Ceti."

"Why would the Emperor attack me?" asked the cat, and waved his paw. "No matter––what happened in another dimension is irrelevant. Perhaps I am a better pilot. Perhaps that version of me knew little about masking radiation signatures. It is fruitless to speculate. I'm here, and that's all I know."

A scream came from inside the medical closet and it rocked back and forth.

"Nistra doesn't like your mictra-whats-it machine," said Amy. "That's all I know."

"Dear me, I completely forgot!" said MacGuffin. "He's been in there too long!"

The cat swiped his paw across a display. The door to the closet burst open and Nistra stumbled out, one claw holding up his spandex pants. He shuffled across the room, jaws open and eyes glazed over.

"I'm no lizard doctor," said Amy, and switched to a Southern accent. "But he don't look right."

MacGuffin snorted. "You're definitely not a sauropod doctor. They don't exist!"

A nearby screen beeped and the whiskered face of Bocephus appeared.

"Are you cats done? You should get up here to the monitor station and have a look. There's some really heavy stuff happening outside the mountain."

MacGuffin waved a paw at the screen. "Don't get hysterical——it's just another storm. If you've seen one dust hurricane, you've seen a hundred thousand dust hurricanes."

"No, Doc——I'm looking at a meteor swarm."

"On my way!"

MacGuffin darted for the corridor, his black tail high and Amy and Philip right behind the cat. All three jumped inside the elevator and watched Nistra shuffle through the laboratory.

"Come on!" yelled MacGuffin, holding the "door open" button with a paw.

"Move it, space pig!" yelled Amy. "Or I'll turn you into space pig luggage!"

Nistra turned and shuffled at a marginally faster speed toward the elevator, the same blank expression on his face and the same hand holding up his spandex pants, although they were too tight to have fallen down in any case. The sauro stepped inside the elevator and stared at the back wall, not bothering to turn around.

"Space pig no like," he whispered. "No like."

MacGuffin smacked a button and the elevator jerked upwards.

"Sounds like a nervous breakdown," he said. "I didn't know that could happen with sauropods. Possibly a repressed memory from the vat-cloning process. Ah, well——live and learn."

Amy touched Nistra's scaly arm. "Sorry about the whole space pig thing. It was a joke."

"No touch!" The sauro jerked his arm away. "Always touch! Always poke, poke, poke!"

Philip stepped between Amy and Nistra. "Watch your manners with the lady, old chap. You may have more teeth than brain cells, but ... sorry, I forgot what I was going to say."

The elevator door swished open. Amy and Philip followed Doctor MacGuffin down a corridor lined with landscape paintings and carpeted in soft blue fabric. After passing through a set of blast doors they found themselves in large circular room. Many levels of bright displays covered one wall, where the calico cat Bocephus sat behind a control panel covered in keyboards and knobs.

Amy, the orange tabby, walked over a pile of cushions in the center of the room and lay down.

"Take it slow, human dude and dudette," he said with a yawn. "Don't freak out. It's just a couple of little meteors."

MacGuffin trotted to the control panel. "I'll be the judge of that. Bocephus, show me the camera feeds."

Amy plopped onto the pile of cushions next to the orange tabby and Philip sat beside her.

"Tell me, Mister Amy," he asked the cat. "How did you find yourself in a place such as this? You don't seem the type of boffin who enjoys working in a lab in the middle of nowhere."

Amy held up a hand. "He's the janitor. That's my bet."

The orange tabby grinned. "I'm picking up what you're putting down, dude––I get it. You're trying to say this is a totally sweet gig, but not my scene, right? When Bocephus and I were first sent here, maybe ten, fifteen years ago, it was a total bummer. Nothing to do but chill, no bros to hang out with, and no hologames. A real let-down, you know? But then Bocephus told me, if karma spits in your face, just pretend it's rain-ing. Totally awesome saying, right? So I look at this as our personal retreat. Lots of meditation, lots of walking around, lots of smoking that nip-nip, if you know what I mean?"

Amy shook her head. "Nip-nip?"

"Catnip. We grow lots of herb here. It's medicinal, but totally has other awesome uses. Like ... uh, medicinal uses!"

"Who would send the two of you here?" asked Philip. "Is this a prison sentence?"

"Sort of, but not sort of. We got arrested by the cops for selling catnip out of the back of our van. That was totally legal because we were living in it, but whatever dude. Our son was totally embarrassed. He made the cops leave us alone, which was cool, but he threw us in a transport and shipped us down here. It's totally cool and everything, like I said. You can't really argue with the Emperor, even if he's your kid."

"Who is?" asked Amy.

"The Emperor."

Amy jumped off the sofa and pointed at the tabby. "Sunflower's dad! Catnip van! Hippie parents!"

The orange cat nodded. "Right on, right on."

"My word," said Philip, standing up. "How did we miss that?"

"Hippie parents," said Amy, and swung her arms wide. "Unbelievable!"

"Yes, dear," said Philip. "I'm shocked that he would banish his family to this desolate cave in the center of a wasteland."

"Don't worry, he didn't send all of us down here. There's still family in Amber. Bankers, mostly, so Sunflower was totally cool with that."

Amy shook her head. "But you look so young."

Sunflower's father gave Amy a broad, fanged grin. "Catnip, baby. Catnip."

A yowl of pain came from MacGuffin at the control panel.

"She's found us," moaned the Siamese cat, rubbing his dark brown ears. "She's going to kill us all!"

Amy and Philip rushed up to the wall of displays.

"Who?" asked Amy.

"The Lady. She's here!"

MacGuffin pointed to a dim camera feed of a meteor crater. As it was still night outside, the deep pit in the earth appeared as a gradation of black against the dark gray of the mountain. Inside the pit, a boulder rolled from left to right.

"A bunch of dead rocks," said Amy. "Nothing worry about."

"Switching to infra-red," said Bocephus.

The screen changed to shades of purple and the boulder flared into fierce red with edges of yellow. The glowing sphere rose over the lip of the crater with a dozen pink lines dangling; the heat signatures of thick, tentacle-like arms.

Amy gulped. "Ah ... maybe it's hot from the atmosphere, and that's space moss hanging from the bottom? Maybe a space octopus?"

"We're on a planet," said MacGuffin. "What's this obsession with adding 'space' to everything? Are you talking about the empty space between your monkey ears?"

"It's definitely one of the Lady's inspectors," said Philip. "That's bad news and no way to shift it. Those things are absolutely mental."

Amy held out a clenched fist. "We can handle an inspector. Didn't we teach the last one a lesson? All we need is some cheese."

Doctor MacGuffin shook his head. "Switch to the independent feeds, Bocephus."

Two dozen of the screens switched to a similar view as the first——either a black boulder or glowing red sphere floating from a crater.

"Good gravy," whispered Amy.

Philip put his arm around her shoulder. "We'd need an entire wheel of cheddar."

"Thirty-one inspectors," said Doctor MacGuffin. "Wait——another impact. Thirty-two. Thirty-three. Doesn't matter. We're surrounded by hundreds of meters of rock. This place was designed to survive the constant lightning columns and dust hurricanes."

Amy raised a hand. "Um, hello? What about the hangar?"

"Hardly a weakness. It's a meter thick and made from reinforced alloys."

Bocephus pointed up. "Uh, oh. Some way uncool stuff happening on camera four."

A line of crackling energy flashed from an inspector toward the massive hangar door. A moment later, a second inspector joined the first and fired its own energy beam. The control panel lit up with blinking red lights.

"Warning," said a computerized male voice from somewhere in the ceiling. "Structure breach. Warning. Structure breach."

"Definitely uncool," said Amy. "No question."

MacGuffin clasped his paws on top of his furry head. "Fizz puffs! I was doing so well, and now this! How long until a total breach of the door?"

Bocephus tapped several buttons on the console. "If all thirty-three attack at the same point, they'll break through in seven minutes."

MacGuffin nodded. "Time enough to grab a few things. Send the start-up instructions to my ship. These blasted inspectors can't chase an interstellar craft."

The calico cat pressed a key and frowned. "Not to harsh your buzz or anything, doc. They'll breach the door in seven minutes, but if we don't open it before that, it's never going to open. They'll burn through the hydraulics for raising the door in five minutes."

"Is the hangar is the only way out of this place?" asked Amy.

MacGuffin shook his head. "Doesn't matter. We'd be dead by morning if we tried to walk across the desert."

"What about the storm we passed while landing?" asked Philip. "Is that going to strike anytime soon?"

"Checking," said Bocephus, tapping on the console and watching a display of swirling clouds.

MacGuffin sheathed and sheathed his claws nervously. "Well?"

"Class-four dust hurricane approaching from southwest. We'll start to get the edge in five or six minutes. Flight will be impossible."

MacGuffin smacked the side of the control panel. "We're leaving now. Set the blast door to open automatically in four minutes. Go!"

Bocephus used both paws to tap dozens of control keys like a concert pianist. "Done!"

"Good. Run for my ship!"

All three cats and Amy and Philip scrambled for the elevator. The door closed and they waited, breathing hard and staring at the levels flashing up the window.

"What about the recombinator?" Amy asked.

"I'm five steps ahead of you," said MacGuffin. "See you in the hangar!"

The elevator door opened to a level filled with machinery, and the Siamese cat ran out like his tail was on fire.

Philip leaned down and jabbed a button to close the door. "Faster, faster," he murmured.

Sunflower's dad turned to Bocephus. "Are we totally ditching this place?"

"Yep. Thinking what I'm thinking?"

The orange tabby punched a button on the control panel and grinned. "Rock on!"

The door opened to a humid floor packed with ultraviolet lights and rows of green plants, and the pair of cats shot out the door.

"See you later, human dudes!"

Philip sighed and pressed the door button. "Alone at last."

Amy grabbed his arm. "We forgot Nistra!"

"Egads, you're right! Where did we leave him?"

"Hit the button marked 'CS.'"

The elevator jerked to a stop, and began to rise again.

Amy clenched her fists at her waist. "I am SO going to kill that space pig."

"An admirable thought, my dear, if we aren't murdered by those inspectors first."

They found the giant reptile staring at the wall of a storage room, still holding the waist of his incredibly tight pants.

Amy grabbed the reptile's arm. "Come on! Inspectors are coming to kill everyone!"

Nistra jerked away. "Space pig! Cargo hold! Space pig!"

Amy poked the lizard in the back. "That was your last chance. Now you're a permanent resident!"

She ran through the level with Philip and back to the elevator. It stopped on the way down and Sunflower's parents jumped inside, each wearing a backpack and holding a leafy green plant in a clay pot.

"Seriously," said Amy. "You're risking your lives for catnip? You know they grow it in other places, right?"

Sunflower's father gave her a fanged grin. "Not these plants, baby, not these."

"Do you know how long we've been locked inside this mountain?" asked Bocephus. "Lots of time spent hybridizing. Breeding and re-breeding. These are the best catnip strains in the galaxy!"

"Right on, right on," nodded Sunflower's father. "The seeds are worth hundreds of woolongs each!"

Amy sighed and leaned against the wall. "Hippies."

"Not to alarm anyone, but we've less than two minutes," said Philip.

Amy smiled and pinched his cheek. "It's a good thing I can run faster than you. Last one to the ship is breakfast!"

Philip kissed her cheek. "Anything for you, my love," he said in a mock-romantic tone. "If I have to give my life as breakfast so that you might live, then so be it."

"Yuck! Gag me with a spoon," said Amy, and slapped the wall. "Is this elevator on the super-slow setting? Come on!"

Sunflower's dad shook his head. "Violence never solved anything, human dudette. Chill out and relax. Stress is way bad for your heart."

"Inspectors ripping your heart out of your chest is also 'way bad' for it!"

"Do you mind if we hitch a ride on your ship?" asked Bocephus. "The doc is kind of a clean freak and he'd probably yell at us for tracking in dust or something."

"No problem. Dust is the last thing on my mind."

The elevator doors swished open. The cats and human teenagers ran pell-mell through the red-lit corridors to the open hangar, where the hundred-meter silver barracuda of the *White Star* and MacGuffin's purple cockroach stood waiting. The airlocks were open, ladders extended, and the engines hummed loud enough to vibrate the stone floor of the hangar. Steam rose from the rear exhaust ports of both ships.

Betsy jogged across the landing area and met them halfway, wagging his brown-and-white tail happily.

"Hello, guys! Need any help?" He noticed the two cats. "Hey——new friends!"

"No time to talk!" Amy sprinted at full speed past the dog and toward the White Star. "Run!"

"Cool," said Betsy. "I like games!"

Eerie clangs and loud scrapes from the blast doors echoed far down the hangar as Amy and Philip helped Sunflower's parents lift their bags and plants up the ship's ladder.

Amy waited until both the cats, Philip, and Betsy had climbed inside. "Seal us up, Blanche!" she yelled to the ceiling of the airlock. "We're launching now."

"I am aware of the situation," said the ship. "I have detected the damage to the hangar door."

"Is that your pilot?" asked Bocephus. "She sounds smart."

The outer hatch clicked shut and hissed, and Amy pulled the lever to open the inner door.

"Yes, she's very smart."

Betsy jumped in front of Sunflower's parents. "Hi, I'm Betsy!"

"Why are you wearing that stretchy red get-up?" asked Sunflower's father. "That's totally not a dog thing."

"It's a ship thing," said Amy. The door to the interior of the ship opened and she jumped through. "Make them wear a uniform, Betsy!"

She ran to the navigation room with Philip on her heels. Inside the navigation room, a mental projection of the hangar's rock walls and runway surrounded the central console.

Philip pointed. "There's MacGuffin!"

The Siamese cat stood below his giant purple cockroach of a spaceship, frantically tossing boxes and bags into an open hatch.

"All systems are ready for immediate launch," said the ship. "Waiting for hangar doors to clear. Hangar doors are clearing."

A staccato of blinding lights flashed around the hangar bay, causing MacGuffin to stop and stare at the blast doors as they crept upward. Outside, the whirling dust storm had turned the night as muddy and brown as a spring river.

"We're not going to make it," whispered Amy.

Sparks flew from the horizontal line of the opening blast door. A pair of silver spheres flew down the kilometer-long hangar bay, metal tentacles trailing behind like strands of deadly steel hair.

"He's still loading crap into his ship!" shouted Amy, and punched Philip in the shoulder. "What's wrong with him?"

"Ow! What' s wrong with you?"

"Blanche, do something! Stop those things!"

"Affirmative, my Lady. Activating electronic countermeasures."

Twin beams of bright yellow energy flew from the White Star and struck both inspectors in a huge shower of sparks. The deadly robots dipped for a moment, but did not slow their frightening approach.

"My Lady, the inspectors are shielded against EMP bolts. I will attempt to hack their control systems. From the design and radiation signatures, these are former battlefield units from Herodotus. I am not likely to succeed."

"We can't just stand here and watch!"

"The inspectors cannot breach the hull, my Lady. You are safe."

"That's not the point. We need that stupid space cat scientist!"

"In that case, I recommend that you turn away, my Lady."

The Siamese cat hurled the last of his bags into the open hatch and frantically climbed the boarding ladder.

"Too late," whispered Philip.

The invisible deck below their feet vibrated as the White Star rose half a meter and glided sideways across the hangar bay.

"She's trying to block them," said Amy. "Good girl, Blanche!"

Two more inspectors joined the first pair, ignoring the steady barrage of yellow EMP bolts from the White Star. All four of the robotic monstrosities shot by as if nothing mattered but the cat desperately scrambling into the airlock of his purple ship.

Amy turned her head. "Now I really can't watch."

"I think you should," said Philip. "My word––look at that!"

Nistra shuffled across the the runway toward them, still gripping the belt of his spandex trousers with a claw. Oblivious to the robotic danger flying toward him, the giant lizard held his jaws open in a numb expression of shock, and no realization of his impending doom showed in his beady eyes or scaly green face.

"Hangar door fifty percent open," said the ship.

"I hope it's painless," said Philip.

Amy sniffed. "You weren't his prisoner like I was. I hope he suffers."

An inspector slowed and hovered above Nistra. A pair of silver tentacles as wide as a human fist wrapped around the arms of the sauropod.

Nistra stared down at the titanium coiled around his biceps and blinked rapidly.

"Space pig," he growled, raising his voice to a scream. "Space pig! SPACE PIG!"

His scaly face transformed into a mask of rage and razor-sharp teeth. The sauro braced his powerful legs and tail, and then jerked his muscular arms down, smashing the inspector against the hangar deck with a deafening crack. Metal shards flew across the hangar and black smoke poured from the cracked shell of the inspector.

"SPACE PIG!"

The sauro grabbed the slack tentacles and spun the dead machine around his head in a huge circle, smashing two of the inspectors and sending them flying lifeless against the hangar walls.

"My word ..." said Philip.

"Gravy on toast," Amy whispered.

The remaining inspector had reached MacGuffin's ship, but the sudden destruction of its colleagues forced it to loop back around. The horrific chrome octopus hurtled through the air toward Nistra, all six tentacles reaching for him. The sauropod dropped the arms of the dead inspector, braced his legs, and charged across the runway. A second later, he roared ferociously and leapt at the titanium sphere, both claws out in front like a flying Godzilla–Superman hybrid.

"SPACE PIG!"

He ripped through the inspector with an explosion of sparks and inky black smoke, the huge chrome pieces bouncing off the walls of the hangar and scattering over the runway. Nistra knelt on the stone floor, his chest heaving.

Amy grabbed Philip's hand and squeezed. "Remind me not to call him that anymore."

"Good show, but I don't think he can do that to three dozen of the blighters."

"Hangar door is eighty percent clear," said the calm voice of the ship. "My Lady, I recommend an immediate departure. Local atmospheric conditions are deteriorating rapidly."

Brown dust whipped through the blast door and down the runway like a hurricane of coffee grounds. In the midst flew a large swarm of silver inspectors.

"Clear a path for MacGuffin's ship," said Amy. "We'll act as a shield on the way out!"

"I have a powerful exhaust stream, my Lady, and it is likely that my thrusters will damage the trailing craft."

"He's going to be a puddle of goo if he stays here! Call the ship's computer and tell him."

The combative Nistra had recovered some of his senses or self-preservation. As MacGuffin's purple cockroach rose on micro-thrusters and rotated to face the rear of the *White Star*, the sauro made a gigantic leap to the side of the craft, opened the airlock, and squeezed inside.

"Craft has replied in the affirmative," said the ship.

Coffee-colored winds swirled across the runway with increasing strength, causing a few of the inspectors to bounce out of control and smash into the blinking navigational lights on each side. Rocks pinged on the sharp nose of the *White Star*. Outside the rectangle of the hangar door, columns of lightning flashed and the sky turned in circles like a swimming pool of Rocky Road ice cream going down the drain.

Amy smacked her fist with her other hand. "Hit it, Blanche!"

The stone walls of the hangar flashed by and the storm became everything. A roar vibrated the silver skin of the ship like the galaxy's largest washing machine on super-spin cycle. Amy and Philip grabbed the console and held on as the ship rocked back and forth. Yellow lights flashed on the control panel and everything around them turned a furious gray-brown. The projection disappeared, replaced by black walls and a scattering of crimson lights. The shaking and unbelievable roar continued for a few seconds and then stopped. The ceiling changed to a black sky full of stars as the exterior projection came back on-line, and in the desert below Amy's feet swirled the wide arms of a gigantic hurricane of sand and dirt and stone.

"Reducing velocity," said the ship. "Minor damage to forward compartments, the navigation array, and offensive systems four, seven, and nine."

"What about MacGuffin?"

"*Cleopatra* is increasing altitude and exiting the local atmospheric disturbance at bearing one-seven-two."

"Just say they're clear of the storm, okay? I don't need a book report."

Behind and below them, the purple cockroach rose above the buffeting winds of the hurricane, black smoke pouring from her nose and streaming behind her.

"She's got riders," said Philip.

Three inspectors clung to the curved hull on top of the ship. Even from high above, Amy and Philip could see their silver tentacles pulling and ripping at the purple skin like dogs on a fallen antelope.

"This is the worst!" said Amy.

Philip squeezed her hand. "Steady on, old stick. Those nasty devils will fall off when he speeds up."

The port side of the *Cleopatra* flashed and more smoke gushed into the night air, adding another black trail. The purple ship rocked and began to lose altitude, dipping her nose toward the earth-colored maelstrom.

Amy stamped a foot. "Do something, Blanche! They've got the recombinator thingy."

"What do you suggest, my Lady?"

"I don't know! Shoot it with your tractor beam, or teleport MacGuffin and the thingy over here."

"Neither a 'tractor beam' nor any sort of 'teleport' are part of my installed equipment, my Lady."

"I've got an idea," said Philip. "Reduce speed and bring us closer to the other vessel."

"Blanche, do what he says."

"Of course, my Lady."

The storm filled everything below as they descended. The hunched purple cockroach of the *Cleopatra* swerved and banked, trying to dislodge the parasitic inspectors even as it struggled to keep a steady altitude. Through the glass of the tiny cockpit, they saw MacGuffin with both paws tightly gripping the ship's control wheel.

"Closer," said Philip. "Lower the undercarriage."

Amy squinted at the teenager. "You mean the landing gear?"

"Yes!"

"Advisory note," said the calm voice of the ship. "Extending struts at this velocity has an eighty-four percent chance of critical damage, five percent chance––"

"Just do it," said Amy. "What's the plan, Phil?"

The teenager pointed down at the stricken *Cleopatra*. "Knock the blighters off with the undercarriage––I mean, landing gear."

"I get it. We'll scrape them off!"

"Reducing velocity," said the ship. "Closing to one hundred meters. Fifty meters."

Plumes of oily smoke trailed from the purple craft and sparks burst within long gashes in the fuselage. The inspectors continued to plunge their razor-sharp tentacles down and rip ferociously at the ship.

"Extending struts."

Amy and Philip held on to each other as the navigation room rocked and vibrated. Both ships skimmed above the surface of the deadly storm at hundreds of meters per second, the twice-as-large mass of the *White Star* only meters above the purple *Cleopatra*.

Designed to support an interstellar craft over a hundred meters in length and twenty in diameter, the five titanium alloy landing struts of the *White Star* were quite suited to the task of knocking the inspectors into the swirling void. The ship banked left and right, loosening the death-grip of the silver monstrosities and sending them flying into the hurricane, but also denting and gashing the damaged upper hull of MacGuffin's ship even further.

"That's the last one," said Amy, pointing at a tentacled sphere disappearing into the brown hurricane. "Pull up!"

As the *White Star* climbed away from the storm, Amy heard a bang from the nose of the ship. A three-meter section of metal and rubber tumbled by and dropped into the storm.

"I hope that wasn't important," said Philip.

"Strut Number One critically damaged," said the calm voice of the ship. "Exterior supports are now retracted."

"Critically damaged?" asked Amy. "Does that mean we can't land?"

"Landing would not be advisable until the damage is repaired."

Philip watched the purple cockroach struggling below. "Are they going to make it?"

"Unknown," said the ship. "If I had direct access to the *Cleopatra*, an accurate analysis could be performed. This would require a brute-force takedown of the ship's security system and infiltration of the navigation control code."

"Whatever works," said Amy. "Do it!"

"Done," said the ship. "Code replaced. Control switching to my command. Efficiency of thrust increased thirty-eight percent. Damage control rerouted. Dumping fuel. Dumping cargo——"

"Don't dump the cargo!" yelled Amy and Philip together.

"As you wish," said the calm voice of the ship. "Increasing altitude. What is our destination, my Lady?"

"Cheezburger."

"The *Cleopatra* has an eighty-one percent chance of landing safely at Cheezburger Central, which has a larger number of emergency apparatus than South."

Beside them, the hunched purple cockroach rose into the night sky and matched the speed of the *White Star*. The trails of black smoke changed to white, and then faded away.

A Siamese cat wearing green pilot goggles flashed to life on a holographic screen.

"White Star! Hailing White Star," said MacGuffin. "The controls of my ship are dead, but somehow I'm still alive. Praise Mittens; it's a miracle!"

"It wasn't a miracle——it was us," said Amy. "Our ship had to hack into your systems and take control, or you'd be rice pudding right about now."

MacGuffin shook his head. "Pudding? What do you mean?"

"I'll tell you after we land. We'll escort you to Cheezburger. Sit back and enjoy the ride."

"How long?"

"Even with damage control working, the *Cleopatra* has lowered velocity and limited non-atmospheric capability," said the calm voice of the ship. "This will increase our estimated travel time. Expected planetfall is four hours, thirty-eight minutes."

A circle of light appeared against the night sky on Amy's left. Sunflower's parents jumped inside the navigation room, both wearing red spandex uniforms and skull cap.

"Yo, human dude and dudette," said Sunflower's father. "We miss anything?"

"The ship was flopping around like a fish out of water," said the calico cat, Bocephus. "We thought we were going to crash. Wait—don't freak me out. Did we crash?"

"It's all fine now," said Amy. "We'll be in Cheezburger in a few hours."

"Right on!"

Sunflower's father nodded his furry orange head. "Awesome."

A scrape of paws came from the corridor. Betsy galloped through the open door and plowed into the two cats, sending them flying. The brown-and-white terrier slid on his back across the invisible floor, stopping only when he bumped against Amy's leather shoes.

"Welcome to the real world," said Amy. "Can I help you?"

The spandex cap on Betsy's head had come free, blinding the terrier and forcing him to speak through one of the eye-holes. He looked up at the sound of Amy's voice.

"Um, yeah! Did I miss anything?"

13

Amy strode through the corridor with Philip, a redwood forest from her memories projected on the walls and ceiling. Even the air felt cold and smelled like morning dew.

"Take a look at the damaged landing gear, would you? Also, make a list of everything on we need to fix after we land."

"As you wish."

"I prefer to repair the damage myself," said the ship. "I'd rather not have a gang of cat mechanics shedding hair and squirming inside me."

"She has a point," said Philip. "I don't think any of us would want that."

Amy spread her arms. "Landing gear is pretty important––it's in the name, you know? I'm not getting out and holding up the nose of the ship every time we have to stop for a Slurpee. These arms are strong with girl power, but that's asking a lot."

"If the spaceport can provide certain pure elements, my nanites can repair the damage in a few hours," said the ship. "Without the necessary materials, construction time will be extended significantly."

"Smashing," said Philip. "Sunflower can shuffle some papers, sign an imperial degree, and you'll be as right as rain."

Amy glanced left and right through the forest. "Speaking of rain, excuse me while I powder my nose and, um ... stuff. Hey––it's the room Nistra talked about. The one we should never go inside."

A round hatch marked "Prive" stood among the redwood trees. Someone had scribbled a symbol on the metal with black marker––long squiggly lines radiating from a triangle.

"It's definitely not a washroom," said Philip. "It looks dangerous."

Amy rolled her eyes. "Doesn't 'privy' mean bathroom? I read that somewhere."

"Perhaps, but––"

Amy pushed on the center of the hatch. "Listen, don't ever stand between a girl and the bathroom. You will die. I'm not saying that to be mean, Phil––I just don't want you to be trampled to death. That would be bad for our relationship."

The hatch spiraled away. Amy stepped inside and the floor turned white, filling the room with a pale glow.

She coughed and waved a hand in front of her face. "Good gravy, this place hasn't been cleaned in forever ..."

Her voice trailed off as she stared at shelves packed with objects and a far wall covered in photos.

Philip stepped through the hatch. "Wizard! A museum." The dark-haired teenager walked to a shelf where a heart pendant and other items were shielded from touch by thick, vertical glass. "But why the security measures for something so common––a necklace? Strange bottles? And this is apparently some sort of confectionary wrapper."

Amy peered inside. "Confecsha-what? It's just bubble gum. Why would anyone save Hubba-Bubba wrappers?"

"This ship belonged to the Lady. Perhaps these objects held sentimental value."

Amy smirked. "The classic story about the half-human mechanical spider creature with a heart of gold? Hubba-Bubba is my favorite gum, but even I wouldn't keep it under glass."

"I say it's a museum of some sort. If the items were special to the Lady, I wager she would have taken them before giving us the ship."

"She's got taste, I give her that. An empty bottle of Diet Coke, a roast beef wrapper from Arby's, a box from a Hostess apple pie——that one better not be empty. Some of the favorite things I've swiped from grocery stores. I mean, 'purchased' from grocery stores. Let's be honest, though——this place is more like a garbage dump than a museum."

"Several tatty old books," said Philip. "*Tom Sawyer, Treasure Island*, and assorted pamphlets."

Amy clapped. "Those aren't pamphlets, those are comic books! It's Namor the Sub-mariner!"

Philip shook his head. "Dear Amy, I don't understand half of what you just said."

Amy touched the vertical glass protecting the shelf. A pin-point light flashed staccato green and the glass whisked up.

"Whoa! How did I do that?"

"I doubt we'll ever know. What I would like to know about is this 'Namor' individual."

Amy pulled a comic book from the top of the stack. "He's like Aquaman, but in the Marvel Universe. No? I keep forgetting you're from jolly old England. Yo ho ho and a bottle of rum."

"Excuse me?"

"Sorry, bad joke. Anyway, Namor is king of the oceans and can swim and fly and talk to fish and crap."

Philip pointed at the cover in Amy's hands. "But that's a young woman."

"It's Namorita, the daughter of Namor. She has all the powers of Namor, can breathe underwater and fly. Namorita is my favorite, and this is one of her best issues!"

"Apparently she's in danger of drowning," said Philip, frowning. "And about to catch her death of cold. Someone has forced her to wear an extremely revealing bathing costume."

The slim blonde on the cover wore an emerald green one-piece swimsuit. Her arms and legs were trapped inside an amorphous black substance, and bubbles streamed from her mouth.

"She can breathe underwater," said Amy. "And you think she's showing too much skin? In California, girls wear less than that at the beach——bikinis and thongs and everything. It's a disgusting meat show."

Philip cleared his throat. "I quite enjoy a sampling of fine, um, meat products. I'd like to visit the seaside in your time."

"I'm sure you would, Casanova. Only for scientific purposes, right? I've got my eye on you."

Amy kissed him on the lips, but a gleam from a lower shelf pulled her away. She bent down, opened the glass in front of the shelf, and picked up a necklace. Tarnish had dulled the silver heart pendant to a smoky white and blackened the metal chain.

"This is exactly like the one I've got back home," she whispered. "My foster mom called it my baby necklace. It was wrapped up in the blanket when they found me." She turned the silver heart in her fingers to look at the back and suddenly dropped it. "No way!"

"What's wrong?"

Philip scooped the tarnished chain from the floor and examined the back of the pendant.

"'To Amy,'" he murmured, reading the inscription. "A common enough name. Not that your name is common, dear heart, it's that the Lady simply found one with your name on it. I daresay if I were strolling through Hyde Park and some tout were selling a hairbrush with 'Philip' carved in the handle, I wouldn't bat an eye."

"Phil," Amy murmured from across the room.

"Yes, love?"

Amy stood frozen, staring at the wall of photos. Some were old, brown, and as curled and dry as dead leaves. Others were made of square plastic, and still others were thin digital displays that showed the subject of the photo in great detail. This subject happened to be Amy Armstrong, in hundreds of stages of life and with dozens of different companions.

"Great Scott," whispered Philip. "Is that you?"

"I could ask you the same thing. Have you been to any of these places? Here's a photo of someone in a spacesuit. Looks like the Moon. Here's one of a woman who looks like an older version of me, sitting on a throne. In this one, I'm wearing a nightgown and holding a baby with blonde hair. I've never met these people or done any of these things!"

Philip pointed at a faded picture. "This one is missing a hand. In another one, she has a hand, but also a scar across her face."

"The Lady said she had been looking for me for a long time," said Amy. "Do you think this is some kind of sick project? Was she some kind of creepy stalker?"

"Perhaps you should ask the ship."

"Fine. Blanche, what's the deal with all these photos?"

"It is a collection of images," said the warm voice of the ship. "A memorial created by the Lady to remember her past."

Amy sighed. "Blanche, I don't think you get it. Why would I be in all the photos if it was about the Lady?"

"Because you are the Lady, my Lady."

"What? I'm Amy Armstrong, not some ancient half-machine spider thing!"

"A journey does not begin at the same place it ends. Amy Armstrong is always the Lady, and the Lady is always Amy Armstrong. It has been this way since the moment I found you."

"Impossible. These aren't me!"

"That is correct. You have your own story to follow, just as the Amy Armstrong in each of these images had her story."

"Multiple dimensions," said Philip, holding out the silver pendant to Amy. "Endless Amy Armstrongs across endless dimensions. The ship seeks out another when the previous passes away."

Amy hugged Philip tight and pressed her face into his chest.

"The Lady kept saying I was special," she said, her voice muffled by the spandex material. "I thought it was because I was smart, or cute, or good at stuff. Not something creepy like this. I'm just her clone!"

Philip stroked her blonde hair. "It may have spent the last two years living on an asteroid with talking cats and dogs, but I think none of this dimensional nonsense matters. Out of an endless number of Amy Armstrongs, you're the smartest, prettiest, and my favorite. I wouldn't switch places with anyone right now."

Amy looked up at Philip with red eyes, and kissed him on the mouth. At last they separated.

"I don't feel any radiation, if radiation even has a feel," said Amy. "Why would Nistra lie about this room?"

Philip took her hand and led Amy out of the room. "I'm not certain, but I think we should keep a close eye on him. He seems like a devilish character and certain to cause trouble for us."

"Good idea."

AMY LAY on the bed in her room, shoes off and hands behind her head, eyes blinking in half-sleep.

"You said I don't have to wash these clothes, Blanche? How does that even work?"

"The nanites that inhabit the fibers clean the garments, my Lady. Nitrates and other waste products of your skin are consumed by the nanites for energy."

"I'm going to pretend I didn't hear that."

She closed her eyes and said nothing for a long time.

"Why didn't you tell me, Blanche?" she murmured. "About my past? About anything?"

"I would have been happy to answer your queries, my Lady, but you didn't ask."

"How could I ask a question about something I don't know anything about in the first place!"

Betsy's furry brown-and-white face appeared on a holoscreen above the headboard.

"Nick's being mean to me," said the terrier. "She hit me with a pillow and said I should go play in outer space."

Amy thumped the headboard with her fist. "I'm sleeping! Don't bother the captain and don't make me tell you again!"

The screen went dark, and she settled back on the bed. "How long until we land?"

"Two hours and twenty minutes, my Lady."

"How's MacGuffin and his purple ship? Still following us?"

"The *Cleopatra* is operating at nominal efficiency. I am confident that it will safely reach the intended destination."

"Thank you, Blanche. Please don't let anyone bother me for a couple of hours."

THE PAIR OF SHIPS crossed the vast suburbs that surrounded Cheezburger and were cleared for landing at the busy central spaceport, their final destination a distant spot of concrete covered with the flashing lights of emergency vehicles.

Brick supports topped by industrial-strength foam cushions had already been prepared for the *White Star* and her damaged landing strut, and the ship touched down at the emergency landing area without a problem.

Amy, Philip, and the rest of the group climbed down from the airlock and walked toward the battered *Cleopatra*. Up close, the ripped purple hull and deep scars from the tentacles of the inspectors were easy to spot. Amy was shocked that the purple craft had flown halfway around the planet.

MacGuffin ran up to her and bowed on the tarmac. "Thank you again for saving my life," said the Siamese cat.

"Don't thank me. Nistra and Blanche did all the work."

"Blanche?"

"Amy's name for our ship," said Philip.

"I see," said the cat. "As soon as I can unload the *Cleopatra*, I will begin analyzing the recombinator matrix inside 'Blanche,' as you call it. As far as my craft goes, I'm afraid it will have to be junked. Far too many holes in the fuselage."

Sunflower's father perked up his orange ears. "Doc, you can't do that! Maybe she's not space-worthy, but tape some garbage bags over those holes and she'll be perfect for cruising around Tau Ceti."

MacGuffin bowed. "So be it. As a token of our friendship, I give you my ship *Cleopatra*."

"Awesome!"

"Rad!"

Sunflower's father and mother jumped at Mac-Guffin and hugged the Siamese cat around his furry neck.

"We're totally out of here," said Sunflower's father.

"Yeah," said Bocephus. "Take it easy, human dude and dudette."

Amy raised a hand. "Hello? Don't you want to see His Imperial Highness Sunflower? He's your son, after all."

Bocephus shook her calico head. "Totally correct, but he's also the one who abandoned us in the middle of nowhere. We're his parents! That was some totally bad juju."

"He's changed. He's literally not even the same cat."

Sunflower's father blinked. "That's cool and everything, but palace life isn't our scene. It never was."

"It might be the last time you'll see him," said Philip.

Nistra shuffled up to the group. "What nonsense," said the lizard. "Every time might be the last time for anything."

Amy patted the sauro on the arm. "Glad to see you're better. We thought you had a stroke or something."

Nistra shivered and pulled away. "Please don't touch me." He blinked and suddenly straightened. "Captain, may I have your approval to load the sauro food I purchased? It is waiting in a shipping container at this spaceport."

"What food?"

Nistra bowed. "Many pardons. My diet is very delicate, and I purchased the food without consulting you. It would be a simple matter of only a few seconds to lift it into the cargo hold."

"Sounds fine to me, as long as it doesn't smell."

"Perhaps a bit. If you are offended by the food, I will eject it into space."

"Sure. Whatever."

Bocephus bowed in front of Amy.

"Thank you for trying to get the family back together, but Sunflower made his choice a long time ago. Our son never wanted a family and never wanted us around. We're not going to fight that."

Amy knelt down to the pair of cats. "Let me call him. I won't tell him you're here, but I can probably get him to pay for the repairs to the *Cleopatra*. He won't have any idea that you're the new owners."

An open holoscreen line was connected to the palace, and Amy convinced Sunflower to approve the significant sums needed for the purple ship.

She waited for Philip to change into his street clothes—an English suit of gray wool—and the pair took an automated bubble taxi to the palace. As they drove away, Nistra supervised the loading of a large shipping container into the cargo hold of the ship, tall and wide enough to theoretically hold a dozen sauropods standing at full height. MacGuffin was hard at work on the transmat drive replacing the recombinator and Betsy and Nick played a cat version of hackysack with Sunflower's parents using a stuffed poona skin.

Amy and Philip returned to the imperial palace and walked through the lush, flowering gardens, their footsteps crunching on the tiny white stones of the path.

"How are you going to convince Sunflower to leave?" asked Philip.

Amy shrugged. "Appeal to his better nature?"

"Does he have one? If I found myself in a dimension where I was king of England, I doubt I would have the courage to leave, even if I knew I didn't belong there. Would you?"

"I'm Amy Armstrong. I don't belong anywhere."

Philip put an arm around her waist. "Poppycock! Everyone has a home. Once the ship is repaired, we'll take you back."

"But ... what are you going to do in 1995?"

"Work in a shop, I suppose, or repair automobiles. I'm fascinated by your stories of amazing machines and everything you tell me about the future."

"That's great and everything, Phil, but you don't have to come with me. Cut your losses and find a nice English girl. One that's not going to turn into a grayhaired robot."

Philip stopped and held both of Amy's hands. "That's quite enough whining! Your future isn't set in stone, dear."

"How do you know?"

"It's what the Lady was trying to tell you. Change the path of your life or end up like her. Nothing is pre-ordained, and a life in California free of flying robots and talking cats and dogs must have a happy ending. At the very least, the knowledge that a wrong choice exists will keep you from following it."

Amy pulled Philip down the path. "But what if SHE knew, and still couldn't avoid it?"

"A pity we can't ask her."

"But we can! The inspectors!"

Philip sighed. "We don't know the origin of those beastly machines. Perhaps they came from the Lady and she has a legitimate complaint against this cat MacGuffin. Even if you could learn something, I recommend against any contact with the Lady or her agents. Don't you recall what happened in London?"

"That was Betsy's fault. He was supposed to scare us into returning, but couldn't control the inspector. The Lady meant well."

Philip smiled. "The road to Hell is paved with the best intentions, as they say."

Amy pulled the tarnished heart pendant from a vest pocket and stared at it.

"I guess you're right," she murmured.

The guards in front of the imperial residence bowed deeply and opened the doors. Amy and Philip entered a large foyer and waited on cushions for several minutes before a patterned interior door slid open. Sunflower emerged with a yellow cape tied around his neck.

"I was eating breakfast when you called," he said in a bored tone. "Did you really have to bother me about some stupid repair bills?"

Amy shook her head. "Stupid repair bills? Did you see the damage to that ship?"

"Not yet."

"Well, don't. I'm sure you're too busy to care about the battle your friends suffered through. Wouldn't want to upset your breakfast."

Sunflower turned away. "That reminds me——I'm still hungry. Give me a call if you need anything else."

"Always nice to have friends that care about you, I always say."

Sunflower looked over his shoulder. "You never say that."

"I just did."

Philip cleared his throat. "Emperor Sunflower of the Western Range, the time has come to abdicate your throne."

"Abdi-what? No, I had that operation when I was a kitten."

"Sorry for the confusion. 'Abdicate' means to leave the throne."

"Fat chance! I've never had so much fun in my life, and I'm just getting started."

"We know," said Amy. "We saw your speech."

Sunflower bared his fangs. "Do you know what's like to be the most important cat in the universe? To have the entire population hanging on your every word? This is my chance to fix cat society——to make it perfect!"

"You don't have that right," said Amy. "You're not really the Emperor, and you don't belong in this dimension."

"None of us belong here." Sunflower lowered his voice to a whisper. "How does place and time, right and wrong matter anymore? The Lady killed the only cat I ever loved, and I'm going to squeeze the last bit of fun out of life while I can."

"She didn't kill your wife," said Amy. "The Lady sent her on a mission to look for the gold Super Nintendo, just like she sent you."

Sunflower flipped the yellow cape over his furry back. "It makes no difference."

"I don't believe this. Are you seriously going to abandon your friends?"

"I'm not abandoning anyone. You can stay in the palace as long as you want. What I'm seriously not going to do is go with you."

A sliding door to Sunflower's left rattled loudly, but stayed closed. A stream of mumbled curses came from the other side, and then a white cat burst through the center of the door in a shower of torn paper and wood fragments.

"Furball!" shouted Sunflower. "What in the name of Saint Mittens is wrong with you?"

"Many apologies, Highness, but we have an emergency!"

"Spoiled soup or a fire in the kitchen? Go find Sooka Black."

Furball shook his head rapidly. "The spaceport is being attacked!"

"Which one?"

"Central."

"Attacked by what? Show us, you fool."

Furball darted back the way he had come with Sunflower, Amy, and Philip scrambling after the long-haired cat. Inside a small closet lined with electronics and screens for security cameras, the cat pointed to a live feed of the spaceport tarmac and the *White Star*. A dozen tentacled spheres swarmed around the ship, firing crimson beams of energy at targets off-screen.

"I don't know how they broke through the air defenses," said Furball. "Maybe disguised as meteorites? That doesn't make sense. Do you think it's an attack by the dog military?"

"They're inspectors, not canine robots," said Sunflower. "You can tell by the two extra tentacles. But where in the name of Saint Mittens did they come from?"

"The Lady must have sent them," said Philip. "Three dozen of the beastly things attacked us at the equator."

A scrabble of claws came from the hallway and Sooka Black appeared with a handful of cat soldiers.

"Your eminence! We're being attacked!"

"Tell me something I don't know."

"Apologies, sire. What are your orders?"

Sunflower rubbed the side of his furry jaw. "What military units do we have in the area?"

A cat in a red beret stood on his hind legs and saluted. "Your Highness! Two regiments of armor, a mobile infantry division, three battalions of anti-air, one full division of regular infantry."

Sunflower slammed a paw onto the security console. "Send in the armor. These second-hand dog robots would chew up our infantry like kibble in a bowl."

"By your command," said the soldier, and darted away.

Sunflower unhooked his yellow cape and stepped out of the security closet. "Let's go."

"To the command bunker?" asked Sooka Black. "A good decision, highness."

"Absolutely not! Take me to the spaceport. I'm not hiding while my friends are in danger."

14

A beam of scarlet energy struck the concrete barrier with a loud crack, spraying bits of glowing rock on the orange tabby and two humans huddling behind it. The air was filled with the dull thud of artillery explosions and the ripping-cloth sound of automatic rifle fire.

"This is the stupidest thing I've ever done!" yelled Sunflower. "I should have stayed at the palace!"

"I thought you were the smartest cat on the planet!" shouted Amy. "That's what you keep telling us!"

"What?"

Amy covered her ears from the deafening noise of battle and peeked around the left side of the concrete barrier.

Normally the spaceport was packed with gigantic oblong cat spacecraft, but almost all had evacuated. The vast expanse of gray tarmac was mostly empty, apart from a pair of burning bubble cars and the scattered bodies of dozens of cat soldiers. The huge silver barracuda of the *White Star* stood parked in the same place Amy had left her. Dozens of metal, octopus-like inspectors hovered over the graceful ship, banging or scraping at her gleaming skin with sharp tentacles. Despite the ferocious effort of these hovering machines, none seemed to have made even a scratch on the fuselage. Several of the robotic monsters flew circles around the stationary ship, firing deadly beams of energy at anything that moved. Amy squinted at the bodies on the tarmac, trying to see if any were Betsy, Nick, or Sunflower's parents.

"Bring us the cat named Cynthia MacGuffin," boomed one of the inspectors in a mechanical voice. "You will not be harmed. Organisms experiencing harm must submit evidence of harm in writing to receive harm-related refreshment coupons."

The inspector shot a crackling beam of energy at Amy, and she ducked behind the barrier.

"Stop doing that!" yelled Philip.

"Sorry!" Amy turned to Sunflower. "I have to tell you something."

"What?"

"Your parents––they're somewhere around here!"

"My what? I can't hear you."

Without warning, the artillery barrage from the cat military stopped, leaving a faint ringing in Amy's ears. A series of distant impacts vibrated the broken concrete under her fingers, the crunch and boom sounding like a giant stomping through his castle.

"Keep your heads down!" yelled Sunflower. "Here comes the armor!"

Amy shielded her eyes from the sun and looked toward the eastern runway of the spaceport, where a group of tiny gray dots curved through the air, causing a faint boom each time they hit the tarmac. As they jumped closer, the gray dots grew in size and the intensity of the impacts increased.

Each armored unit was the size of a large sedan and shaped like a mechanical tiger, smoky gray in color with black stripes painted down the steel flanks. The four legs smacked into the tarmac with a thud, and the ferocious machine leapt high, jump-jets on either side firing brightly and pushing it up and forward through the air. Sharp teeth were painted on the blunt "head" of each machine, above and below a narrow, curved window. Inside the jaws and behind the glass, Amy thought she saw a white helmet. The armored tigers thumped into the tarmac and flashed by with a roar, as fast as a horde of gigantic fleas.

"Crikey!" shouted Philip.

"Pride of the empire!" yelled Sunflower. "They'll rip those inspectors apart!"

A few hundred meters from the *White Star*, the armored cats unleashed a barrage of missiles from pods on their backs, firing white trails of smoke at the apex of each jump. A second before impact, the missiles burst into halves and drilled into the silver spheres with a dense, uranium-tipped rod. Many of the inspectors fell to the tarmac, tentacles limp and black smoke pouring from their metal shells. The remaining spheres fired back at the armored units, sending dozens of scarlet energy beams crackling through the air. The closest armored units were struck multiple times. Halfway through a leap, one armored tiger tumbled head-over-heels and crashed into the tarmac, flame and smoke pouring from the wreckage.

The ground shook violently and tossed Amy into the air. A steel-gray tiger with "L047" painted in white on its left side stood ten meters away, legs spread on the newly-cracked tarmac and white fangs painted on the nose. The turbine engines whined loud and blew shimmering heat from large exhaust tubes on either side of the tail.

The machine clanked forward, each step vibrating the concrete, until it stood next to the barrier. A high-pitched breeze blew Amy's hair in all directions. Behind the glass cockpit at the mouth, a cat pilot touched the front of his blue helmet.

"Stay down, your highness," crackled his voice from a speaker. "I am here to protect you."

"Good!" yelled Sunflower.

The deadly beams of the inspectors had brought down another armored tiger, which lay on its side, legs askew and black smoke pouring from the charred metal. Too close for missiles now, the rest of the armored cats leapt at the inspectors, using their diamond-tipped claws and tons of weight to pull the tentacled monsters down to the tarmac. Once on top of the enemy spheres, the armored machines used their front and back legs to rip them apart like kittens on a ball of yarn. Within less than a minute the fighting was over, and all that could be heard was the whine of turbine engines and the crunch of armored footsteps on the concrete.

Amy looked around the side of the barrier. "Looks like the coast is clear. All the inspectors are dead."

"Not too soon, either," said Philip.

Sunflower looked over the barrier. "Betsy!"

"Wait!" shouted Amy.

Before she or Philip could grab him, the orange tabby leaped over the top of the concrete wall.

On the tarmac not far away, the Jack Russell terrier had squirmed out of whatever rock or crate he'd been hiding under and trotted with his tail wagging toward the smoking ruin of an inspector. The dog was oblivious to the still-twitching tentacles, one end of which glowed scarlet.

Amy pushed Philip's hands away and vaulted over the wall after Sunflower. The cat made it to Betsy and yelled in the face of the happy terrier, just as the armored tiger flew over Amy, the hot breeze of his engines blowing her skirt and hair. It landed with a deafening crash on the body of the charred, half-dead inspector, but the end of one tentacle still glowed, and still pointed at the arguing Sunflower and Betsy.

Amy sprinted harder and leapt at her friends Pete Rose-style, pushing them out of the way with both hands. A heavy force smashed her in the chest—hard and hot, like a ball of lava flung from a volcanic pitching machine. She curled up and screamed.

HANDS MOVED under her shoulders and lifted her off the tarmac. Sounds and smells whirled around her in the darkness: the clank and thump of armored tigers, the shouts of sergeants to their cat soldiers, the acidic smell of charred plastic and carbonized steel.

"Please don't die, Amy," whispered Philip. "Please don't die. Please don't die."

"She's dead," said Sunflower's voice.

Amy groaned. "Ow ... ow ow ow. Who's licking my hand?"

"Sorry!" came Betsy's voice. "Sunnie said you were dead. Can I have your stuff if you're dead?"

Amy opened her eyes and looked up at Philip's face. The teenager held her in his lap.

"Am I dead?"

Philip smiled. "I'm not a doctor, but I think you'll be fine. Your blouse is a bit worse for wear, however."

Amy felt the edges of a ragged hole in the center of her blouse, fist-sized and right over her heart. A perfect pink circle marked the skin of her chest above her bra, bright and fiery like a bad sunburn. Amy touched the moist burn and gasped.

"Ow! Holy mother that hurts."

Sunflower peered at the wounded skin. "It's probably going to make a scar and be super embarrassing. Maybe you can draw a happy face on it?"

Amy groaned. "If it doesn't go away I'll kill every cat in the galaxy, starting with you!"

"The bigger question is, how did you survive?" asked Philip. "The energy from those machines can cut through steel."

"I don't know. Maybe the power supply was dying and the beam wasn't at full power."

MacGuffin stuck his furry Siamese face above Amy's. "Is she dead?"

"No!" shouted everyone.

"Blessed Saint Mittens, I was just asking a question! You can't always tell with Centaurans." The cat touched Amy's blouse. "This cloth saved her life, that's my hypothesis. Certainly more tests are in order. Many, many tests." He rubbed his paws together. "So exciting!"

Amy shivered. "No tests, especially if it means shoving me into a tiny closet and lots of machines poking me in rude places!"

MacGuffin frowned and twitched his whiskers. "Science doesn't have rude places, young lady."

"This is a weird conversation," said Sunflower. "What exactly did you people do at the equator?"

The rumble of fusion engines came from overhead, and everyone looked up. The *Cleopatra* landed next to the *White Star* and the airlock hissed open. An orange tabby and a white cat with calico patches jumped out.

Sunflower froze. "Mom? Dad? What are you doing here?"

The pair of cats glanced at each other, and then walked up on all fours, tails drooping and heads bowed.

"Sorry," said Sunflower's father. "We don't want any trouble, son. We'll leave as soon as the ship is gassed up."

Bocephus smiled uncomfortably. "It was getting so cramped and boring down at the station. These humans showed up and brought us here, but don't blame them. It's our fault for escaping. If you're going to lock us up again, could it at least be somewhere nice? A little beach house would be perfect."

Sunflower shook his head. "What are you talking about? I didn't send you anywhere. I've only been Emperor for a few days, and haven't had time to lock up anyone except my old geography teacher."

Amy took a deep breath and winced at the pain. She held out an arm and Philip helped her to stand.

"Remember, this is not your dimension," she said. "Sunflower the Emperor——the one who disappeared——was ashamed of his parents. He sent them to that research station on the equator so nobody could find them."

Sunflower jumped forward and hugged both his father and his mother.

"I love both of you," he said. "Whatever happened in the past wasn't me. I'm a completely different cat."

His father nodded his furry orange head. "So I guess we can hang out with the emperor now? Totally awesome!"

"Not exactly. I'm leaving."

"What?" Betsy scrambled up to them. "No! Can I go with you?"

Sunflower shook his head. "You idiot. You're coming with me."

"We're going somewhere? When did this happen?"

"I'm glad you had a change of heart," said Amy.

Philip nodded. "It's hard to tell at times, but Sunflower really is a first-rate chap."

"Don't push it with that squishy stuff or I'll change my mind," growled Sunflower. "Besides, you bunch of shaved monkeys and galactic rejects are all useless without me. Every one of you would choke to death on a cheese sandwich or brush your teeth with plutonium if I weren't there to show you how everything is really done."

Bocephus hugged Sunflower. "What about us? You finally care about your parents and you have to leave?"

"I don't belong here. I know that doesn't explain anything, and I'm sorry. Let's just say that I am your son but I'm also not your son." Sunflower stood on his hind legs and looked left and right. "Sooka!"

The brown cat ran up to Sunflower. "Sire, all of the invaders have been nullified. I respectfully suggest that Your Highness retire to the safety of the palace."

"That won't be necessary. Bring me an official document creator and the seal of office. Also, load one of those armored cat-tanks into the White Star. Should be fun to play around with if I get bored."

Sooka Black clapped his paws, and a black-and-white tuxedo cat scampered up with a wide satchel on his back.

"That was fast," said Amy.

"The seal and document creator must always be near the emperor," said Sooka Black solemnly. "If he wishes to make a proclamation, there must be no de-lay."

"If he finds certain geography teachers still alive, for example?"

Sooka pulled an electronic tablet and a pouch of red velvet from the satchel. Sunflower took the tablet from him, scribbled a few short sentences on the electronic screen with his paw, then took a brilliant diamond from the pouch.

"My word," said Philip.

"You read my mind," said Amy. "Can I borrow that rock? I promise to bring it back in a few hundred years."

"Absolutely not."

Sunflower pressed the top of the diamond into a socket on the tablet, and a light flashed green beside it.

"There you go," he said, handing both items to Sooka Black. "I have abdicated the throne and passed it to a commoner. The new Emperor and first sovereign of the Seven-Leaf Dynasty is Amy."

"What? I'm not a cat!"

"Not you––my father, the other Amy!"

Sunflower's father hugged him with tears in his eyes. "Son, I'll try to be as awesome as you."

"Take care of yourself and always be groovy," said his mother, and kissed his furry cheek.

"Cut it out with that hippie emotional stuff," said Sunflower. "Sooka, please carry out my last proclamation."

The brown cat bowed. "Your will is my command, sire."

The group stood in a circle, staring at each other and shifting their weight from foot to foot.

"This is awkward," said Amy. She leaned on Philip's shoulder. "Take me to the ship. I really need some aspirin. Take care everyone, and thanks for all the fishy water!"

Amy and Philip waved all the way to the airlock ladder.

"Betsy, come on!" yelled Sunflower. "This way."

The terrier had been following Sooka Black and the official seal carrier, but at hearing Sunflower, he turned and darted across the tarmac.

"I thought I was staying," said the dog. "I always get confused."

"I think your knowledge implant came loose. Let me find something big and heavy to knock it back into place."

"Thanks, Sunflower," said Betsy, as he climbed the ladder. "You're the best!"

15

Crates and oddly-shaped tools littered the floor of the transmat chamber. MacGuffin stood in front of an open wall panel, holding a pair of metal paddles on either side of an obsidian sphere the size of a basketball. A column of blue energy rose from a cylinder in the wall, passed through the floating sphere and into another cylinder above, generating a thick, acrid smell and a hiss and crackle like milk poured into a giant bowl of rice cereal.

Amy stepped into the room and stumbled over a box. "Whoa, MacGuffin! Didn't your mother teach you to pick up your toys?"

The Siamese cat bared his fangs, but kept the paddles steady on either side of the black sphere.

"Do not disturb me at this critical juncture," he hissed. "This procedure is far too dangerous."

Amy sighed and clasped her hands behind her back.

"Do not tap your feet," said MacGuffin. "Do not whistle. Do not make a sound."

"Sorry."

"That was a sound."

Amy stood quietly and tried not to move a muscle. After several long minutes, MacGuffin stepped on a button near his foot and lay the paddles in a cushioned metal case.

"Done."

Amy let out a huge sigh. "Great. What are you doing that's so important?"

"Calibrating the recombinator so that you may return home."

"I guess you're staying with us, then? That would explain the forty-thousand boxes in the corridor. Believe me, I counted."

The Siamese cat grimaced and closed the lid on the case at his feet.

"Only as long as it takes to fix the transmat drive. I am depending upon your goodwill, and hope you can take me to Alpha Centauri. The Lady would never look for the most celebrated scientist that Meowie University has ever produced among the most backward species in the galaxy."

"What exactly did you fix?"

MacGuffin waved a brown paw at the sphere. "The recombinator matrix. Completely replaced." He closed the wall panel and tugged the handle of another panel nearby, but it remained shut. "I've temporarily wired an elemental chamber behind this compartment. One second, please."

Amy picked a tool from the floor that looked like a black-handled Philips screwdriver, and began flipping it over and over in one hand.

"What's an elemental chamber?"

The cat rubbed his paws together and pulled at the door handle again.

"If you have a sufficient quantity of pure atoms from a dimension, theoretically you can return to that dimension. Gold and other dense metals would be the only feasible candidates, given the size constraints of our equipment."

"This is different from the way the Lady does it?"

MacGuffin shook his head. "The Lady creates a link with the Spacebook network before transmatting, and can return using the information from that signal. This is completely different. The Lady only wants her operators to transmat into a dimension, steal an object of extreme value, and remat back to her ship."

"I'm trying to get back to where I came from in the first place," said Amy, still flipping the screwdriver.

MacGuffin gestured to the door. "Could you please give me a paw with this?"

"Give you a paw. That's funny."

Amy jerked open the wide metal panel, and a golden light streamed into the transmat room. The gold Super Nintendo glowed inside, covered in silver mesh and a web of red and black wires.

"Whoa," she whispered.

"A temporary fix," said MacGuffin. "I had to route the transmat drive of the entire ship through this block of metal, and disable the security override. It's amazing if you think about it! This entire ship can travel through dimensions."

"I know," said Amy. "I've done it."

"Close the panel, please. I just told you the overrides are disabled, and the drive could misfire if anything touches it."

"Stop yelling, okay? You're like my mom."

Amy casually flipped the screwdriver into the air, but fumbled the catch on the way down. The screwdriver bounced into the elemental chamber and wobbled to a final resting place on the silver mesh.

"Blessed Saint Mittens and his three legs!" screamed MacGuffin, hopping up and down. "Don't touch it!"

Amy shrugged. "Take a chill pill. Nothing exploded or anything. It's okay."

The Siamese cat pulled at his ears with both paws. "You *poona* brain! Centaurans really are the dumbest creatures in the universe!"

"I'm not from Alpha Centauri, I'm from ...
Earthhhh ...."

The universe slowed to a crawl as Amy spoke the last few syllables. The air thickened into a soup of aquamarine honey that boiled on her skin and tasted of burnt toast. The searing heat became a chill that flashed through her body and turned everything around her to white nothingness. Amy inhaled the sweet, burnt soup and closed her eyes.

She opened them a second later and blinked at MacGuffin.

"Um ... what just happened?"

The Siamese cat shook his head. "That was the worst experience I've ever had in my life, and I've been married twice!"

Amy pushed blonde hair out of her eyes. "It felt like a demat––like we crossed into another dimension." She looked up at the ceiling. "Blanche, did we just do what I think we did?"

"I cannot read your mind, captain," said the ship calmly. "I assume you are referring to our recent dematerialization of twenty-five seconds ago. This would not have happened if a particular override had been in place."

MacGuffin stamped his foot. "I wouldn't have disabled the override if I knew that a clumsy human would have been dropping things everywhere!"

"Sorry."

MacGuffin sighed and searched through his scattered tools. "Your apology changes nothing. I suggest you stampede down to the navigation room with those huge monkey legs and discover our precise location in the galaxy."

***

PHILIP AND AMY stood surrounded by space, the unmistakeable blue-and-white marble of Earth below their feet.

Philip squeezed her hand. "Home at last, dear."

"Right on!" Amy hugged the dark-haired teen around the neck and kissed him. "Blanche, plot a course to California," she said. "Pacific Grove."

"As you wish, my Lady."

Amy shook her head. "She keeps calling me that even though I hate it."

A circle of light opened in the stars, and Sunflower, Betsy, Nick, and Nistra stepped into the navigation room from the corridor.

"Not this place again," said Sunflower, catching sight of the blue planet. "I mean——'yay.'"

Betsy barked and jumped in the air. "I love Old Earth! This is Old Earth, right? Not the Earth with lots of craters and radiation and scary mutants?"

"Honestly, I can't tell the difference," said Sunflower.

Nick buzzed across the room to Amy. "Ooo, time for girls to go shopping," said the tiny sprite. "Promise me we'll go shopping?"

Amy smiled. "I promise. No boys allowed."

"There certainly is much water," said Nistra. "Vast farms for the purpose of raising *poona* would be easy on such a planet."

"Don't get any ideas," said Amy.

The ship matched the Earth's rotation and carved a path through the upper atmosphere, slowly descending through a dozen orbits to ensure a safe entry. Amy and the crew didn't mind, as they watched the continents and swirling clouds pass far below their feet.

"Rain over England, as always," said Philip.

Amy squinted at the continent of Europe. "I thought we'd see more cities and bridges and crap. Everyone's always talking about how you can see this or that from space. I don't see anything!"

"What about the Great Wall? We saw that when China passed below."

Amy shrugged. "Sure, but what about the cities?"

The air grew thick and whipped over the silver skin of the ship. Night fell as they descended toward the Baja coast of Mexico and turned north to follow the California coast. Near Big Sur the moon turned the Pacific Ocean white, creating a stark contrast with the the dark, rocky shoreline. Beyond the mountains Amy saw the Monterey Bay——a huge, curving divot in the rocky coast, carved out by the galaxy's largest ice cream scoop.

"There's the lighthouse! On the southwest side edge of the bay. See the rotating light?"

The ship dropped in altitude. Amy felt something inside her stomach fall as well.

"Where are all the streetlights?" she whispered. "There are trees everywhere and barely any houses!"

Philip pointed out a collection of wooden buildings standing along an orderly grid of dirt lanes.

"Look at those fine houses. Nothing to sniff at, by Jove. It's a small village with more trees than citizens, I suppose, but would be a pleasant area to call home. From the way you described it, love, I imagined a mad circus of men and machines all stacked on top of each other. Ah yes! Look there——you can see the smoke from a steam train, even after dark. How refreshing to know that some things never change."

Amy stamped her foot. "Philip, it's not my home! We're in Pacific Grove, but it's not the right year!"

EPILOGUE

The middle-aged woman applied mascara in a small mirror held by the sharp, talon-like fingers of an artificial hand. No attempt was made to disguise the mechanical limb or disguise it with flesh-colored material. The polished metal bones and twisted black and red wiring lay exposed for anyone to see as the joints clicked and spun with oily efficiency.

She had Amy's face, but with thirty more years of fine lines, stress, and sagging eyelids. Time and practice with makeup helped to conceal some of those imperfections, but she made no effort to hide a terrible wound that slashed the left side of her face. The ragged scar started in the blonde hairline above her left temple, dropped over the highest point of her cheekbone to the edge of her mouth, and tapered at her chin. Marbled pink and white, the ancient injury contrasted sharply with her deep red lipstick, mahogany eye shadow, and the black mascara she applied with a curved pen. The woman set down the applicator and picked up a hairbrush.

She wore a white silk blouse and a skirt the color of wet sheep. A matching gray jacket hung from a hook on the wall next to several lockers and a full-size bed covered in a dark gray blanket. The rooms were efficient, cold, and gray, with all the character and joy of the control room on a nuclear submarine.

The woman stopped brushing in mid-stroke at the sound of a faint warbling. The sound grew louder as she walked through the bedroom into a small office, where a red light flashed on top of a steel desk. The woman pressed a button next to the light.

"Yes?"

"Captain, the target has dematerialized," said a young female voice. "You wanted to be notified if that happened."

"Did the tracker repeat the signal?"

"Yes. We have the information."

"I'm coming up."

The woman ran the brush once more through her long blonde hair and slid her arms through the jacket that matched her gray skirt, taking care not to rip the fabric with the talons of her artificial hand.

She strolled through an extremely narrow corridor, stooping to avoid brushing her head on the low ceiling. Along her path, cats in black berets swung open a series of oblong metal hatches for her, saluted with paws to their berets, and closed the hatches as she passed.

The woman stepped through the last hatch and into a large, spherical compartment. A series of large screens formed a line across the curved walls, each displaying a different view of a cloudy brown planet tipped with green at the north and south poles. A human-sized chair padded with black leather stood in the center of the floor, behind two rows of cats and dogs at miniature terminals. Another row of cats and dogs were seated at terminals above the display screens, with a metal ladder on either side. The room was silent apart from the hum of electrical equipment and the soft click of paws on keyboards.

The woman smoothed the back of her skirt with her human left hand and sat in the central chair, crossing one leg over the other. A gray shorthaired cat wearing a headset timidly approached the chair from behind, the pink bow of a plastic barrette pinned to the fur on top of her head.

"Show me the data," said the woman.

The gray cat handed her an electronic tablet. The woman scanned through rows of numbers for a moment and handed it back.

"Good," she said. "Open comm lines to Two, Three, and Four."

"Yes, my Lady," said the cat, her voice wavering.

"And get rid of that pink thing on your head," said the woman. "Ridiculous."

"Of course, my Lady."

The large displays flickered and split into the images of three women, all of whom might have been a twin of Amy Armstrong if it weren't for the noticeable difference in age. The woman on the left was older, with wrinkles below her blue eyes and gray streaks in her shoulder-length blonde hair. In the center, the young blonde in the white tank top must have been in her late teens, but the pierced nose, black lipstick, and tattooed arms made her seem older. The woman on the right screen had dyed her hair and eyebrows black, and wore dark-rimmed glasses and a black turtleneck. She held a cigarette in the European style; between the thumb and index finger of her black leather gloves.

"We've found another one," said the scar-faced woman in the chair. "Good data this time."

The punkish version of Amy hooted with laughter. "Took you long enough!"

"When was the last one we found?" asked the Amy in black. "Not that I haven't had fun these last few months, but it's been a while."

"It doesn't matter how long," said the older Amy on the left screen. "Show us the proof."

"Thank you, Two," said the scar-faced woman. "For the record, it's been exactly three months and four days. Here's a video of the new copy. Check your data feeds."

An image of Amy in a white blouse, plaid skirt, and black tights snapped to life, sprinting toward the camera. She jumped and pushed an orange cat out of the frame. The screen flashed scarlet and faded to black. The three women reappeared on screen.

"Certainly looks like one," said the older blonde. "How did you find her? A search on SpaceBook?"

"Waste of time!" scoffed the punkish Amy. "That's why everyone makes me do it!"

"No, Three," said the black-haired twin. "It's because you're good at wasting time."

"Shut up, Four!"

The scar-faced woman raised her mechanical hand and the other versions of Amy became quiet.

"It was blind luck," she said. "I was tracking down a thief on Tau Ceti when this one turned up out of the blue. One of the inspectors tagged their ship with a tracker, sucked the data when they transmatted, and here we are."

The older blonde nodded. "Impressive."

"Don't mess with One; she knows her stuff," said the punkish teen in the center.

The woman in black took a slow drag from her cigarette and blew smoke from the side of her scarlet mouth. "Do we turn her, or burn her? I say, burn."

"Turn," said the older blonde.

The scar-faced woman smiled faintly. "First we try to turn her. I suggest the burden fall on Three. She's the closest in age to the copy, and will have the best chance at drawing the girl into a friendship. I'll provide you with an escape pod. Once you're inside, find some way to disable their ship. That will give you time to trick them into joining us."

The punkish blonde nodded. "Right on."

"If that doesn't work, we'll have to do it the hard way. Meet me at Tau Ceti immediately and we'll coordinate the transmat."

All of the displays snapped back to a view of the swirling brown planet. The scar-faced Amy swiveled her chair around to face the small gray cat.

"What do you think, Miss Nakamura? Do you think she'll join us?"

"I don't know," said the cat softly. "I just hope no one gets hurt."

The scar-faced woman smiled broadly, showing perfect white teeth. She reached out and prodded the gray cat's chest with a fingernail painted deepest red, like the color of blood from an opened vein.

"Someone always gets hurt," she whispered. "That's the best part."

END

Next in the Series

SpaceBook Awakens

The third book of the adventures of Amy Armstrong finds the heroine and her friends stranded in 1910 California. Separated from her friends and her ship, Amy is forced to work with a dimensional twin of herself against an army sent to destroy both of them.

Available October 2016!